THE VILLA OF SECOND CHANCES

JENNIFER BOHNET

Boldwood

First published in Great Britain in 2022 by Boldwood Books Ltd.

Cover Design by Debbie Clement Design

Cover Photography: Shutterstock

A CIP catalogue record for this book is available from the British Library.

Paperback ISBN 978-1-80162-273-8

Large Print ISBN 978-1-80162-274-5

Hardback ISBN 978-1-80162-272-1

Ebook ISBN 978-1-80162-276-9

Kindle ISBN 978-1-80162-275-2

Audio CD ISBN 978-1-80162-267-7

MP3 CD ISBN 978-1-80162-268-4

Digital audio download ISBN 978-1-80162-270-7

Boldwood Books Ltd
23 Bowerdean Street
London SW6 3TN
www.boldwoodbooks.com

For Oli with love

PART I

THE LAST WEEK IN MAY

Marcus Jackman and
Freya Jackman

Request the pleasure of

. . . .

On the occasion of
their wedding

on June 27th at 2pm
at Villa Sésame, Antibes.

1

'What did you say? No don't repeat it,' Rebecca West held up a hand in protest. 'I heard you the first time. You can't mean it? Not after all the work, all the years. It's something I never expected to hear you say.' Her voice trailed away and her shoulders drooped as she looked at her sister in shock.

The two of them were sat at the wrought-iron table on the balcony of Rebecca's private suite at the top of Villa Sésame, with its panoramic view of the Antibes Mediterranean coastline and the Esterel mountains away to the right. Rebecca had plucked up the courage to challenge her sister about the strange mood she'd been in recently. Learning the truth, though, had been devastating. The remains of supper – crab salad – and empty wine glasses littered the small table.

'Why? You're not ill are you? You aren't hiding anything from me?' Rebecca pressed.

Delphine sighed. She'd known this conversation was bound to be difficult but hadn't realised how difficult. Villa Sésame had been their joint life for the past twenty-five years. Deciding to tell her sister she wanted out was a decision she'd taken several months to make. Although Rebecca's horrified reaction to the news had been expected, her own guilty feelings that she was letting her sister down by wanting to retire, were harder than ever to push away. But she needed to explain.

'No, I'm not hiding anything and I'm not ill, but I do want a different life. It's been hard since André died and working here has saved me in many ways, but I'm tired and I want a life not dictated to, and ruled by, a timetable of weddings and functions.' Delphine looked at Rebecca. 'I'm not suggesting we sell the place. I don't need you to buy me out either, André's insurance has left me comfortable and I've got savings. I just want to become a sleeping partner – in more senses than one.'

Rebecca rubbed a hand over her face. She knew André's death a year ago had hit her sister hard. 'How about a six-month sabbatical starting after summer? October to March?'

Delphine shook her head. 'No. Look, I'm not planning on leaving you in the lurch. I'm sure Christine would jump at the chance to be full-time, so really all you need is to find a new chef. Easy!' She smiled at Rebecca, but Rebecca remained downcast.

'If only it were. You know how difficult it is. Top-notch chefs tend to want to work in bigger establishments – and the salary they want is huge.'

'We could take on a trainee for the summer, somebody finishing catering college this year. I'm giving you four months' notice, I can teach somebody a lot in that time,' Delphine suggested. 'This summer will be business as usual, but October the first is the day marked in my diary as the beginning of my new life.'

'But what are you going to do exactly?' Rebecca asked, still trying to understand Delphine's momentous decision.

'Sleep, read, paint, sit by the sea, travel a bit. Maybe get a dog, make new friends.'

Rebecca leant back on her chair and, placing her hands on the back of her head, sighed as she regarded her sister. 'So no discussion? You've simply decided to retire and leave me to it?'

'Yes.'

'I can't imagine this place without you here, but you've clearly given it a lot of thought, so I have to accept it's what you want and it's going to happen.'

'Good,' Delphine said, standing up. 'Time I went home.'

'Did you talk to Bart about this before he left for Corsica?'

Rebecca knew her son, Bart, was close to his aunt and would be concerned too about why she was making this decision.

'Of course not. I needed to speak to you first. You can tell him when he returns in a couple of weeks.'

'You do realise that I shall take every opportunity to make you change your mind?' Rebecca said, giving a small smile as she began to collect the dirty crockery together.

'You should know by now, when your big sister says she's going to do something, she does it. So don't waste your breath.'

'And you should remember too, your stubborn little sister is unlikely to take that advice.' Rebecca laughed. 'It's going to be a fun summer.'

Her smile faded as Delphine disappeared into the sitting room, waving a hand in the air as she opened the apartment door and left. In truth, Rebecca couldn't bear the thought of running Villa Sésame without Delphine at her side. The two of them had worked hard together to make their mark as one of the top places to hold intimate special events.

The summer Rebecca had finished college, Delphine was offered a job in Antibes working for a three-star chef. After several discussions, it was decided she would accept it and the two of them had moved to France. Delphine to immediately start work and Rebecca to do a French immersion course in Nice and to decide what she wanted to do career-wise. Whilst on the course, she had met a couple of girls who were working on the yachts and decided she'd enjoy that too. Delphine adored cooking and feeding people, while Rebecca preferred the front of house, the organising side of things and making sure people were happy.

It didn't take long for the dream of owning their own place to take root in both their heads. At first, they thought of a modest restaurant with rooms or similar, with Delphine running the kitchen and Rebecca managing everything else, but gradually, as their savings mounted up, they'd gone for the big dream – a villa on the Côte d'Azur.

It had taken them years to save and fund the purchase of the run-down belle époque villa nestling in the hills between Antibes and Cannes, overlooking the Mediterranean. For Rebecca, it had been over ten years working on the large luxury yachts that rubbed buoys with each other in the marinas all along European coastlines. During those years, Rebecca had risen from lowly deckhand to chief stewardess, squirrelling her large salary away. Delphine, a trained chef, had worked in the best restaurants in St Tropez, Monaco and Cannes, while all the time they were searching for the right place to set up a venture of their own.

They were both in their thirties, Rebecca thirty-one and Delphine thirty-seven, when they had walked into the shell of what had once been a beautiful belle époque villa owned by an Italian princess. Like a number of the older villas along the Côte d'Azur, Villa Sésame had changed hands several times since the beginning of the twentieth century as fortunes fluctuated and large properties fell out of favour because of the expense of maintenance. Rebecca could still remember the moment they'd both looked at each other and said, 'This is the one.'

Delphine had met and married the love of her life, André

Blanchet, a few years before they found Villa Sésame. By this time, there was enough money saved for a substantial deposit but they both knew the renovation of the villa would be expensive so Rebecca had signed on for one last season on the yachts. And then, during that exciting year when all their dreams and plans were starting to come true, Rebecca had found herself unexpectedly pregnant. Being a single mother was something that had never figured in her plans and definitely not then, when the future was so promising. However, there was nothing to be done but get on with it and the care of baby Bart, when he arrived, was shared between the two sisters as they took a hands-on approach to renovating the villa.

In the beginning, they did enough work on the run-down villa, with its views down towards the Med glistening in the distance and the town of Antibes away to the left, so that they could open as a restaurant and get some cash flow to slowly renovate the rest of the villa. They concentrated on installing a commercial kitchen, the saloon with its ornate cornices and French doors opening on to the terrace became the restaurant, a smaller room was turned into a cloakroom, and the rutted driveway up to the villa was resurfaced.

They'd started cautiously. Opening at first for lunches and Saturday dinners, but as the villa and the surrounding grounds, with the olive grove, gradually came back to their full glory, they were asked more and more to cater for weddings. Ten years after they originally opened, they rebranded and did a relaunch as a wedding venue. With its twelve bedrooms, infinity pool and outstanding views, it quickly became known as *the* venue on the Riviera for intimate events: birthdays, anniversaries and, of course, weddings.

Now, twenty-five years on from when they'd first opened as a small restaurant, a fully restored Villa Sésame was regarded as a special place and one of the most sought-after wedding venues in the area, renowned for the hospitality and the degree of privacy offered to their clients.

Thoughtfully, Rebecca loaded the dishwasher in her compact kitchen before pouring herself a small cointreau as a nightcap and returning to the balcony. Sitting there as the sky darkened and the evening turned to night, she tried to sort out her feelings. Despite the age difference of six years, she and Delphine had always been close and after their parents were killed in a boating accident when Rebecca was sixteen, they'd clung to each other, growing even closer. With no other family, the two of them had comforted each other and Delphine had taken the role of protective big sister up several notches.

André, when he'd married Delphine, had realised it was a question of 'love me, love my sister' and Rebecca had come to regard him as her big brother. Much to their mutual relief, with his accountant's hat on, he'd taken over Villa Sésame's bookwork, and had been a sounding board for the way the business evolved, but the sisters took the final decisions.

The heart attack that had taken him out of their lives had broken Delphine's heart and devastated both Rebecca and Bart, whom André had thought of, and treated as, the son he and Delphine had never managed to have.

Rebecca sipped her cointreau. Delphine was sixty-four later this year, maybe she was right in wanting to stop working so hard and enjoy life more. But making the decision without discussing it was unlike her and Rebecca couldn't help feeling that there was more behind it than her sister was telling her.

The summer ahead of them might be a busy one but any opportunity she got, Rebecca resolved she would do her utmost to get Delphine to change her mind. She didn't want to run Villa Sésame without her sister.

* * *

Delphine closed the door of her cottage, tucked away in a private part of the villa's grounds, with a sigh of relief. The hardest part was done. She'd told Rebecca her plans to become a sleeping partner. She knew that her sister was upset that there had been no discussion between them, that she'd presented it almost as a *fait accompli*, but that had been a deliberate tactic on her part. Throwing her plan to retire out into the open made it more real, more likely to happen, than just letting it go round and round in her mind. It was a step forward into the future. An unknown future that should have been full of promise, except it was stretching away in front of her like an army assault course that she would never in a million years have any desire to tackle. Cheerfully telling Rebecca all the things she and André had intended to do in retirement had been hard because they had been plans made by the couple they were, not the single person she had become.

Making her way upstairs to the main bedroom, Delphine slipped out of her clothes and stood under a cooling shower in the en suite bathroom, gathering her thoughts. It wasn't that she didn't love the business she and Rebecca had built together – she did. But guilt had seeped into her mind, taking over her thoughts, since André's sudden death. He'd retired at sixty-five and had wanted her to retire when she reached sixty but she hadn't wanted to – she enjoyed her working life too much. She'd compromised, delegated more, trained up the kitchen staff to take more responsibility and worked less hours so they had spent more time together in that last year, although still not as much as André had wanted. He'd asked her to promise him she would retire on her sixty-fourth birthday and then they would do some travelling together.

Her biggest regret would always be the fact that she'd been unable to give him the family he'd wanted, but not retiring on her sixtieth birthday as he'd asked her to and spending more time with him, was also now eating away at her conscience.

While André would never know that she was keeping her promise to finally retire, hopefully retirement would somehow ease her guilt. She would do all those things they'd promised each other they'd do together one day, albeit alone and with a heavy heart. She could only hope too, that the pain of losing him so unexpectedly would eventually go away. She was determined not to tarnish her memories of their happy life together by dwelling on the fact that the rest of her life was likely to be lived as a lonely single woman.

2

Clementine Vaughan, Clemmie to her friends, adjusted the last handmade red silk rose a fraction before stepping back to regard it critically. Satisfied, she glued the ostrich feather stems into place so that their champagne-coloured plumes floated around and above the posy of flowers on the hat's brim in a protective manner. Carefully, she crossed over the room and placed the hat on a spare mannequin head and stood back to look at it. A real 'mother of the bride' statement hat this one, with its large brim, pleated silk and over-the-top flower decoration. It was a calmer, smaller version of the client's original request that Clemmie had tactfully persuaded would suit her better during several fitting appointments. Hopefully, she would adore it when she collected it later.

One last look and Clemmie closed the door of her workroom and made for the kitchen overlooking the garden and the River Dart shimmering in the distance. She picked up the post from the front doormat on her way. She'd risen with the sun that morning, forgoing breakfast to get straight to work. Now, at ten o'clock, she needed food and coffee.

Five minutes later, she was sat at the kitchen table happily munching her way through cereal, toast and marmalade, drinking a mug of coffee and sorting the post. Opening the envelope with its familiar writing and French stamps, she smiled with delight when she saw the card with its watercolour background of the Côte d'Azur and the beautifully styled calligraphy of the words written on it. She reached for her phone and pressed Freya's number, which was on speed dial.

Freya answered immediately and Clemmie guessed that she'd been waiting for the call.

'At last, Marcus is making an honest woman of you again. Why didn't you tell me last time we spoke that this was on the cards?'

'Wanted to surprise you,' Freya said. 'You are free on that date, aren't you? I know it's short notice, but you have to be here. It's going to be a quiet affair, no more than twenty guests, if that, for the actual wedding, probably a few more for the evening party.'

'I'm definitely coming.'

'Good, because I want you to be my bridesmaid again – Angela too, if she comes, which I hope she does. And please will you make me a hat.' There was a short pause. 'What about a plus-one?'

'In my dreams,' Clemmie laughed. 'Although...' she hesitated and Freya jumped straight in.

'Have you met someone?'

'I might have, but it's early days. You'll be the first to know if it turns into more than friendship,' Clemmie promised, smiling to herself.

'Okay. You can tell me more when you get here. The other thing is, I want you and Angela to come and stay with us for a few days the week before the wedding and for a couple of days afterwards. Marcus has booked Villa Sésame for our exclusive use for eight days. It's a wedding present for me instead of a honeymoon. You wait until you see the place – it's wonderful. There's enough room for family and close friends. So the plan is we'll stay there from the Monday, you and Angela can join us there, say, Tuesday or Wednesday, and we can have a good old gossip like the old days. Mum will join us on Wednesday and everyone else will arrive at various times on Friday, ready for the pre-wedding dinner that evening. Marcus is meeting up with a few mates, Thursday evening, so we can have a girly night round the pool then. We're due a five-year reunion, so it's perfect.'

'Gosh, is it five years since our last one?' Clemmie said, thinking how young they'd all been when they'd promised to always keep in touch as they'd left Dartmouth in their teens for various colleges. Freya to art school down in Falmouth, Clemmie to the London College of Fashion and Angela to do an English degree at Bristol.

'Yes. Paul's funeral last year doesn't count. We need to make some new happy memories for Angela.'

Clemmie sighed. It had been an awful day.

'I'll definitely make you a hat and coming over earlier to stay for a few days would be lovely, but bridesmaid at my age? I think that might be a step too far. What about Madeleine? Won't she claim daughter's privilege? And what about your granddaughter, Lily, as a flower girl?'

'Madeleine has said she'd rather not, as she's currently suffering from morning sickness with this second pregnancy and feels dreadful most days. As for Lily being a flower girl, we'll see when they get here. She's not quite shaken off the terrible twos yet, she could disrupt things. Effie has already asked why I'm bothering to get married again at my age. Honestly, you think she'd be happy for me.'

Clemmie laughed at Freya's words. Effie, shortened from Alfreda, Freya's mother, had never been one to mince her words.

'Anyway,' Freya continued, 'I used the wrong word. In France, the word is witness. No groomsmen or bridesmaids here. Please, Clemmie.'

'Okay, but this is the last time I'm playing the role of bridesmaid, witness whatever, for anyone, understood?' Freya was her oldest and dearest friend, how could she refuse? 'Do I get to choose my own outfit?'

Freya laughed. 'I promise marrying Marcus will be my last outing as a bride. You can buy and wear whatever you like. I know you'll look fabulous. Perhaps you can make yourself a hat too?'

Clemmie could hear the teasing note in Freya's voice and took the bait. 'Not even for you. As you know full well, I hate wearing a hat and these days I don't.'

'And you Milliner of the Year 1997.'

'Yes, well, that was a long time ago. Email me with details of the sort of hat you want. Please don't say a fascinator,' she added.

Freya laughed. 'Definitely not. I was thinking maybe slouchy. Think Bianca Jagger's wedding to Mick back in the early seventies. Something like that would be perfect. A bit of a vintage look to go with the creamy silk trouser suit I'm thinking about.'

'Sounds very French. I've got a couple of hats to finish off in the next week for clients, but I'll work on a few designs and pop the drawings over on email.'

'Thanks, Clemmie. Got to go. You take care.'

Freya ended the call just as Clemmie quietly asked, 'What about Verity?'

Clemmie looked at her phone thoughtfully before replacing it on the table – 1997. A different century and she had been living a different life back then.

She'd never truly enjoyed those days when she was riding high in the fashion world. Remembering them even now made her shudder. Always a private person, she had found being in the spotlight difficult. Back in that decade, her hats had been on the heads of anyone who was anyone, being shown off by celebrities at Royal Ascot, society weddings, garden parties. Her work diary was full of illustrious names with appointments for fittings. Money had rolled in with people desperate to get a Clementine Vaughan hat on their heads. Money that she had no time to spend and enjoy mounted up in her bank account, which, in the end, had proved to be a blessing when her marriage had broken down some years later. Accepting the accolade of Milliner of the Year that evening, decades ago, in the Dorchester Hotel, she'd had no idea that she'd ever end up leaving London.

Now, all these years later, her life had come full circle and she was living not only back in her home town of Dartmouth but in the family home she'd inherited from her parents. Of course, she wished certain things could have been different, who didn't from time to time? Not choosing to marry a serial philanderer would have been a good start. The four years since she'd finally said 'Enough is enough' and kicked him out had been hard in many ways, but her life had definitely improved since their divorce. Lucy, their daughter, had been living at home then, so she hadn't been on her own, but then Lucy had met Jake and moved to Australia to be with him. Video calls and zoom meet-ups, however frequent, couldn't disguise the fact that Lucy was no longer close by and that she, Clemmie, had been sidelined from a position of utmost importance in her daughter's life to a smaller part in the wings.

Clemmie smothered a sigh. She had good friends here in Dartmouth and her hat business kept her occupied and her bank manager happy, even though the heady days of making hats for the rich and famous had all but disappeared. It was the thought she was doomed to spending the rest of her life alone that frightened her. It was a thought she found herself pushing away more and more these days. But where there was life there had to be hope and, as she'd just admitted to Freya, she had met a man recently whom she liked, and no one could ever truly know what the future might hold?

But was her life about to be disrupted again by a certain person she'd been avoiding since she was a teenager and had hoped never to see again – Verity Stoppard, Effie's niece and Freya's only cousin? Had Freya heard the question and deliberately hung up or was it a case of genuinely not hearing her. Mmm. Given their best friends status, Clemmie was ninety-nine per cent certain that Freya had heard her and didn't want to answer. And that could mean only one thing. An invitation to the wedding had been sent to Verity. Which Clemmie understood – a cousin was a cousin and family was important to Effie. Besides, weddings were usually family affairs. Next time she spoke to Freya, though, Clemmie vowed she would make sure she received an answer to her question. She needed to be prepared.

3

After finishing the phone call with Clemmie, Freya stifled a guilty sigh, before slowly climbing the three and a half flights of stairs leading to the roof terrace of the town house Marcus owned on the ancient ramparts of Antibes. Pushing open the French doors, she stepped out onto the terrace with its potted palm trees and a rampant purple bougainvillea in a large terracotta olive oil urn covering the back wall. She stood for a few moments breathing in the sea air, watching the activity out on the water – big yachts, small yachts, a large cruise ship in the distance and fishing boats returning to port with seagulls wheeling and diving over them in the wake. The seascape scene in front of her made her fingers twitch for a pencil and her sketchbook and she glanced over to the far corner, where her easel leant against the wall, a pencil and pad propped into the ledge at the bottom. The moment she'd set foot up here for the first time, Freya knew she'd never tire of sketching or painting the scene before her and she'd already done numerous sketches and watercolours of it. Marcus's friend, Hugo, owned an art gallery in the centre of town and he was keen to hold an exhibition of her work after the wedding.

When they'd divorced after seventeen years of marriage, Marcus had left the UK declaring, 'New life, new start, new country, new house.' At the time, Freya had wondered whether the term new wife would be added to the 'new' list. Thankfully, it turned out it hadn't.

Five years ago, their daughter, Madeleine, had married. An occasion that had thrown her and Marcus together as 'parents of the bride' and proved to be life-changing as they both realised, while they presented a united front in their assigned roles, they still got on rather well. There was still a spark between them, much like when they'd first met and before the stresses and strains of Marcus's career with the Foreign Office proved too much for Freya to live with. She happily accepted a 'no-strings' invitation for a week's holiday with him in Antibes.

That first time Freya had visited and seen the house after Madeleine's wedding, she'd understood completely why Marcus had purchased the place. It was a gem of a house, even if it did have an inconvenient layout with its four floors. The roof terrace alone, however, made it irresistible Besides, all those stairs did a good job of keeping you fit, Freya reasoned. And, of course, the terrace now held another special memory.

Marcus, not generally the most romantic of men, had chosen a night when the terrace was bathed in moonlight from a full moon and the sea had a silvery sheen to it as they listened to its rhythmic lapping at the rampart walls as he gently asked, 'Will you please come and live with me in France?'

Freya remembered catching her breath at the question. Give up the life she'd struggled to build for herself since the divorce? What would happen if it fell apart again? Was she brave enough to try? Marcus's next words though, 'I've never stopped loving you. Not having you by my side feels like I've lost a limb. We'll get it right second time around' had decided her. She'd felt exactly the same when they'd divorced – only in her case she hadn't lost a limb, her heart had broken.

It took time for her to sell up in England and move across, but now, two years later, it was as if they'd never been apart. When Marcus had asked her to marry him again, there had been no hesitation. She was looking forward to her future again as Marcus's wife and hoping it would be a long one, but it couldn't be taken for granted, they were more baby boomers than millennials these days.

When she'd told Effie she and Marcus were remarrying, her mother had rather waspishly enquired why on earth she was bothering getting married again at her age.

'Everybody assumes you're married anyway, you've got the same surnames, and besides, nobody expects people your age to be living in sin.'

Freya had smiled and shrugged. The first time she'd married, she'd expected the 'until death do us part' to be the way of things. She'd never stopped loving Marcus and this time would be different if only because they were both mature, older versions of themselves. And as Marcus had officially retired, he wouldn't be constantly on call from a demanding government department. Yes, Marcus was right. This time around it would be better than before.

A door slammed below. Marcus was back. Freya sighed happily.

'Freya, darling?' Marcus called.

'On the terrace.'

Five minutes later, he appeared, two glasses and a bottle of rosé clutched in his hands.

'Good sail?' Freya asked, moving across to kiss him.

'Not enough wind really, but it was great to be out on the

water,' Marcus replied, pulling the cork out of the bottle of rosé. 'You're looking pensive? What's up?'

'Clemmie phoned. She's definitely coming to the wedding, happy to be bridesmaid and she's making me a hat.' Freya paused, taking the glass of wine and clinking it against Marcus's glass.

'And now you're worried about the Verity issue,' Marcus said.

Freya nodded, not wanting to admit she'd cut Clemmie off when she'd asked about Verity, rather than answer her. The fact that Clemmie had asked the question told her that she was worried about her presence at the wedding. It would be only fair to warn her. The next time they spoke she'd tell her, but admitting to something that would be bound to upset her would be difficult.

'I'm hoping the RSVP from Verity will say, thanks but no thanks, and I won't have to tell Clemmie, but...' Freya shrugged. If the invite was accepted, telling Clemmie, face to face, when she arrived the week of the wedding would be better – better perhaps, but still, oh so difficult. Effie had insisted on Freya sending an invitation to Verity – family was family and her dear departed sister, Hyacinth, would want her daughter included. Hopefully, it would be declined and Clemmie need never know it had been sent – or come face to face with her long-ago nemesis.

* * *

To her own surprise, Verity Stoppard was finding herself bored with her life these days. Since she'd taken the decision nine months ago to sell her estate agency business and retire, life had been a social whirl for a while and she'd relished the freedom from routine and the tyranny of office hours, not to mention dealing with increasingly demanding clients, but over the last few months her freedom had developed a routine of its own. There were weekly visits to the gym, hairdressers, nail boutique, golf lessons, tennis and lunch at The Ivy three or four times a week. And now Verity was realising there was a limit to how much golf a woman could play, however enthusiastic she'd been in the beginning, and retail therapy didn't quite hit the mark for her these days. There wasn't enough space in the built-in wardrobes in her dressing room any longer to squeeze in another empty hanger, let alone one with clothes on. As for her shoe and handbag collections that she'd insisted were investments to her accountant when he'd queried the amount of money she spent on them, even the thrill of adding another Hermès bag to the shelf had paled. After all, there was no one to leave them to – no children and therefore no grandchildren.

Being a lady that lunches had lost its appeal too. Her friends – acquaintances really, she'd lost contact with close friends years ago when she was too busy climbing the career ladder – were all still working and interesting men were at a premium during the middle of the day. More and more, she began to regret not staying on as a consultant rather than cutting herself adrift so eagerly.

Verity poured a generous measure of her favourite artisan plum and vanilla gin into a cut-glass tumbler and sniffed it appreciatively before adding a splash of Fever Tree Mediterranean tonic. Five o'clock in the afternoon might be regarded as too early in some circles to have a drink, but so what – somewhere the sun was setting. It wasn't as if she was becoming dependent on alcohol to lift her spirits. That was a road she'd vowed never to go down, unlike her mother. The thought of her mother would have brought a frown to her Botoxed forehead if it could. No, she could go without a drink any time if she had to. But not this evening.

Verity glanced across at the mantlepiece in her dining room where she placed all the square card 'stiffies' she received, on display for any visitor to see how busy her social life was, with weddings throughout the summer, invites to parties, launches of products in prestigious hotels. Her glance lingered on the latest one. Trust Freya to go all arty with a drawing and fancy writing. She'd planned on turning it down as soon as it arrived, when Aunt Effie had told her to expect an invitation. So why was she hesitating?

She had a perfectly good excuse for refusing, because a little further along the mantlepiece was the grand embossed wedding invitation to what was already being talked of as the society wedding of the year on the same date, an invitation she had already RSVP'd to accept.

Glass in hand, Verity wandered out into the large conservatory she'd had built five years after she'd bought the house. With its umbrella-shaped glass roof, French door windows, it was her favourite room in the house. Standing in front of those windows looking out over the garden that a team of gardeners kept weed-free and pristine, she took a long drink of her G & T and tried to put her thoughts in order.

It was a long time since she'd had a holiday in the south of France and now that Freya and Aunt Effie both lived down there, it was an ideal opportunity to visit. If the invitation was to be believed, she'd be a welcome guest at her cousin's wedding. On the other hand, if it had only been sent because of Aunt Effie's insistence that 'family was family', it would be better to refuse. But... Should she risk it for old times' sake? Or would going be like opening up a Pandora's Box of old grievances, regrets and hurts, changing nothing in the scheme of things?

Verity drained the last of her G & T and turned to go back to the kitchen to refill the glass. To go or not to go? That was the first question. If she did accept the invitation and go to the wedding, a second question sprang up: how would a certain person who was sure to be there react? Badly, without a doubt.

Getting on with people businesswise was easy for Verity: she'd adopted the part of successful business woman as her own and simply acted it out – it was family and a certain ex-friend she had a problem with. And while she would have to admit it was her own fault, it was family she regretted missing out on more and more. These days, as she rattled around alone in her big house that would have made a wonderful family home, she was beginning to realise that family was important. Maybe she should think of Freya's wedding as an opportunity to try to correct the wrongs of the past? It would be a start, if nothing else, but whether it would embrace a certain long ago incident with Clemmie remained doubtful.

4

As Angela Hamilton opened the door of her car ready to drive Will, her son, to Totnes station to catch the London train, Tom, the village postman, crossed the road and handed her the mail.

'Just junk mail for you today, apart from this. Looks like a party invitation,' he said, holding out a square envelope. 'Good to see you, Will.'

'Thanks, Tom, How's Sally?' Angela asked.

'Well, as she's nagging me to help her sort out the garden, I reckon she's almost back to normal.' Tom replied with a smile.

'That's good news. Give her my love. I'll try to pop round to see her one day this week.'

Sally, Tom's wife and her friend, had had a fall a few weeks ago, breaking her leg and spraining her wrist and Angela felt guilty she hadn't done more than three or four measly visits with magazines and chocolates. Tom had assured her they were being overwhelmed with help and cooked meals, and at the time, Angela had accepted he was telling her the truth and stepped back with relief. But now the guilt was beginning to eat away at her for letting her friend down. After all, Sally had been one of the first to help Angela at her own time of need.

Throwing the junk mail and the white envelope onto the dashboard, she got into the car and smiled up at the postman.

'Sorry, got to dash or Will's likely to miss his train.'

* * *

Half an hour later, Angela drove into the station car park and stopped the car.

'Your train's due in two minutes. We'd better get you across to the platform,' she said.

'No, Mum, don't bother to come into the station. Let's say goodbye here and I'll run across the bridge.'

'It's not a bother,' Angela protested. It would give her an extra few precious moments with her son.

Will leant across and kissed her cheek. 'I'll ring at the weekend as usual and Steph and I will be down together in a couple of weeks. She was sorry she couldn't make it this time.' He hesitated. 'Maybe you'll have made a start on getting rid of some of Dad's things by the next time I come? I know it's hard and I wish you'd let me help when I'm here, but you won't. It's not helping you get over the accident. You need to sort things in the house.'

Angela fought back the tears and nodded as she turned to give him a kiss on the cheek. 'You take care up there in London and don't forget to give Steph my love,' Angela said, ignoring his words and forcing a bright note into her voice as Will got out of the car. 'Can't wait for you both to visit.'

She sat there watching as Will made his way into the station, ran across the bridge and smiled as she saw him stride onto the platform for the London-bound train. Looking at him as he joined the small crowd of people waiting, she gnawed at her bottom lip. She'd always been determined never to be one of those mothers who lived their lives through their child, but here she was, desperate to hang onto Will. Having him at home, even for such a short time, gave a purpose to her days and life. A purpose that was missing from her normal routine these days.

As much as she wished he was staying longer, she knew it wasn't fair to expect it of him. At twenty-four years old, his life was in London now and he was happy. That was the main thing, even if she did still miss him dreadfully.

The London train pulled into the station, blocking her view of the far platform. Through the rain and dust-stained carriage windows, she could see people searching for seats throughout the train. She thought she spied Will find his place in a mid-train carriage but couldn't be sure.

Grown-up Will was good company and fun to be with. Over the past weekend, Angela had revelled in her son's presence, wishing it would never end. When he'd been job hunting after uni, she'd secretly been hoping he'd find something locally and come back home to live. But the offer of his dream publishing job in London couldn't be turned down and away he went. When Paul was still alive, it had been different and the two of them had enjoyed being empty nesters... before things had changed so dramatically. If only Paul had never...

Angela smothered a sigh. The nightmares had receded, mostly, but during the day her thoughts still repeatedly returned to memories of Paul. Particularly that last day they'd had together. She shook her head and concentrated on finding Will on the train.

Minutes later, the train drew away, leaving a deserted plat-form in full view – and Angela with tears pouring down her cheeks, frantically searching for a tissue, grateful that Will had missed this latest meltdown.

Once she'd wiped her face, blown her nose and stopped crying, she sat there for a few moments pulling herself together. Sitting there, the square envelope caught her eye. French stamps meant that it was from Freya, one of her oldest friends. Half-heartedly, Angela opened the envelope, wondering what it could be. Not a party invitation, a wedding invitation – and a note mentioning a reunion, urging her to come, reminding Angela of the Beatles song they'd all sang along to after swearing lifelong devotion to each other, 'Will you still love me when I'm sixty-four.' Despite her current feelings, Angela smiled. They might be in their late fifties, but they weren't quite that old yet.

She'd forgotten their younger promise to each other. The three of them – Freya, Clemmie and herself – had been insepa-rable in those long-ago days, convinced they would never lose touch. And if they did, they would meet up in the dim and distant future when they reached that age. Of course, life had got in the way. Marriages and christenings had been celebrated, but contact had diminished to birthday and Christmas cards and the occa-sional meet-up with one or other of the friends. Rarely had the three of them been able to get together. The last time had been Paul's funeral, eight months ago.

To go or not to go? It would be good to see Clemmie and Freya again, but... She sighed. She wasn't ready. Going to a wedding, mixing with other people, making social small talk, were all normal things to do and in the past she'd enjoyed them. But her life was no longer normal and she doubted she could convince anyone, or make herself believe, it was. She was still struggling with the loss of Paul and the guilt. Guilt that she knew her friends would winkle out of her and she'd have to tell them the truth.

Facing the condemnation that she knew they were bound to share could mean losing their friendship. Best not to go.

Angela put the card back in the envelope and started the car to drive home. Reaching the T-junction at the end of the car park exit, she hesitated. The whole empty day stretched ahead of her. She could do anything, go anywhere she liked. Why go home straight away? She glanced at the signpost in front of her. 'To the coast.' Why not?

Half an hour later, Angela pulled into a parking area above a small cove tucked away off the tourist route that had been a favourite summer haunt when Will had been young. June might only be a day away, but a cold on-shore breeze was blowing as she got out of the car and she was glad to pull on her thick fleece before making for the beach and walking along the curve of the bay.

The grey overcast sky echoed her mood as she trudged along the empty beach, lost in nostalgic thoughts. It had to be more than ten years since she'd been down here. Both Will and his best friend, Ben, had declared the beach to be boring once they were teenagers and wanted to do different things, bringing the era of them all spending summer days here to an abrupt end.

Passing a securely boarded-up wooden shack with weather-beaten posters advertising cold drinks and ice creams hanging from it, Angela smiled to herself. No shack of any description on the beach in those long-ago days. She and Zoe, Ben's mum, had always had to bribe the boys with the promise of ice creams on the way home to get them off the beach and into the car. Life had been good when Will was young. Better than it was now, that's for sure.

Angela picked up a flat pebble and skimmed it into the sea, watching it bounce once before disappearing into oblivion under the water. Rather like the way she'd become invisible to the rest of the world after Paul's death. Last Christmas and New Year, just a few weeks after the accident, was the first she'd spent as a widow. She'd put on a good face while Will was home, but once he'd left, she had slipped back into despair.

She knew she was guilty of having wallowed in grief for the last few months, doing zero to make a new life for herself. But the thought of the next twenty years being like the past eight months, without a real purpose to life, made her shudder. She knew she had to get a grip, get on with her life – and let Will live his without her clinging on to him. Living alone, though, felt strange and wrong. Sometimes, when she caught herself talking to herself, she feared for her sanity in a lonely old age. Another stone hit the water and sank without trace.

How to change things though? What could she do? She'd always considered herself lucky that Paul had been a high earner and she'd been happy after gaining her degree, to leave uni, marry Paul and become a stay-at-home wife and mother. It was something her own mum in particular had been disappointed about and had tutted over the waste of her 2.1 English degree for years. Three decades on, it was too late to hope it would open any employment doors now. Two days a week as supervisor in the local charity shop wasn't exactly what employers liked to see on a CV. Maybe she could do a course in something. Retrain as a... As a what? Perhaps signing on with a temping agency as a filing clerk. Although weren't offices supposed to be paperless these days? So many obstacles. So little point to anything.

Angela crouched down and picked up another stone, realising as she did so she'd walked the length of the beach. She skimmed the pebble and counted as it made one... two... three...

four bounces across the water before disappearing. Not bad. Could she do it again? Selecting another flat stone, she sent it on its way. Yes. Another four bounces.

Turning to make her way back along the beach to her car, Angela smiled. Maybe she should take the bouncing stones as a positive sign moving forward. As difficult as it would be, she had to try harder to put Paul's tragic death and the last year behind her and get her own life back on track. She had to stop feeling guilty for being alive. Maybe she could make a list of the things she felt she could actually tackle and tick them off one by one? Baby steps. It would at least be better than stagnating like she'd been doing for the last eight months. She owed it to Paul, she owed it to Will and she owed it to herself.

Back sitting in the car, Angela found a beaten-up biro in the door pocket. On the back of Freya's envelope, she began to make a list: clear the spare room; tackle the garden; charity shop; get a haircut...

And she'd think about going to the reunion and Freya's wedding.

5

The early-morning air was sweet and fresh as Delphine took her wicker trug from the hook behind the door of the kitchen storeroom and made for the chickens and the kitchen garden. Villa Sésame had been full of surprises in the early days of renovations and one of the most welcome had been the discovery of the old kitchen garden tucked away down a path at the back of the villa. André had been thrilled and had insisted it was his project to recreate it.

'I am an accountant by necessity, but my heart and my fingers love to garden,' he'd said. 'And we shall have *les poulettes* for *des oeufs*. When you are working in the kitchen, ma chérie, me – I shall be busy out here.'

It had taken time to establish, but now, as well as a prolific vegetable patch, the soft fruits – raspberries and strawberries – as well as the apple, pear, lemon, orange and grapefruit trees were all flourishing in the kitchen garden.

Over the years, André had single-handedly recreated a kitchen garden for the villa. He'd discovered where the original walls had been, uncovered the paths that had intersected the area and found the remains of a glasshouse against the back wall where peach trees had once grown. He'd had hopes of renovating it, but the remains had been declared unsafe and he'd sadly overseen the demolishing of the rusty ironwork and the earth below cleared of antique broken glass. Afterwards, that area of the garden, and a small orchard where there were a couple of ancient apple and quince trees still producing fruit, had been declared perfect for a chicken enclosure. Fenced off from the rest of the garden, it was now home to a mixed brood of hens and their spacious chicken coop.

As she wandered up through the garden, Delphine could hear the soft clucking of the chickens waiting in their hut to be released for the day.

'*Bonjour, les filles,*' she said as she unhooked the door of the coop and tied it back. André had, of course, always spoken French to them and it came naturally to her to do the same rather than use English. '*C'est une belle journée aujourd'hui* – perfect for dust baths if you feel the need.'

After André's heart attack, she'd spent a lot of time out here with his hens, talking to them, her tears dropping onto their feathers as she cuddled one or two of the tamer ones. Cleaning their hut out, replacing the straw in the nesting boxes, filling the feeders, checking the water – things that André had shown her how to do down the years – all became her job. Even now, she refused to let anyone else take on *les poulettes*, although that day would arrive soon. It wasn't just the eggs they produced, it was the comfort she gained from spending time with these simple animals knowing how much joy they had brought her husband. *And now you're thinking of abandoning them at the end of summer*, a voice niggled inside her head. Sighing, Delphine wiped her tears from the feathers of Blanche, the hen she was cuddling, and carefully placed her on the ground, as she mentally promised they would always be looked after.

Making sure all the hens were out wandering around and scratching the ground, Delphine gave the nesting boxes a quick check and picked up three eggs, knowing there would be more at midday. Closing the enclosure gate behind her, she walked towards the raised herb garden that André had set up years ago. It was another real treat to come out here in the mornings and pick the fresh herbs she wanted for the day.

'*Bonjour,*' a voice called out and Delphine turned to wait for the man striding towards her. She'd forgotten today was a Joel day. Never having had to find a gardener before, they'd soon realised after André died that they would need to find someone quickly. Carla, an English friend who ran a small guest house in Antibes, where they suggested people stayed when they themselves were full, had come to their rescue, ringing to offer condolences from her and her partner, Joel, who was a freelance gardener, she'd said.

'You are not to worry about the grounds or the kitchen garden, Joel will be coming to help you until you find someone permanent. He knew and liked your husband, says it's the least he can do for you.'

The sisters had both heaved a sigh of relief, accepted and expressed their gratitude.

A week or two after the funeral, Delphine and Rebecca had thanked Joel for his help and asked if he could, would, continue to look after the villa grounds and the kitchen garden on a free-lance contract basis. He'd agreed and since then he'd appeared once or twice a week and the villa grounds André had loved and devoted so much of his time to, continued to flourish.

After exchanging a few words with Joel, Delphine made for the kitchen. She'd buzz Rebecca and see if she fancied joining her for breakfast. The three fresh eggs in the trug were calling out to be made into scrambled eggs for the two of them. The summer would pass in a blur of weddings and other events and she was determined to make the most of any spare moments and spend them with her sister. October would arrive soon enough.

6

A couple of days after speaking to Freya, Clemmie emailed a few hat sketches to her. At least sending an email meant she didn't have to talk to her, ask about Verity. Besides, she could anticipate what the response was likely to be from Freya's reluctance to answer.

Let me know which you like – as it's summer, I think the choice is probably between chiffon or straw rather than felt. Both hat brims are unstructured so are floppy, but I can adjust the floppiness. I've still got your head measurement, so no worries there. If you decide on the chiffon one, I'll need to know the colour you want. Love Clemmie. xx

Clemmie pressed send and glanced at the time – twelve o'clock – before closing her laptop. Time to walk to the Dartmouth Yacht Club at the far end of the South Embankment where she was meeting Jonty for lunch. Knowing Jonty's liking for a cold lager, he was probably there already and would have secured one of the outdoor tables for them.

Although still early summer, the embankment was busy with

holidaymakers strolling along enjoying the sunny weather and stopping every five paces to watch the activity on the river. Tourist boats and private yachts were making their way either downriver towards Dartmouth Castle or upstream towards Dittisham and Totnes, while giving way to all three ferries which were busy toing and froing across the river between Dartmouth and Kingswear.

Clemmie took deep breaths of the sea air as she half walked, half ran, conscious that the loitering crowds were hampering her progress but determined not to let them upset her. July and August were the months when the crowds really became impossible to cope with and then she took to staying home, except for early-morning or mid-evening strolls along the riverfront.

Jonty was chatting to a couple of holidaymakers at the table next to him when she arrived and stood up to welcome her as she weaved her way between tables set out on the wide embankment pavement. As she sank down onto a chair, a waitress turned from serving a table of four and held out a menu.

Clemmie shook her head. 'Thanks, I don't need that. A glass of rosé please and a platter special. Jonty?'

'A platter for me too please, but lager instead of wine,' Jonty said, smiling at the waitress. His ever-present phone, which he'd placed on the table in front of him, pinged. A quick glance and he sighed as he replaced it on the table.

For a few moments, they watched the lower ferry on its journey from Kingswear getting closer before manoeuvring itself into position for a safe lowering of its ramp and the disgorging of its cargo.

'How was your trip to Bristol?' Clemmie asked.

Jonty shrugged. 'Put it this way, I'm glad to be home.'

'I have some news,' Clemmie said, turning to Jonty as their view of the ferry disappeared behind the old building at the end of the embankment, but before she could say more, the waitress returned with their drinks and platters and set them down in front of them. 'Bon appétit.'

Clemmie continued when the waitress had moved off.

'I'm off to France in a couple of weeks. Freya, my oldest friend, is marrying her husband again.'

Clemmie registered the puzzled look on Jonty's face.

'Freya and Marcus met and married years ago, had a daughter, divorced after about seventeen years, and got back together again about five years ago at their daughter's wedding. Like you do.'

'Like you do,' Jonty echoed. 'Which part of France?'

'Between Cannes and Antibes on the Riviera. Do you know it?'

'I've sailed around the Med a lot,' Jonty said, breaking a piece of bread off the baguette on his platter. 'Antibes was always a favourite harbour.'

Clemmie waited for him to say more, but he'd turned his attention to the serving of olives, smoked meats and tomatoes in front of him. She sighed. They'd become good friends, but in the five months since they'd first met, Jonty had never been very forthcoming about his past or his personal life. Beyond learning that he was divorced, had one daughter and had recently taken early retirement, she knew little about his previous life. Or even how he'd ended up living in Dartmouth. His reticence to talk about himself she'd put down to, a) he was a man and everyone knew that men were notorious for 'keeping it all in' and, b) everyone was entitled to their secrets. Which meant, in turn, that she hadn't talked much about her past to him either, other than to tell him she was a widow and her only daughter lived in Australia.

Although Dartmouth being the small town it was, there was

no doubt several people who would have mentioned her past to him on her behalf whether he wanted to know about it or not. Given him a comprehensive rundown on her most embarrassing moments, from birth to the day she left home. And, of course, he had only to google her name to learn even more – not that she had a great social media presence these days. Googling his name out of curiosity had produced just one profile, which most definitely was not the Jonty she knew.

Being an unknown stranger in town gave Jonty a distinct notoriety, the gossips knew nothing about him, so it was only rumours and speculation that occasionally reached her ears. One outrageous rumour whispered several times was that he was an 'undercover agent for MI5' – an idea that had made Clemmie burst out laughing the first time she'd heard it and she didn't believe it for one moment. A week or so ago, when she was helping him varnish a Redwing sailing dinghy, she'd asked him outright about another rumour she'd heard.

Jonty had looked at her, his eyebrows raised and laughed. 'Seriously, do I look like a diplomat?'

'Well, obviously not right now,' Clemmie had said, looking at his cut-off jean shorts splattered with sticky varnish and his faded black 'Queen' T-shirt. 'Maybe you did back in the day. You're very upright, you dress well, you're polite and quite diplomatic over things. And you have a certain *je ne sais quoi* going on.'

But even then, he hadn't volunteered the information of who, or what, he actually was. He'd just laughed, shaken his head and gone back to varnishing the boat. Clemmie hadn't tried to press him again. After all, neither of them had discussed their relationship as such and it seemed intrusive to ask questions about his past when they were still navigating the early days of their friendship, having met just months before.

They'd met on the coastal path out by Dartmouth Castle,

Jonty had been frantically trying to catch a young Westie puppy, who, having slipped his collar, was intent on mischief and mayhem. When the dog ran up to her, Clemmie instinctively bent down and scooped him up and held him tight while he licked her face.

Once the collar was back around the dog's neck and the lead firmly wound round his hand, Jonty had thanked her and introduced both himself and Hamish.

'He's a rescue dog that my daughter has adopted for her sins. Obedience training hasn't figured in his life so far.'

'He's very sweet,' Clemmie had said. 'He'll get better as he gets older, I'm sure.'

They'd fallen into step alongside each other as they'd started to walk the road towards Warfleet and on into Dartmouth, with Hamish walking to heel as if it was the most natural thing for him to do. In South Town, Jonty had stopped at the top of a flight of steps leading down towards the river and Bayards Cove.

'Maybe I can buy you a drink sometime to say thank you for your help with this monster?' he'd said, indicating Hamish. 'Not right now, unfortunately, because I have to meet someone in the next half-hour. How about tomorrow evening on the Yacht Club terrace? Seven o'clock?'

And that was how their friendship had begun. It was a friendship of spasmodic meetings – the occasional lunch, an evening drink on Bayards Cove, walks with and without Hamish, and that one-off time helping varnish the dinghy. Whilst Clemmie secretly longed to be invited for a sail, so far it hadn't happened. Weeks could pass without them seeing each other. Clemmie would be busy meeting clients and making hats and Jonty – well, Jonty would disappear from time to time, usually to Bristol where his ex-wife, Victoria, and his daughter, Emma, lived. But when they did meet up, they slipped easily into the relaxed friendship that had established itself between them from day one.

'So, France,' Jonty said, picking up his glass of lager. 'You and your friend go back a long time?'

'There are three of us actually – Freya, Angela and me. We all grew up together here. We could have been the prototype for Donna and the Dynamos.' Clemmie looked at Jonty questioningly. 'You know the film *Mamma Mia*?'

'I have a daughter, of course I know the film – even sat through it. That's a long friendship, the three of you must be close?'

Clemmie took a sip of her rosé. 'We are, although sadly we don't see much of each other these days. Freya's in France, I'm here. Angela is only about forty miles away, which these days might as well be four hundred. Which makes me feel guilty, but getting to the outskirts of Dartmoor from here without a car is nigh on impossible and Angela has shut herself away recently.' She sighed. 'The last time we were all together was for Paul's funeral late last year. Angela's husband. Motorbike accident,' she explained quickly. 'Anyway, Freya wants us both to go over early and have a reunion meet-up before the wedding. Create some new happy memories for Angela.'

Clemmie was silent for a few seconds, remembering how close the three of them had been before life took them away from each other.

'I'm happy to drive you out to Dartmoor if you want to go any time,' Jonty said. 'Love the freedom of the place.'

'Thanks, I might take you up on that. These platters are good, aren't they?' Clemmie said, wanting to change the subject away from Angela. 'Could almost be having lunch in France already with this weather and the view. A couple of weeks and I'll actually be there.'

Jonty nodded. 'Great time of year to go, late June. It won't be too hot or too crowded.'

'One of the best bits for me is going to be staying in a villa somewhere near Antibes. Marcus has booked it exclusively for close family and friends for the week before the wedding. Can't wait. Freya has asked me to make her hat for the wedding so it will give me time to fit and finish it.'

'Almost wish I was coming with you,' Jonty said, reaching for his lager.

'Are you going anywhere this summer?' Clemmie said, swallowing the impulse to say, *'Why don't you? I can take a plus-one,'* as she glanced at him.

'Not sure,' Jonty shrugged. 'Depends on Hamish, dog-sitting duties. Emma and the kids are supposed to be going to Scotland with Victoria sometime, but as usual, Victoria is being difficult to pin down with dates.'

Clemmie gave a sympathetic smile. Jonty had never specifically badmouthed his ex-wife, but she was beginning to realise how difficult a woman she was without him putting it into words.

'Oh, look at that yacht. Isn't she beautiful?' For several moments, they both watched as the impressive-looking schooner motored its way from the castle upriver towards one of the large mooring buoys with just the jib sail raised.

Jonty's phone gave another ping. This time when he picked it up and looked at it, he swore quietly before replacing the phone in his pocket.

'Sorry, but I'm going to have to go. Something has come up. I'll settle the bill at the bar as I leave.'

'Victoria again?' Clemmie asked as Jonty pushed his chair back and stood up.

He gave a brief nod. 'I'll see you around.'

'See you around,' Clemmie echoed as he left. This wasn't the first time he'd been called away unexpectedly by Victoria when Clemmie was with him. For an ex-wife, Victoria still had a strong grip on the strings of marital connections: Victoria had a problem – ring Jonty; Victoria needed advice – ring Jonty; Victoria needed him to talk to Emma – ring Jonty. Sometimes these requests were a prelude to Jonty disappearing for a while, other times he rang Clemmie within hours to apologise.

It was none of her business, and even if she was getting to like him more and more as they spent time together, she and Jonty were friends, not a couple having a relationship, so she shrugged it off philosophically when their arrangements were disrupted. She couldn't help wondering, though, whether Jonty would ever be free to start a new, close, relationship with anyone. Was the spectre of Victoria always going to be in the way of him meeting a new love?

7

Rebecca sat at her desk in the small office at the back of the main entrance hallway of Villa Sésame and switched on the computer. On the wall in front of her were two large calendars. One showing the bookings for the year, the other staff timetables for the coming summer months. On the side wall was a huge whiteboard with a lengthy to-do list covering its surface.

Whilst Rebecca waited for the computer to boot up, she opened the bulky A4 events folder laying on the desk entitled 'Jackman Wedding' and stuffed with important information about the event. She knew everyone laughed at her somewhat old-fashioned habit of printing out everything and keeping paper records as well as on the computer, but for her it was peace of mind: always accessible and far better than any cloud device. She'd insisted too, that Christine, her PA, had a folder for every event with all the printouts.

Freya Jackman was due at eleven o'clock for a penultimate pre-wedding meeting and glancing through the various papers in the file, Rebecca knew she was able to assure her that everything was on schedule. Just one or two things needed to be clarified and finalised. This wedding was a particularly intimate event, with only twenty guests, compared to the usual fifty of previous ones at Villa Sésame. But with Marcus and Freya staying at the villa for eight days and various family and friends joining them at different times before the weekend, ready for the pre-wedding evening dinner on the Friday night, it was likely to be a hectic few days.

Bookings like this were a mixed blessing. Being available 24/7 to guests staying before and after the wedding inevitably brought problems. Most guests were lovely, but occasionally there were one or two who were more than demanding. Managing Villa Sésame between them, both Rebecca and Delphine needed to be able to anticipate and be ready for any possible problems.

The first time she'd met Marcus and Freya Jackman when they'd come to see what Villa Sésame had to offer, Rebecca had assumed they were the parents looking at the venue for a daughter's wedding as they'd struck her as a particularly happily married couple. They were so comfortable together. To learn that it was their own remarriage they were planning had made her smile. At that meeting, Marcus had told her he wanted to celebrate big time and he was certainly going all out to do that. They were such a lovely couple that Rebecca was equally determined this second wedding celebration would be as perfect as she could make it for them,

Rebecca glanced at the diary open on her desk. The next booking after the Jackman wedding was just over a week later – a fourth of July evening party for thirty ex-pat Americans celebrating Independence Day. So everyone would have time to recover from what was going to be a busy eight days with the Jackman wedding.

Rebecca sighed. She planned on using the time afterwards to find a replacement for Delphine – if that was even possible. She still found it hard to believe that her sister was so determined to become a sleeping partner. She deliberately hadn't pressed her any more on it, as deep down she was hoping that Delphine would change her mind. Right now though, she needed to concentrate on being fully prepared for the meeting with Freya. Having seen for herself how much Marcus and Freya loved each other and knowing it wasn't often anyone got a second chance at love and a happy ending, she was resolved to do her utmost to give them the best possible wedding day.

Rebecca smiled to herself as she began a final check through of the things that Freya was sure to ask about when she arrived.

* * *

Freya arrived promptly at eleven o'clock and Rebecca picked up her folder and notebook and led the way out onto the terrace, where Delphine was already placing plates, cups and a small selection of petits fours on the round wrought-iron table.

Delphine gave Freya a friendly 'Bonjour' before returning to the kitchen for a cafetière of fresh coffee.

A few minutes later, as she placed the coffee on the table, she looked at Freya and asked, 'Was there anything extra you wanted to discuss with me regarding the menus or the cake?'

Freya shook her head. 'No. It all sounds absolutely perfect. You've given us so much choice, thank you. And the layered cake you're making sounds stunning.'

'In that case, if you'll excuse me, I'll get back to the kitchen,' and Delphine turned to Rebecca. 'Buzz me if you need me.'

Puzzled, Rebecca looked at her sister's retreating back for a few seconds, before pulling herself together and pouring Freya a coffee. Delphine always sat in on meetings; why not today? Was this an attempt to get Rebecca used to the idea of her not being there?

As Freya sipped her coffee, Rebecca opened the file and began to update her with all the finalised arrangements so far. 'The photographer is booked for the Friday evening pre-wedding dinner and for Saturday from midday. We did agree you didn't want any photos of you and your friends getting ready, didn't we?'

'Definitely not. Photographs when we're all looking our best are good for morale – we're all of the age when we need flattery and soft lights, I think, rather than before and after pics.' Freya laughed.

'Okay. You have the use of our specially adapted Butterfly Room, where all the brides and their attendants have their hair and make-up done before being helped to dress. The hairdresser and make-up artist are booked and confirmed for you, your mother, Effie, and Clemmie and Angela, your witnesses, and Madeleine, your daughter. Is there anyone else?' Rebecca paused, her pen hovering over the page.

Freya shook her head. 'No. Oh, there might be. No. Forget it. She hasn't accepted yet, but even if she does come, she isn't one of the guests staying here.'

'There are still a couple of bedrooms free, so any extra guests won't be a problem,' Rebecca assured her. 'That reminds me. I need a guest list for place names, et cetera. And also if they have any particular dietary requirements. Any vegans among your friends?'

'There's a couple of vegetarians and Delphine has put several vegetarian choices on the menu, which is great. I'm not sure about vegans. I'll check and let you know.'

'I've booked a local trio for the evening party, and I'll need an update on numbers for that,' Rebecca said, consulting her list again. 'We've used the trio several times before and they play anything from swing and jazz to modern pop and more romantic pieces.'

Freya smiled her thanks at Rebecca. 'Anybody ever told you that you're a super-efficient wedding organiser? If not, I'm telling you now. You've taken all the hassle and made it look easy. I can't thank you enough.'

* * *

An hour later, as she drove back down to the centre of Antibes, Freya found herself thinking how different this wedding was going to be from the first time she and Marcus had married, all those years ago. They had been an on-and-off couple since the time they'd met when Marcus was training as an officer at the Britannia Royal Naval College. He'd gone off to sea at the end of his time at Dartmouth and Freya had concentrated on her own career as an artist and managing an art gallery. They'd always planned on getting married, but it wasn't until she was twenty-nine that the time was right and they finally named the day.

The chosen day had been bathed in blue skies and April sunshine. Her dad had been alive then and had proudly walked her down the aisle of St Petrox Church – the ancient church out on the Dartmouth headland. Clemmie and Angela had been her bridesmaids, and Marcus's boyhood friend, Rufus, had been his best man. Marcus's fellow officers had formed the traditional archway of swords for the two of them as she and her new husband took their first steps together as man and wife. The reception at the now defunct and much-missed iconic Gunfield Hotel on the banks of the Dart had been a wonderful, relaxed affair.

They'd been so happy that day, and for so many years afterwards. It wasn't until Marcus had left the navy and joined the

Foreign Office that things had started to fall apart. He was away so much, sworn to secrecy, she never knew where he'd been until he returned – if then – and in the end she couldn't cope with the stress and worry his job stirred in her. Now Marcus had retired, he was so much more relaxed and life together had, in a way, returned to those heady early days of their marriage when they couldn't bear to be apart.

After parking the car in the large underground car park, Freya strolled down through Antibes, past the newly refurbished Place Nationale and on up to the market, where she was meeting her mother for lunch at one of their favourite restaurants.

When Freya had moved over to live with Marcus in Antibes two years ago, she'd encouraged her mother to think about moving to the Riviera as well. As an only child, she didn't like to think of her mum getting older all alone back in the UK. Effie had hummed and hawed, but in reality, when Marcus had shown her the perfect ground-floor flat in one of the modern complexes near Boulevard Albert Premier, it hadn't taken her long to sell up in Dartmouth and a year ago she'd moved over.

Freya had worried that she would find it difficult to make friends, but within a couple of weeks Effie had enrolled herself on to a French for beginners class, found a yoga teacher so she could continue with her beloved hobby and had met up with Cecily, who lived in the same apartment block and who insisted Effie joined the bridge club to meet people. After which her life became a social whirl. These days, Freya rang her mother every evening to check on her but only saw her when Effie could fit her in to her busy schedule. Today's lunch was one of those times.

Effie was already sat waiting for her when Freya reached the restaurant, a bottle of rosé in the cooler on the table and a glass already in her hand. Freya bent and gave her mum an affectionate kiss on the cheek before sitting down.

'Have you been here long? Sorry if I'm late.'

'I was early,' Effie said. 'How was your meeting?'

'Rebecca has everything in hand – she is so organised. Apart from giving her numbers for the evening party and finding out if anyone is vegan, there is nothing left for me to do. Except go clothes shopping with you?' Freya raised her eyebrows at her mum. 'Or have you found something already?' Picking up the bottle of wine, Freya poured herself a glass. '*Bon santé.*'

'Cecily and I are thinking about going to Monaco one day this week. If we do, I thought I'd have a look around their posh shops,' Effie said. 'Although, in reality, I've got enough frocks hanging in the wardrobe.'

A waiter arrived, ready to take their food order.

'Usual Niçoise salad? Or do you fancy something different?' Freya asked.

'My favourite lunch happens to be the plat du jour today,' Effie smiled.

Freya glanced at the blackboard marked up with the menu, before turning to the waiter. 'Two *magret de canard* with dauphinoise potatoes please.'

As the waiter moved away, Effie turned to Freya. 'So, what's happening with Verity?'

Freya stiffened. 'I've sent her the invite, as you wanted me to, but haven't heard anything. To be honest, I'm hoping that it's too short notice for her to come. She's probably spending the summer on some Greek island or the latest "in" place she's discovered.'

'She's family,' Effie said. 'Hyacinth would be turning in her grave if she knew her daughter was persona non grata at your wedding.'

Freya sighed. 'She's not exactly persona non grata, but even you have to admit Verity can be difficult. She's never been the easiest person to get on with. If Aunt Hyacinth were still alive, it would be different.'

Effie nodded. 'The two of them looked out for each when they were together, that's for sure. Verity would make sure Hyacinth didn't drink too much and Hyacinth stopped Verity from...' she paused.

'Being a pain,' Freya laughed.

'Yes. If she does accept, she'll expect to stay with you and the others at the Villa Sésame. Is there room?'

Freya hesitated before shaking her head. She knew Effie would be cross when she told her the truth, that she was deliberately not mentioning the villa arrangement to Verity because there was no way she wanted her cousin spoiling the run-up to the wedding for the others.

'There could be room, but I don't want her staying there with us. Mum, I'm sorry. I know you worry about Verity because she's your niece, but you know what she's like, she's always been like a chameleon let loose with a blunderbuss with us. One moment she's being charming to everyone, the next she's spitting out her hateful comments here, there and everywhere. The few times I've seen her since Hyacinth died, she was a complete nightmare. I'm the only cousin she has, but she has made it clear down the years that we'll never be close.'

Effie gave a resigned nod. 'Hyacinth and I always hoped you and she would get on better as you both got older, but sadly it hasn't happened. Such a shame she never married. Good, here's lunch,' and Effie smiled at the waiter as he placed their lunches on the table.

Freya too, smiled and said 'Merci,' to the waiter, glad of the reprieve from talking about Verity.

'Clemmie is definitely coming?' Effie asked as she picked up her cutlery.

'Yes, and Angela.' Freya had her fingers firmly crossed as she answered. No way did she want Clemmie backing out because of Verity's presence, if indeed, her cousin decided to show up.

'I'm really looking forward to having time to catch up with them properly – especially Angela, after all she's been through with the accident and Paul's death. Clemmie says the last time she saw her she was still a shadow of her former self. Only to be expected, I suppose, and it will take time. I'm hoping the invitation to Villa Sésame has given her something to look forward to.

8

Two weeks after she received the wedding invitation, Verity was starting to feel irritated with herself. She'd always taken pride in being the kind of person who made snap decisions and stuck to them, even if, when, they turned out to be a mistake. She simply put it behind her and got on with life. Dithering about a silly wedding invitation was so unlike her. Why was she letting the past intrude into the present? Especially as she'd already written to the parents of the bride whose invitation she'd already accepted, apologising for the fact that she was now unable to attend their wedding due to an unforeseen family commitment. The invitation to which she was still thinking about and dithering over her reply.

She and Freya had been close growing up and as young cousins they'd been thrown together at various family events, and every year her mum had driven her down to spend the summer with her sister, Alfreda (Aunt Effie) and Freya. Those summers had mostly been fun and she'd enjoyed playing with Freya and her friends, Clemmie and Angela, until her teenage hormones had kicked in and she'd scornfully told the other three, who were all a year or two younger than her, that they were babies and she wasn't going to play their silly games any more.

From then on, it had been a case of one-upmanship on her part, to show them what they were missing, having to live in a sleepy Devon town, while she lived in London, where everything was so much better. It had all gone wrong when she was sixteen and fourteen-year-old Clemmie had challenged her about how much better life was in a big city. Shouting at her that she should stay up there in that case because nobody liked her down in Dartmouth. In a fit of pique, Verity had shoved Clemmie in the chest and she'd lost her balance, falling off the embankment into the river. Before she'd reached the water, Clemmie had banged her head on one of the concrete landing steps, knocking herself unconscious. All hell had broken loose at that point, with people rushing to pull Clemmie out and get her to the hospital. Verity's summer came to an abrupt end and she was dispatched home without seeing Clemmie again.

The next year, rather than face everyone, she'd managed to talk her mother into allowing her to get a job during the summer and the long Devon holidays with family came to an end. Part of her had welcomed the fact she didn't have to face any of them, particularly Clemmie, but another part had secretly felt peeved about missing out on holidays. Effie had sent a round robin a couple of times a year, telling her how she and Freya were and hoping she was well, and she'd visited occasionally, but she and Freya had never managed to get over their differences stemming from the time of the accident.

She had, of course, been invited to Freya's first marriage to Marcus but had been too busy to take time off work – at least that had been her excuse. So why was she dithering about going to the repeat performance all these years later?

Verity picked up her phone and pressed Effie's number.

Talking to her aunt would maybe make up her mind one way or the other. Effie picked up after only a couple of rings and sounded happy to hear from her.

'How are you, Effie?' The title aunt had been dropped years ago.

'I'm good. Are you coming to the wedding?'

Verity smiled to herself. Effie was straight to the point as usual.

'I'm definitely thinking about it. Spend some family time with you and Freya. We had some good times together, didn't we, especially before Mum died? If I do come, is it okay if I stay with you?'

There was a second's pause before Effie answered.

'Of course you can stay here if you want to, but there's the wonderful Eden Roc hotel on the Cap – much more your scene, I'd have thought.'

'I know the Eden Roc. I've stayed there several times and it's truly lovely but this time I'd rather stay with you. Catch up properly on family news. Besides I haven't seen your new place yet.'

'The thing is I won't be here,' Effie said. 'I'll be with Freya, Marcus and everybody up at Villa Sésame from the Wednesday. Marcus has arranged it for us.'

'Playing happy families, no doubt.' Verity said quietly, unable to keep the bitterness out of her voice.

'I'm sorry. But you're welcome to use my apartment.'

'I'll ring the Eden Roc and reserve a room,' Verity replied. 'At least as a paying guest, I'll be made to feel welcome there.' She sighed as she ended the call with her aunt. So much for spending some family time with Effie and Freya. Her cousin didn't really want her at the wedding. The invitation had come, as she'd thought, because Effie had insisted.

Why had she thought for a single moment that going to Freya's wedding would be an ideal opportunity to try and right the wrongs of the past? It would be easier all round if she stayed away. But if she was serious about making her peace with Freya – and others – which she realised she was, she needed to be there. Decision taken.

She wouldn't phone the Eden Roc hotel. She'd had a far better idea.

A few minutes later, the internet had given her all the contact information she needed. Verity took a deep breath, picked up her phone again and tapped out the number, drumming her fingers on the table as she waited for it to be answered.

'Good evening, Villa Sésame. Rebecca speaking. How may I help you?'

'I understand you are organising the wedding of my cousin, Freya Jackman. I'm planning to surprise her and hope, a) that you can help me and, b) that you can keep a secret from her.'

'I'll certainly do my best. How would you like me to help you?'

Five minutes later, Verity ended the call with a satisfied smile on her face. As far as she was concerned, the twenty-seventh of June couldn't come quickly enough. She was fed up of being the odd one out. It was make or break time with her only relatives.

9

Angela roamed through the house restlessly. It was all well and good making lists and taking decisions to get her life back on track, but putting them into practice was another thing altogether. She paused on the upstairs landing. The door to the master bedroom was firmly closed. When all those months ago she'd finally come home from the hospital, she hadn't been able to bear the thought of sleeping alone in the king-sized bed. Instead, she'd moved into the small guest bedroom with its nun-like single bed. Where she still slept. Slowly, she turned the handle of their old bedroom and pushed it open.

The large bed was unmade, its pillows and bedding folded neatly and placed on the mattress by the headboard. Guiltily, Angela looked at several black bags dotted around the room on the cream carpet. Her friend, Sally, had given her a hand bagging up Paul's clothes and things for the charity shop before Christmas, but Angela had left them there, sitting in the room, since then, unable to find the energy or the willpower to let them go. Remembering Will's words in the car about getting rid of Paul's things, she hurriedly grabbed one of the bin bags and carried it downstairs, placing it in the hallway. There. That was a first positive step. Within minutes, it was joined by four others and the box containing a mixture of trainers and shoes. She'd take them to the charity shop in town tomorrow.

Pleased with her efforts, she returned upstairs and closed the bedroom door again. She preferred the room at the back of the house now – it was quieter for a start, no street noise to keep her awake and worry her. She'd always hated being in the house at night by herself when her imagination tended to run away with her. Angela gave a wry smile, remembering how Paul had often teased her about having the house lit up like a funfair whenever he came home after working late on winter evenings. These last months, she'd even reverted to the childish habit of having the landing light on all night.

She crossed over the hall and looked out of the window at the top of the stairs at the overgrown garden. The garden had been a joint effort in the main. Angela looking after the pots on the patio and the small flower bed at the front of the house, whilst Paul had cultivated a vegetable plot, mown the lawn and supervised the pruning and shaping of the shrubs and the large oak tree that stood at the end of the garden. Now everything about it was looking neglected. She'd pushed the mower around a few times before the wet weather made it a no-go area and had ignored everything else.

Looking at the weeds and the brambles that had sprung up in the flower beds, Angela realised the garden was an absolute tip. Old Mr Chambers, whose next-door garden was a riot of colour, with not a weed in sight and a green lawn sporting the latest in crew cuts, would start complaining soon if she didn't do something about it. When she took the bags to the charity shop, she'd look for a new pair of gardening gloves. She'd sort the garden out this summer – there, that was another decision made. She was getting good at this.

A motorbike revved in the next road, instinctively Angela braced herself as she heard it. A sound that she had previously loved to hear, but not these days.

Angela had actually welcomed the changes Paul's midlife crisis had made to their lives. When Paul had said he fancied buying a motorbike, Angela had even said it was a good idea and helped him to choose the model. Growing up with two brothers who were bike-mad, she knew he'd relish the freedom, not to mention the adrenaline high, riding it would give him. She'd almost bought herself one too, but in the end they'd both decided two was an expense too far and riding pillion would be more fun for her.

Paul had loved his bike. For a few precious months, they'd reverted to the kind of couple they'd been at the beginning of their relationship years ago. He stopped working such long hours and together they'd taken off on summer evenings and at weekends. They'd had a lot of fun in those months. Their only argument being the ponytail he'd wanted to grow, which Angela had flatly refused to countenance, saying she couldn't bear that hairstyle on middle-aged men. If only she'd banned the bike and allowed the ponytail, Paul would still be alive. And she wouldn't be standing here shaking as the noise of the unseen bike faded away.

* * *

The next morning, once the bags were in the charity shop, Angela slammed the boot of her car shut and said goodbye to the volunteer who had helped her unload them. Driving back through town and out into the countryside, she hesitated for a few seconds more than normal at the T-junction before tightening her grip on the steering wheel and turning left, taking the route around the village, away from home and out of her comfort zone.

This route also took her uncomfortably close to where the accident had happened, which was the true reason why she hadn't visited her friend, Sally, recently – she lived in the last house officially still in the village in this direction. The cemetery and the Remembrance Garden were also situated on this side of the village. Places she'd avoided for months, coming with Will when he was home and just occasionally on her own.

Angela glanced at the tin on the passenger seat. She'd finally arranged to see Sally for coffee this morning and had baked her a lemon drizzle cake, knowing it was her all-time favourite, as a small way of saying, sorry I haven't been there for you.

But before coffee at Sally's there was something Angela was determined to do now that she was so close to the Remembrance Garden and a few moments later she parked the car in front of the wrought-iron gates outside the church. Getting out and locking the car, she walked slowly down the gravel path towards the church.

Taking a deep breath to steady herself, Angela pushed open the heavy oak door and walked into the cool sanctuary of the ancient church. All Hallowes In the Field had been built back in the mid-nineteenth century to serve the parishioners of the surrounding villages, but these days it was simply known by the locals as the funeral church. There hadn't been a wedding or a christening within its hallowed walls for nearly fifty years.

Angela hadn't been inside the church since Paul's funeral, but today there was something she wanted to do. Once her eyes were accustomed to the dimness, she made her way towards the side where pamphlets and hymn books were stored. Nearby was a small bank of candles where half a dozen candles were flickering.

Angela dropped a handful of change in the box, before taking a candle, lighting it and placing it carefully in an empty holder. She stood watching it for several seconds before moving away and sinking onto a pew.

Never an overtly religious person, she didn't kneel, she simply sat, closed her eyes and concentrated on emptying her mind.

Leaving the church ten minutes later, Angela walked slowly along one of the paths into the Remembrance Garden. Created half a century ago and incorporating the ancient cemetery, it was a refuge of peace and tranquility, especially in summer when the perfume from roses and other flowers filled the air, and bees and butterflies flitted from one plant to the next. The silvery ash trees, the lichen-covered gravestones, the low beech hedges dividing the garden into sections, the soft cooing of the doves flitting from the trees to the small dovecote and the tweeting of numerous smaller birds – tits of all sizes, sparrows, thrushes – it had become an oasis of calm.

Narrow brick paths wound their way throughout the acres of garden in a series of confusing twists and turns. The first time a grief-stricken Angela had wandered around the garden, she'd got hopelessly lost. These days, the correct path was engraved on her brain: left at the first willow tree, a hundred metres and then right at the rose bed, straight on until she reached the small pond with its water lilies and the wooden bench dedicated anonymously to 'A Wonderful Mum', before taking a final left turn into the section of the garden where the modern memorial plaques were placed in lieu of actual graves.

As she neared Paul's bronze plaque, she was pleased to see it was already being shielded by the olive tree sapling she'd requested to be planted in his memory. Sadly, there were several more plaques placed in the ground nearby since her last visit.

She stood in front of Paul's plaque and tried to relax. She'd read in one of the grief-counselling papers someone at the hospital had handed her months ago that saying your thoughts aloud to the person you'd lost helped in the healing process, even though there was never a reply. Until now, she hadn't felt able to actually put her thoughts into words, but since her decision a few days ago to try to start living her life again, she found there were some things she wanted to say. Glancing around now, making sure there was no one within hearing distance, she took a deep breath and began to speak softly.

'Paul, darling, I miss you so much, much more than I ever thought possible. I should never have encouraged you to buy a bike, although we did have fun for a few months, didn't we? I just wish I could turn the clock back and I would definitely veto buying a motorbike, the jury is still out about growing a ponytail though. And I'm not sure I'll ever stop feeling guilty. Maybe when the nightmares stop completely, the guilt will go away too.'

Angela raised a hand and squeezed her eyes tight, willing herself not to cry.

'I wanted to tell you that Freya and Marcus are remarrying soon in France and I've been invited to be a bridesmaid again. Remember their first wedding? Such fun. I've said I'll go, but I'm not sure I can face it if I'm honest, not without you at my side. Clemmie will be there on her own, of course, so maybe we can console each other. If only I wasn't so terrified of breaking down in public. Anyway, I'm going now, but I promise I'll come back soon. Love you always.'

As she turned to leave, a groundsman appeared wearing protective gear – sturdy boots, leggings and a face shield currently pushed up on to his head. He glanced up and gave her a quick nod and a brief smile as she passed him, before pulling the shield down into place and beginning to carefully strim a nearby overgrown patch of grass.

Angela stumbled as she gave a half-smile in return. She didn't know him and yet she had this unsettling feeling that maybe she did. The look in his eyes as he glanced at her had seemed familiar in the split second before he'd pulled the shield down over his face and turned away to concentrate on his work. Maybe on a previous visit here with Will she'd seen him?

No, mentally Angela gave a shake. The few times she'd come with or without Will the gardens were empty of people, no groundsmen or mourners wandering around. But she couldn't get the thought out of her head that she knew him from somewhere. And from the look of recognition in his eyes when he greeted her, it seemed as though he knew her too.

10

'Ready about,' Jonty shouted from the helm as he prepared for a tack.

'Ready,' Clemmie said and ducked as the boom of the Redwing dinghy with its large red mainsail swung over from port to starboard as Jonty changed course to catch more of the wind. Seconds later, the boat picked up speed again as the wind filled its sails and Clemmie pulled the jib sail line tight before catching it around the cleat.

Early evening and they were on their way back downriver from Dittisham after an exhilarating sail. As they passed Greenway, a heron on the bank took a low flight before landing again a hundred metres or so downriver. A few moments later, Clemmie saw the warning lights flashing on the ferry slip by the unmanned 'Britannia Halt' railway line on the east side of the river to stop the cars leaving the approaching ferry. Shortly afterwards, she watched as a steam train chugged along the line from Kingswear filled with tourists taking the scenic coastal route to Paignton.

Jonty's invitation to join him for a sail this afternoon had been unexpected but one Clemmie had accepted with alacrity and delight. She'd always loved being out on the water, ever since her father had encased her in that first cumbersome life jacket for a sailing lesson. Sailing was something she'd done throughout her childhood and into her twenties, when moving away had meant the river was no longer on her doorstep and sailing became a hobby she only did on rare occasions. Even now she was back and walked by the river every single day, the opportunity to get out on the water was hampered by the lack of her own boat. Being back on the river this afternoon had been wonderful, especially with such a good sailor as Jonty.

As Jonty carefully steered the dinghy as close as he could get to the public slipway alongside the Higher Ferry, Clemmie jumped out and ran for the launching trolley they'd left ready for their return. Ten minutes later and Jonty was pulling the trolley, with the dinghy safely secured on it, across the road into the Coronation Park dinghy storage area.

'Thanks for the sail,' Clemmie said, still on a high from the experience. 'Redwings are such special dinghies. I remember when I was a kid, there were several of Dad's friends who owned one. I think there was a weekly race in summer, when the fleet of red sails made a real splash of colour out on the water. You're lucky to have one, they might be old now, but they're expensive.'

'Not mine sadly. Belongs to a friend who's given me the long-term use of it so long as I maintain it – hence the bottom cleaning and varnishing the other week. You're a good sailor. When you return from France, we must try for a regular sail.'

'I would love that.' Clemmie hesitated. 'Fancy a cold supper at my place? Home-made ham and broccoli quiche, salad, cheese and crusty bread. Nothing special. Might even find a lager in the fridge for you.' She held her breath, waiting for Jonty's answer. It would be the first time he'd been to her cottage for a meal. They'd always met for lunch in town, or an evening drink in one of the pubs when he'd walked her home afterwards, but nothing as intimate as a meal prepared and served for just the two of them at either of their homes.

'Sounds like the perfect ending to a good day,' he replied.

Clemmie gave him a happy smile, ridiculously pleased at his acceptance.

Half an hour later and the two of them were out on the terrace at the back of Clemmie's cottage in Above Town, with its view out over the river and down towards the castle at the head of the estuary.

Jonty helped her carry things out and place them on the large rustic-looking wooden table.

'Great table.'

'My dad made it. It's played a big part in my life. Had some lovely meals around it with friends and family down the years,' Clemmie said, placing the food on the table, as Jonty put crockery and glasses down.

'Your dad was a carpenter?'

'Boatbuilder at Phillips across the river officially; jack of all trades in truth. He loved being busy, but he also loved going fishing and coming back here, lighting up the barbecue, cooking his catch and relaxing with family and friends.'

'You had a good childhood here in Dartmouth?'

'Looking back, I was very lucky. Lots of laughter and love. Dad taught me and my friends to sail and I was given so much freedom. Children today don't get a quarter of the freedom. How about you? Where did you grow up?'

'In the wilds of West Wales,' Jonty said. 'And, like you, I had a lot of freedom.' He concentrated on pouring Clemmie a glass of chardonnay before opening a lager for himself. They clinked glasses and Clemmie waited for him to say more about his childhood, but the subject appeared to be closed with his next words. 'Victoria, Emma and the children have finally booked for Scotland today,' he said.

'When are they off?'

'The week before you go away for a fortnight.'

'What's happening with Hamish? Are you dog sitting?'

'No. Emma told her mother that she wouldn't go if Hamish didn't go as well. Said he was part of the family and a dog called Hamish deserves to go to Scotland for his holidays. Surprisingly, Victoria agreed.'

'So you're free for a week or two,' Clemmie said, biting back on the words, '*no urgent trips to Bristol to see the ex-wife.*'

Jonty nodded as the look on his face told her he knew exactly what she wasn't saying. 'Yes. And I intend to make the most of it by sailing every day if possible.' Jonty grinned at her. 'You game for more crewing before you go to France?'

'You going to let me helm occasionally?' She smiled when Jonty nodded. 'In that case, definitely. We could even enter a couple of races in the regatta, haven't done that for decades.'

Sitting there eating supper together, Clemmie felt a sense of contentment creep over her. Jonty, always good company, seemed happier and more relaxed today than she'd ever seen him before. Was it the effect of knowing Victoria was off his back, so to speak, for a couple of weeks, or something else? As he helped himself to another slice of quiche with the words, 'Best quiche I've had', she toyed with the idea of asking him to be her plus-one for Freya's wedding. But pushed the idea away.

It wasn't until Jonty was leaving later and bent to kiss her gently on the cheek as he thanked her for a wonderful sail and supper that Clemmie heard herself say. 'Now you're free for a few weeks, would you like to come to France with me for the wedding? Not as my plus-one of course, just as my friend?' And immediately regretted asking as she felt Jonty stiffen and step back from her. 'No, of course not. I shouldn't have asked, only I'm rather dreading being on my own there in case...' her voice trailed away, as she berated herself for babbling. 'Anyway, forget I mentioned it,' and Clemmie gave him a bright smile.

'May I give you an answer at the weekend?' Jonty said. 'I need to think about it, but a few days in the south of France sounds good.'

Another kiss on the cheek and he was gone.

Clemmie closed the front door. Had she just embarrassed herself and ruined a beautiful new friendship? And why would he need to think about it? Surely it was as simple as saying 'Yes, I'll come' or 'No, sorry, not my scene?'

After Jonty left, Clemmie wandered through to her work-room. Half an hour making a start on Freya's hat would help clear her head before bed. In the email Freya had sent with her choice of design, she'd said her new engagement ring was a lovely square-cut aquamarine and she wanted her hat to complement it. Searching through the large double wardrobe with fitted shelves where she kept her material stock, Clemmie had found the ideal material. The palest of aquamarine chiffon, the equally pale silk for the lining and she'd put the sinamay that would shape the crown of the hat over the block, ready to start shaping it. It wasn't a compli-cated hat – she'd made so many similar ones down the years – but she wanted to put a couple of special touches to it just for Freya.

Clemmie was deep in thought as she cut the chiffon to size when Angela rang.

'Hi, how are you doing?' Clemmie asked.

'Oh, you know. Good days, bad days.'

'Yes, I do know,' Clemmie said, remembering the bleak days

after her divorce. Not quite the same, but hard to live through. 'It will get better,' she said.

'You are definitely going to Freya's, aren't you?' Angela asked.

'Yes.'

'Good, because I'm not sure I can and one of us needs to be there.'

'We both need to be there,' Clemmie said gently. 'Why aren't you sure about going?'

'I saw a stranger, a man, the other day that brought the whole accident spinning right back.'

'Any idea why a strange man would have that effect on you?'

'I called him a stranger because I don't know his name, but...' Angela paused and Clemmie could hear the hesitancy in her voice as she spoke again. 'I saw him in the Garden of Remembrance, but it wasn't until I got home that I realised who he was. He was the first person on the scene after the accident. And now I can't get him, or the accident, out of my mind again. Freya's wedding will be emotional enough and I'm terrified I'll break down and embarrass everybody – myself included.'

Clemmie thought quickly. Angela was clearly still fragile and time away with friends would be a good thing for her. 'I think a change of scenery and getting away for a short break would be good for you. How about if we fly down together? Would that help? Have you booked your ticket yet?'

There was a short pause before Angela answered.

'Yes, it would help. And no, I haven't booked yet. I keep putting it off.'

'Freya really wants both of us there. I think she sees it as a good omen for this time around, repeating the same line-up, so to speak.' Clemmie gave a short laugh. 'Are you up to driving here, picking me up and driving us both to Bristol? If you'd rather I came to you, I can ask Jonty to drive me out to you.'

'Yes, I can manage the drive to you on my own and the rest of the journey with you will be fine. Who's Jonty?'

'Just a friend,' Clemmie answered, ignoring the note of curiosity in Angela's voice. Now wasn't the time to tell her about Jonty, especially as he hadn't given her an answer about joining her in France. 'I'm booked on the Monday morning flight to Nice. If I can't get you on that one, I'll book the first flight I can for both of us, okay?'

'Thanks, Clem. I'm sorry to be such a pain in the proverbial.'

'You're not. I don't know why I didn't suggest we travel down together before. Email me your passport details and I'll get on with it.'

Finishing the call, Clemmie turned off the workroom lights, closed the door and went through to the kitchen, opened up her laptop and began the laborious task of changing her flight and booking them both onto another one. An hour later, she sent Angela an email.

Booked us on the Wednesday afternoon flight. You need to be here about ten to give us plenty of time to get to Bristol. Drive carefully.

Clemmie sighed. Cutting the stay at the villa short by almost two days was a pity, but being there and helping Angela through a difficult time was more important.

After sending a quick email to Freya telling her of the change of plan, Clemmie thoughtfully switched off the laptop. Why had seeing a man she only knew from the scene of Paul's accident upset Angela so much? Was it all the memories of that terrible day being brought back into focus? Or was there something else?

11

_____

Clemmie glanced at the suitcase on the spare-room bed. Freya's hat, which she planned on putting the finishing touches to once she was at the villa, was already in place, its crown stuffed with scarves to keep its shape, wrapped in tissue paper and its brim firmly wedged flat into position with a strategically placed paperback or two. Clemmie knew from experience that a quick steam and press on arrival would have the hat looking pristine after its journey. Now all she had to do was choose which clothes to take for six days on the Riviera.

Her 'witness' dress for the wedding was ready to go in at the last moment, together with her favourite cashmere pashmina. White jeans, a striped Breton top, a couple of T-shirts, a skirt or two, a sundress, her denim jacket, shoes and a small clutch bag. Her travelling toiletries bag was full with new and unopened miniature tubes of toothpaste, moisturiser and shower gel and a new toothbrush. Still plenty of room in the case for her tablet and e-reader and a pair or two of shoes.

Swimsuit! Almost forgot. The luxury of having the use of a

pool was to be made the most of, and Clemmie pulled open the
drawer where she'd thrown her trusty black swimming costume
at the end of last summer. A bikini she'd bought a couple of years
ago and never worn was in the same drawer. Should she take that
instead? It was the Riviera after all. A knock on the door startled
her and she threw both items into her case to decide later and
hurried downstairs to open the front door.

'Morning,' Jonty said, holding out a bag. 'Doughnuts with
coffee?'

'Sounds good. Come on through.' Clemmie gave him a
curious look. She hadn't seen or heard from him since the night
of their supper. She remembered him saying he'd let her know by
the weekend – well, it was the weekend now. Were the doughnuts
going to turn out to be some sort of apology for when he turned
down her invitation?

'I need coffee first,' Jonty said, acknowledging her look.

Five minutes later, with coffee on the table in front of them,
Clemmie took a bite of doughnut and sighed with pleasure.

'Why are these so delicious and so bad for one at the same
time?' she said, licking her lips clean of the sugar she knew was
there. 'No answer needed. But you do need to tell me why you're
here. Did you come just to feed me with doughnuts?'

'I came for two reasons. First, I got the feeling that you were
worried about going to your best friend's wedding for some
reason? Am I right?'

Clemmie nodded. 'I think Verity – someone I fell out with
years ago – will be there and I'm dreading coming face to face
with her.'

'The second reason I came was to say I'd like to be your plus-
one at the wedding.'

Clemmie looked at him, stunned that he'd used the phrase

'plus-one', rather than friend as she'd suggested. 'Are you sure? Only there has been a slight change to my plans since the other evening.'

Jonty looked at her and raised his eyebrows. 'You are still going?'

'Yes, but almost two days later than planned and I'm travelling down with Angela. You remember I told you about her husband? Well, she's had a bit of a wobble about being on her own and I've promised I'll be moral support.'

'Any reason we can't do that together?'

Clemmie smiled and shook her head. 'No.'

'Okay. I do need to qualify certain things. I'll happily spend time with you on Friday, accompany you to the pre-wedding dinner and to the wedding, but I won't stay at the villa.' Jonty held his hand up as she went to protest. 'I feel it would be taking advantage of your friends' generosity when they don't know me. I have friends in Cannes, which is only twenty minutes away, and I'll stay there. It's an opportunity to catch up with them too. If there is time, maybe I can even introduce you to them.'

'Okay. Thank you. So I can expect to see you sometime Friday?' Clemmie said.

'I'll fly down on Thursday, hire a car and see you at Villa Sésame Friday morning.'

Clemmie smiled at him. 'Sounds like a plan.'

* * *

Freya put the finishing touches to the painting on the easel, placed her palette knife and oil palette on the table at her side and stood back to stare at her work critically. Hugo had asked her to do a couple of abstract paintings for the exhibition and at first she'd demurred – abstract was not in her comfort zone. She'd promised to try but didn't hold out any hope for the paintings to be any good.

The first abstract she'd painted was small and almost totally blue. In her mind, she'd visualised the blue of the moving Mediterranean Sea darkening slowly as it reached the azure blue of the sky with its suggestions of non-defined vapour trails. In the end, she'd been pleased with it and surprised at how much she'd enjoyed the process, although she was unsure as to whether it was good enough for the exhibition. That was down to Hugo.

The one in front of her now, though, had been inspired by a quick visit to her neighbour along the Ramparts – the Picasso Museum. There she'd stood in front of Picasso's famous 'Still life with Bottle, Sole and Ewer' absorbing everything she could from it. For days afterwards, she'd tossed around different ideas in her head, sketched out pencil drawings, until finally she was ready to start painting a still life she'd entitled, 'Communication'. Like Picasso's masterpiece, it was a geometric composition, but with a broken computer screen in the central section, pens, a damaged mobile phone, a diary, fuzzy letters and numbers haphazardly visible in the various sections.

Standing back looking at it, Freya resisted the urge to touch it up in places. It was finished, she had to let it go. Once it was dry, she'd ask Marcus to help her take the two paintings round to Hugo's gallery to join the ones already there for the exhibition. Time to concentrate on the wedding now.

Freya's phone vibrated in the pocket of her painting smock, bringing her back to the present. As she answered it, Marcus appeared on the terrace and she flashed him a smile.

'Clemmie! Everything okay? Angela all right?'

'I think she's rather relieved about travelling down with me rather than on her own, but there is still something not quite right. I'll try and wheedle it out of her on the flight down, although when I tell her my news, she might be a bit cross with me.'

'Why? What news?'

'A friend would like to join me at the wedding, if that's still all right? Not a plus-one, okay? A friend. His name is Jonty and he has friends in Cannes where he'll stay. So is it all right if he comes to the Friday dinner and to the wedding?'

'Not a problem,' Freya said as a smile spread across her face. 'He's welcome to stay at the villa too. There's plenty of room. Looking forward to meeting him.' After a little more chat, Freya ended the call with a cheerful, 'See you and your friend next week then.'

Putting the phone back in her pocket, Freya turned to look a Marcus.

'Clemmie has found herself a partner for the wedding, would you believe? His name is Jonty and she insists he's a friend, not a plus-one. He's going to join us for dinner on Friday evening and come to the wedding but will be staying with friends in Cannes. Clemmie says he doesn't want to impose as we don't know him. Shame. If he stayed up at the villa with Clemmie, it might be the start of something serious.' Freya gave a wicked smile. 'Maybe we can give it a little nudge over the weekend.'

Marcus gave her a warning look. 'Let's wait and see what this Jonty is like before you start pushing Clemmie into his arms.'

* * *

Antibes was busy that Saturday afternoon when Rebecca drove into the large car park near the marina. She and Delphine had given themselves the afternoon off before the Jackman wedding took over their lives for the next week. Rebecca, desperate for a lungful of sea air, planned a walk around the marina and the harbour.

'Are you joining me for a look around the boats?' Rebecca asked as she locked the car.

Delphine shook her head. 'No. *Bibliothèque* first to change a couple of books and then I'm going shopping for a pair of new walking boots. I need to be ready for October,' she added when Rebecca pulled a face at her words.

'Okay. See you at The Blue Lady later,' Rebecca said, naming their favourite meeting place.

The windows of the *capitainerie* with its harbour master's office overlooking Port Vauban glinted in the sunlight as Rebecca made her way slowly through the marina. Now the biggest marina in Europe, it had been so different when she'd first left this port all those years ago as a lowly stewardess on board one of the smaller luxury yachts. It had taken her three years to rise to chief stewardess and graduate to one of the large superyachts now confined to the secure International Quay – affectionately known as Billionaires Quay – away to the right and closed off these days to both curious locals and sightseeing holidaymakers.

Those last few years working in the luxury end of yachting had been rewarding in a monetary sense as they finally led to Villa Sésame, but so exhausting. Standing by the stern of a motorboat similar to one of the earlier boats she'd worked on, she glanced across at the seventeen superyachts on the secure quay. That last year working for a Russian prince on what at the time had been the most expensive superyacht ever built had almost killed her, with the exhausting schedule and rigid protocol demanded of its crew. Knowing that her final salary and bonus at the end of the season was her ticket to freedom and to Villa Sésame had been the only thing keeping her there to the bitter end. But it had truly been worth it. Rebecca smiled to herself. If she had abandoned ship before that last UK port of call in Dartmouth, not only would she have sacrificed a large salary, she also wouldn't have met the love of her life. Or had her son, Bart.

Rebecca wandered on down through the marina deep in thought. Bart, growing up in Antibes, had gravitated naturally to the boats and a life involving them. He was happy to help out when he was home and Villa Sésame was full with guests. Bartender, waiter, breakfast cook, groundsman even, he did anything that was required, before escaping back to his yacht delivery business with a wave and a cheery 'See you soon'.

He used his old bedroom when he worked evenings or early mornings at the villa, but these days he rented a studio apartment down near the marina, saying it wasn't fair to disturb guests at the villa with his comings and goings especially when he arrived back in port in the early hours. He'd promised to try to be home in time to help with the Jackman wedding next Saturday, then maybe she'd have a chance to talk to him about the future afterwards? Would he perhaps be willing to help more when Delphine retired in a few months?

Mentally, Rebecca dismissed the thought. Bart had his own life to lead. Besides, even if he did become more hands-on at the villa, she would have to employ a top-notch chef. The more she thought about it, the more she became convinced that without Delphine at her side, it was inevitable that the whole ethos of the villa would undoubtedly change. And did she really want to carry on without her sister? Perhaps it was time for her to take a break or even move on herself. There was no disputing the fact that it was hard work running a prestigious hospitality business. And that was before Delphine even left.

Rebecca side-stepped a couple about her own age who were happily swinging a little girl between them as they all walked along the pontoon, the little girl squealing 'again, Grandy' every time her feet touched the pontoon. The thought slipped into her mind that it would be years before Bart made her a grandmother and then she'd be a singleton grandparent, like she had been a single mother.

Rebecca smothered a sigh. She'd never stopped hoping she'd meet someone special, get married, maybe have another child or two and a proper family life as well as a successful business. But that ship had sailed and she had to stop feeling sorry for herself. Bart and Delphine were her family and Bart was living proof that she had met someone special, even if it had turned out to be only for a short time.

Leaving the marina, Rebecca crossed the road and began to make her way into town to meet up with Delphine.

Her sister was already at the cafe when she arrived, coffee and a slice of cheesecake on the table in front of her, two or three bags at her side.

'Looks like you had a successful shop?' Rebecca said, glancing at the bags. 'Waterproof jacket and boots?'

'Not to mention jeans and trainers. I've ordered coffee and cake for you,' Delphine said, smiling at the girl behind the counter and indicating Rebecca was there now.

'I've been thinking,' Rebecca began. 'Maybe it's time for me to do something different as well. We could sell up and go travelling together. If you want a travelling companion, that is?'

Delphine forked the last of her cheesecake up and ate it before pushing her plate away.

'It could be fun, but I'm not sure joining me is the right thing for you to do. The timing is wrong. I'm six years older than you and André was on at me before he died to retire and live a little before it was too late. You are too young to retire. Besides...' Delphine hesitated. 'Strangely enough, I'm looking forward to spending some time on my own.'

Rebecca glanced at Delphine. Was she regretting how entwined their lives had always been? Surely not? 'The business is healthy, the villa is in good shape and property has increased in value. If we sell up, we would both have a healthy bank balance and no money worries for the future,' Rebecca added.

'What would you do though?' Delphine asked. 'You'd be bored within three months of not having the villa to organise.'

'I could start crewing for Bart on yacht deliveries. I always did like the seagoing life – it was just the diva-type owners that spoilt it for me. Money in the bank would mean I could choose – we both would have more choice. Maybe I'd buy my own boat and sail around Europe.' She paused. 'Bart's unlikely to want to take over the business so there's no one to leave it to,' Rebecca continued quietly. 'I could even write a tell-all book about running Villa Sésame.' She grinned at Delphine. 'We've both got a few tales to tell about that.'

Delphine gave her a serious look. 'If you really want to change your life, then yes we can think about selling up. We'll have to give it some serious thought over summer. Make some discreet enquiries as to what the market is like. But understand it's on the condition that it's not a knee-jerk reaction on your part to me wanting to become a sleeping partner. And whatever we decide, I'm still retiring on the first of October.'

The waitress placed Rebecca's coffee and cheesecake in front of her at that moment and Rebecca gave her an absent smile as she said 'Merci.' Now the idea of selling Villa Sésame had been voiced she couldn't decide whether the churning in her stomach was due to nerves or excitement at the thought of changing her life. A life that she'd expected to trundle along the same path for several more years was now in danger of coming to an end. And she wasn't sure how she felt about that.

PART II

THE WEEK OF THE WEDDING

12

Monday afternoon and Freya and Marcus were taking advantage of their first day at Villa Sésame and enjoying the pool. After swimming a few lengths each – a sedate breaststroke for Freya, a water-thrashing front crawl for Marcus – they were now relaxing on recliners at the side of the pool, cold drinks on the low tables alongside them.

'Hiring the villa for a holiday before the wedding was a brilliant idea of yours, thank you,' Freya said. 'It's going to be wonderful having all our favourite people here. Combining our wedding and honeymoon like this is wonderful.' She reached out a hand and Marcus caught hold and squeezed it.

'With your exhibition coming so soon after the wedding, I knew you wouldn't want to go away. And we live in such a beautiful place. Plus, it's lovely to be able to treat friends and family, thank them for all their support over the years. Talking of family – Verity?' He raised an eyebrow at her.

Freya sighed before she answered. 'The last time Mum spoke to her she said she'd book a room at the Eden Roc. But whether she did or not, who knows?' Freya shrugged. 'At least staying at the Roc, she wouldn't be up here causing trouble. Mum rang her for me last week to try to get a yes or no for definite from her, but there was no answer. Which could mean one of two things: Verity is being anti-family, as usual, and will simply turn up on Saturday. Or she's taken offence at not being invited to stay here and isn't coming. If she does come, with luck, we'll only see her for the Saturday.'

'Such a shame Madeleine, Sean and Lily aren't arriving until Friday because of work,' Marcus said.

'At least they're staying on until Wednesday and coming back to the house with us for a couple of nights.' Freya smiled happily. 'I can't believe little Lily is nearly three already. I love that age. And we're going to be grandparents again before the year is out? Wonder if they'll have a boy this time? So excited about that.'

Marcus glanced across at her. 'D'you wish we'd had a bigger family?'

'What's the old saying? If wishes were fishes,' Freya said, shaking her head. 'Not really. It was hard enough with just Madeleine at times. Another child in the mix might have broken me when we separated.'

Marcus squeezed her hand again in a conciliatory gesture as she continued.

'I never stopped loving you. I just couldn't cope with... with all the outside demands of your job. Stuff that no longer exists, thank goodness, now you've retired. But you know that. We've talked it all through before.'

'I never stopped loving you either. I couldn't understand at the time why it all fell apart. I do now in hindsight. I can't wait to marry you again and I promise, you, Madeleine and our two grandchildren will be my priority hereon in,' Marcus said. 'Life, Mrs Jackman, is going to be wonderful again.'

Freya smiled. 'When is Rufus getting here?' she asked,

knowing that Marcus was looking forward to seeing his old friend for the first time in several years.

'Sometime on Thursday. He's driving down rather than flying. It's great he's going to be here for the evening "non-stag-do" dinner in Antibes with Hugo and the others.'

'You've got a lot of catching up to do,' Freya said. 'I'm looking forward to our girly session around the pool that evening too. Thankfully, Clemmie and Angela managed to get organised enough to travel down together on Wednesday. I thought we could maybe go to Cannes on Thursday, do a spot of shopping in rue d'Antibes. I'll see what the two of them want to do.'

'So we've got this place to ourselves for tomorrow and most of Wednesday,' Marcus said. 'Time to relax and look forward to the pre-wedding dinner on Friday, our wedding and the party on Saturday. And then we can concentrate on enjoying the rest of our lives together.'

13

Clemmie, not sure how Angela would react to hearing about Jonty being at her side for the wedding weekend, had delayed telling her until they were in the air and on their way to the south of France on Wednesday afternoon. There was less than twenty minutes left of the flight when she finally told her.

As expected, Angela looked upset and Clemmie hastened to reassure her. 'Honestly, it won't make any difference to me being there for you if you have a wobble, okay? I'll be one side of you and Jonty will be the other. You'll like him, I know.'

'How long have you known him? And how much do you like him?'

Clemmie hesitated, unwilling to admit, even to Angela, how much she did like him when she wasn't sure about his feelings towards her.

'Not long, but we get on really well. I've even been sailing with him,' she added, knowing that Angela would recognise the significance of that. 'He's got the loan of a Redwing, imagine. Remember all those years growing up watching them on the Dart, wishing I could be out there? Taken until now for me to actually crew on one.' Mentally she congratulated herself on changing the subject away from Jonty.

Angela smiled. 'I remember the arguments we used to have. You defending the traditional Redwing and me longing for a modern fibreglass Laser of my own – they were so much faster. I wanted to be out on the water by myself. I always thought sailing a Laser would be like speeding on a motorbike – only quieter. Mum stopped me having a motorbike, saying she worried about the boys with theirs and couldn't cope with me having one as well.' Angela bit her lip. 'Who'd have thought all these years later, I'd be counting the cost of finally having a motorbike in my life.'

'It's hard, I know, but it's still early days. I know it's not the same, but when Sam and I divorced, I was in pieces for months, blaming myself for not being enough for him, but deep down I knew whatever I did would never ever be enough. Once a philanderer, always a philanderer,' Clemmie answered quietly.

'The accident is eating me away inside,' Angela said, fighting back the tears. 'I could have prevented it. He could have grown his hair, which I vetoed. I should have vetoed buying the bike instead.'

'Angie, Paul's death was a tragic accident and you have to try to move on,' Clemmie reached out to gently touch Angela's arm. 'Paul enjoyed those months when he finally realised his boyish ambition of being, not exactly a boy biker, but certainly a man who loved the freedom of the open road.' She took hold of Angela's hand and squeezed it. 'I know it's a dreadful cliché to say it takes time, but it's true. Grief is slowly overtaken in a way by a feeling of acceptance, you become grateful for the love you had. It's not easy, but you do need to take a step forward every day, so this weekend we'll try to make some happy memories for you.'

'I know you're right but...' Angela closed her eyes and took a deep breath before looking at Clemmie. 'I'm not sure I'm ever going to get over loosing Paul the way I did.'

An hour later, walking through into the Arrivals Hall at Nice, Clemmie breathed a sigh of relief to see Freya waiting for them. Angela hadn't said a word since and Clemmie was at a loss to know what to do. Hopefully, once they were settled in at the villa and wedding preparations took over, she and Freya together should be able to bolster Angela up and help her to enjoy the weekend. Hopefully too, she would finally be able to confide in them about whatever it was troubling her, because there was definitely something.

That was the hope anyway.

* * *

As Freya parked back at the villa, Rebecca and Christine came out to welcome the new arrivals, and show them to their rooms.

'I'll see you both out on the terrace when you're ready,' Freya said. 'Champagne and nibbles will be waiting. Effie arrived earlier too; she's looking forward to seeing you both again.'

Clemmie was the first to join Freya and Effie on the terrace. After her welcome hug from Effie, Clemmie sighed with happiness.

'What a fantastic place,' she said, gazing out at the view. 'I'm surprised you haven't got your sketch pad out – the Mediterranean in the distance, the gardens, the villa itself.'

'No sketch pad at the moment, but I do have this,' and Freya waved her phone at her. 'So lots of pictures.'

'She's told you about her exhibition after the wedding?' Effie said.

Freya laughed. 'I've told everybody I know about it, I'm so thrilled and excited.'

'Brilliant news,' Clemmie said.

Freya glanced around. 'So, quickly, before Angela joins us, how is she?'

'Definitely not good. May I help myself?' Clemmie asked, pointing to a platter of salmon blinis. 'I'm starving. No food trolley on the plane today.'

Freya held the plate out to her and waited while she ate a blini.

'Delicious. Right, Angela. On the plane coming over, I told her about Jonty joining me here and it set off a bit of a meltdown. Something has knocked her right back and she can't get the accident out of her mind. I think we need to ply her with wine and get her to open up about whatever it is that's wrong, because there is definitely something.'

Freya sighed. 'Difficult, but I agree we have to try to help.'

'Maybe the villa will work its magic on her and she'll talk to us without us probing. Isn't Sésame supposed to have magical properties?' Clemmie said. 'As in Open Sésame. I mean, look at this place,' and she gesticulated around with an open arm. 'It's awesome. Already, I feel happy and relaxed and I haven't been here for an hour yet.'

Freya laughed. 'It does feel like a special place – not sure about magical though.' She turned as she heard footsteps. 'There you are, Angie, come and have some food and a glass of champagne.'

Angela too was enveloped in a welcoming hug from Effie before being allowed to accept the glass of champagne Freya held out.

'What a wonderful place,' Angela said. 'Thank you so much for inviting me to stay. It's going to be five days of living a different life. I don't think I'll ever want to go home.'

'You're more than welcome. And don't forget now Marcus and

I are based in Antibes, you can visit any time, there's always room for you. Although I have to warn you, the house is not up to this standard of luxury.' As Freya spoke, she pulled her sunglasses down from the top of her head, where she'd pushed them earlier and her aquamarine engagement ring sparkled in the sunlight.

'Love your ring,' Angela said.

'Thank you. Marcus insisted on buying it for me as I'd given the first one to Madeleine and I didn't feel I could ask to have it back.' Freya glanced at the third finger of her right hand, where she'd worn her original wedding ring ever since the divorce. 'At least I've still got my gold ring – just got to remember to give it to Marcus before Saturday.'

'I think the hat is almost a perfect colour match for your ring,' Clemmie said. 'I'll fetch it down later and do the finishing touches. Where is your outfit? Not hanging in your room for Marcus to see, I hope?'

Freya laughed. 'No. Rebecca has locked it away for me in the Butterfly Room where we'll be getting ready. I'll show you later and we can put the hat with it and the things you both plan to wear.'

'So do we have any plans for the next couple of days?' Angela asked. 'Personally, I'm quite happy to crash out and stay by the pool for the next forty-eight hours.'

'There will be time for that,' Freya said. 'But you can't come all this way and not do some sightseeing. Tomorrow, I thought we'd go to Cannes – anyone up for a spot of retail therapy along rue d'Antibes? And then tomorrow evening, when Marcus and a few mates go for what he's calling "non-stag-do dinner" down in Antibes, we can have a swim and a girly pizza hen evening around the pool. How does that sound?'

'Like a perfect day in the south of France,' Clemmie said, holding out her glass. 'I'll drink to that.'

14

_____

Rebecca and Christine were in the office on Thursday morning catching up with the mountain of paperwork that the villa seemed to generate every week. All the guests, with the exception of Marcus, were out for the day and the villa was quiet. The only noise was that of the cicadas chittering away in the trees under a cloudless blue sky and the heat, already nudging twenty-nine degrees, was building quickly, rendering the gentle breeze coming off the sea incapable of defusing it. The chambermaids had been and gone for the day, and Delphine was busy in the kitchen helping to prepare the pizzas, salad and desserts ready for the girls' night down by the pool.

With all the women currently in his life out for the day, Marcus had been left to his own devices and was relaxing by the pool, waiting for a special guest of his own to arrive. His best man and oldest friend, he'd excitedly told Rebecca as they'd waved the women off earlier.

'Haven't seen him for a few years, so we have a lot of catching up to do.' He'd also asked her to arrange for a bottle of champagne to be served with their lunch. 'Need to celebrate.'

Christine had just left her to check on supplies in the kitchen
with Delphine and Rebecca was on the phone to the wine
merchant when she heard a car door slam. Finishing the call, she
moved across to the mirror on the wall for a quick 'ready to
welcome guest' check on her appearance and to refresh her
lipstick when she heard Marcus greeting his friend.

'Rufus, you old bugger. Great to see you.'

Rebecca paused, lipstick poised. Unusual name. She'd known
a lovely man called Rufus once upon a time.

'You too,' a quiet voice answered.

A wave of nausea hit Rebecca, freezing her body, as she heard
the unseen man respond to Marcus. His voice was stirring some
long-ago memories that she'd shut down for years.

'This place looks as good as you described it.'

'Freya's taken the girls and Effie off out for the day, so we'll get
you signed in and then we can spend the next few hours catching
up.'

A knock came on the office door before Marcus opened it and
poked his head around. 'Rebecca, my guest has arrived. Come
and meet my best man, Rufus Whelan.'

Rebecca put the cap back on the lipstick, took a deep breath
and, as Marcus opened the door properly, stepped out into the
foyer.

'Hello, Rufus. Welcome to Villa Sésame,' she said as she held
out her hand.

'Becky?' The stuttered word and the shock on his face showed
her that he recognised her instantly as he took her hand.

'You two know each other?' Marcus said, looking at them
both.

Struggling to regain her composure, Rebecca managed to
keep her voice level as she answered. 'We met once a long time
ago. It's good to see you again, Rufus, and it's Rebecca these

days. Now, please excuse me, I need to check on something. I'll buzz Delphine to come and show you to your room.' And she turned back into her office, closing the door behind her, trying to calm her rapid breathing. There was no way she could go through the usual motions of helping a guest to settle in – not when that guest was Rufus. A man she had indeed known in the past.

After buzzing Delphine for immediate help, Rebecca waited in the office behind the closed door until she heard Delphine arrive and take both Rufus and Marcus upstairs to his room. She slumped down onto her office chair and, putting her elbows on the desk, buried her face in her hands. How on earth was she going to deal with this? After all these years, Rufus turning up here at the villa wasn't something she'd ever given any thought to. And how the hell had she missed seeing the name Rufus on the guest list? She remembered asking Freya for a final name list, but she didn't remember receiving one.

She opened the paper file and flicked through and found the list – the name Rufus clearly visible at the top. So either Freya or Marcus had handed one to Delphine or Christine and they'd dealt with it, not bothering to mention it to her, just ticking 'seating place names' off the to-do list.

She was still sitting there when Delphine quietly opened the door and walked in.

'You okay? Are you going to tell me what's going on?'

Rebecca took a deep breath. 'Marcus's guest? Rufus Whelan. I... I knew him a long time ago.'

'And?' Delphine said, giving her sister a serious look. 'A welcome visitor from the past or is he going to be a problem?'

Rebecca shrugged. 'I don't know. Could go either way.'

'Well, for the sake of the Jackman wedding, I suggest you delegate everything possible to me or Christine and stay out of his way as much as you can until Monday afternoon when everyone has left.'

Rebecca nodded. 'Good idea. I'll do that.'

Even as she agreed, though, she suspected that there would be no hiding place from Rufus now that he knew she was the owner of Villa Sésame. He would be sure to seek her out, if only to talk about their shared past. Well, as someone famously said, 'The past is a foreign country' and a return visit there simply did not feature in her plans any more. It had been impossible before and now was far too late. Even if meeting Rufus again had figured in her dreams for more years than she cared to count.

* * *

'What's the name of those islands out there?' Angela asked, looking out towards the Mediterranean as Freya drove them along the *bord de mer* towards Cannes.

'Îles de Lérins,' Freya answered. 'No time this visit, but next time you come we'll have a trip out there. Both islands are lovely, but Saint Honorat is my favourite, with its ancient monastery. There's such a feeling of tranquillity over the entire island, which is wonderful. Visiting there, you get a sense of detachment from the modern world, which we all need sometimes.'

'I could definitely do with some of that,' Angela said.

Freya risked a quick glance at her but decided it was not the moment to start probing with questions as to what was wrong. Clemmie clearly agreed with her as she pointed out the famous Palm Beach Casino complex they were now passing. 'Shame we don't have time for a flutter in there,' she said, skilfully turning the conversation away from Angela.

Ten minutes later, Freya had parked in the large underground car park and the four of them made their way up and out onto the Croisette. Although still relatively early in the day, the temperature was climbing into the high twenties and they were all glad to feel a gentle, if warm, breeze blowing off the sea as they joined the tourists making their way towards the Palais des Festivals. Standing looking at the famous flight of twenty-four steps with its red carpet, Clemmie pulled out her phone.

'Photo opportunity. Effie, please will you?' And she handed Effie her phone. 'We'll do a selfie with all four of us in a moment, but I'd love one of the old gang back together.'

Standing a few steps up, with Freya in the middle, Clemmie and Angela automatically put an arm around her, kicked a heel out behind themselves and smiled for the camera. Angela's smile was a little forced, but she managed to keep it in place until the camera clicked and the three of them moved apart.

'We'll have a quick wander along the Allée des Étoiles du Cinéma and have a look at who's left their handprint on the star-studded ground. There should be a couple of new ones after last month's Film Festival,' Freya said. 'And then we'll head for the shops before finding somewhere for lunch. Okay?'

Rue d'Antibes was busy and the shops were full of temptation, but Clemmie was the only one who gave in to it when she bought a pair of docksiders. 'I do need a new pair if I'm going to go sailing regularly with Jonty and I know I can buy these at home but...' she shrugged. 'It's a souvenir in a way. Every time I wear them, I'll remember today and this holiday.'

Over lunch at a fish restaurant Effie recommended as being one of the best, if not the best, in town, Clemmie glanced at Freya.

'Remember the fish and chips supper we had in Dartmouth the evening before you married Marcus for the first time?'

Freya laughed. 'How could I ever forget? Hen nights were a lot quieter in those days, but we had fun.'

'I remember we kept bumping into Marcus and the others

when we were supposed to be avoiding them,' Angela said, smiling. 'When we all ended up in The Royal Castle, Paul came over to us and said they were going to The Floating Bridge next and would stay there, so we had the town to ourselves. I think we stayed at The Castle though.'

Silence greeted her words and she looked at them.

'What?'

'That's the first time you've brought Paul's name up in conversation,' Freya said gently.

Angela flushed. 'It's hard.'

'The more you do it, the easier it will become,' Clemmie said quietly. 'We're more than happy for you to reminisce.'

Angela bit her lip. 'Every time I say his name, I feel sick with guilt and want to turn the clock back.'

'Which you know you can't,' Effie said, putting her hand on Angela's arm. 'But it could help you so much if you would only talk to your friends, who are ready to listen to you, about Paul and the accident.'

'But aren't we trying to turn the clock back right now, sitting here and thinking about the past when we were all a lot younger,' Angela said, her voice rising with impatience as she deliberately ignored the invitation behind Effie's words. 'And wishing we could reinvent time.'

'No, that's not what is happening here,' Effie interrupted. 'We're simply remembering the good times you all shared and looking forward to more this weekend and in the future. Freya and Marcus's wedding is not re-enacting the past, it's a new beginning for them, even if the supporting cast of bridesmaids and best man are the same.'

'I didn't realise Rufus was coming too,' Angela said. 'He and Paul used to keep in touch, but I...' She shook her head. 'What's he up to these days?'

'I don't know, to be honest, but I'm sure he'll catch us up on his plans over the weekend,' Freya said, realising that Angela would welcome a change of subject and wondering how she could help her friend overcome her sorrow over Paul's death.

Delphine was deep in thought as she returned to the kitchen after she left Rebecca in the office. Why was her normally placid, 'take everything in her stride' sister, so agitated by the arrival of their latest guest? Someone whom she confessed to having known in the past but for some unexplained reason she was clearly wary of renewing their acquaintance.

Mechanically, Delphine slipped her arms through her white chefs' jacket and fastened it.

For the next hour she moved around the kitchen doing things automatically as she prepared lunch. Two cheese and onion flans were soon cooling on the marble slab at the side of the kitchen and were quickly joined by a mozzarella and tomato salad. Marcus had asked for a light lunch for him and his best man as they were dining out that evening, so Delphine prepped a fresh crab salad for them, followed by a bowl of strawberries and cream. As she went to set the table out on the terrace for the two men, she could see and hear laughter as well as the murmur of their voices down by the pool. Would Rebecca agreeing to delegate everything she could and to stay out of the way of the wedding party as much as possible, upset their normal well practised wedding routines? Tomorrow, Friday, with the pre-wedding dinner party officially marking the start of the weekend celebrations could possibly pose the first problem. Thankfully, they had plenty of staff working tomorrow evening so Rebecca should find it easy to stay out of sight behind the scenes. Saturday, the wedding day itself though, could prove to be more of an issue. Rebecca, as the person responsible for making sure the day went smoothly for the bride and groom, spent a lot of time with the bridal party and greeting the guests as they arrived. There was no way she could hide away until the evening party was underway.

Delphine gave a soft groan as she buzzed her sister in the office to tell her lunch was ready. Whilst she knew that Rebecca would do her utmost to avoid any disruption to the wedding weekend, she could only hope and pray that Marcus's best man would feel the same and wouldn't spoil his friend's special occasion.

15

It had slipped Rebecca's mind that as part of the wedding package Marcus had asked for a taxi at seven thirty and back again at eleven the night of his non-stag-do dinner with friends down in Antibes for himself and his single male guest at the villa. By the time Rebecca remembered, the only person available to drive them and collect them later was herself.

She smiled at Marcus, avoided looking at Rufus and slipped into chauffeur mode, glad that Marcus had sat in the front passenger seat. Rebecca concentrated on her driving and the drive down to Antibes was silent until they reached the traffic jam on the coastal road.

'I'd better let Hugo and the others know we may be a little late,' Marcus said, getting out his phone.

Sitting there waiting for the traffic to move, Rebecca made the mistake of looking in the rear-view mirror, where she was accosted by Rufus's eyes staring into hers, and she quickly turned her gaze back to the road.

Ten minutes later, Rebecca stopped near Port Vauban Marina

and, after promising to pick them up when Marcus rang later, watched them walk the short distance to the restaurant. It was then that she registered Rufus's limp for the first time and briefly wondered how he'd received it.

* * *

Back at the villa, with all lights lit in and around the pool, the mood was relaxed. The sun, setting behind the red volcanic rocks of the Esterel mountains, had turned the sky into an intense inferno of scarlet. The four women had swum, eaten pizza and were now lying on sun loungers in the balmy evening air enjoying glasses of Prosecco and watching the vivid red sunset.

'That sky is something else,' Clemmie said. 'I've never seen a sunset like it. It's quite frightening – like the world is on fire behind the Esterel mountains.'

'Sunsets like this occur regularly. I've tried to paint one a couple of times,' Freya said. 'But it's hard to capture the true intensity of those reds.'

'Let's hope the old saying "red sky at night, shepherd's delight" holds true over here and the weather is beautiful again for the weekend,' Angela said.

'It will be, it's June and it's the south of France,' Freya answered confidently. 'Either of you have any plans for tomorrow, apart from Clemmie introducing her plus-one to us all? So looking forward to meeting him.' She threw a mischievous glance in Clemmie's direction.

'He's a friend,' Clemmie protested. 'Nothing more.'

'I've got a few last-minute things to sort out in the morning, but I'll be around afterwards,' Freya continued, acknowledging her friend's words with a knowing smile and a nod.

'I thought I might go for a wander around Antibes,' Angela said. 'Effie, would you like to join me? Give me the guided tour, as you're a local now?'

'I'll even treat you to lunch at my favourite restaurant,' Effie said.

As they all lay there, a comfortable silence surrounding them, they heard a car travelling up the gravel drive towards the villa.

'Rebecca's back from dropping off the men,' Freya said. 'Sounds as though someone has followed her in.' This as they all heard another car arrive and doors slam and the departure of a vehicle down the drive.

Five minutes later, they could hear Rebecca talking as she was clearly accompanied by someone as they both made their way down towards the pool. Freya was the first to sit up and, as Rebecca and her companion came into view, swore loudly.

'Freya, language,' Effie admonished quietly.

'You have a surprise guest,' Rebecca said, her happy smile fading away as she sensed a sudden tension descending. She glanced from a furious Freya to a smiling Verity, who had assured her she was family and would be welcome, but clearly wasn't. Why, oh why, hadn't she at least mentioned the phone call to Marcus?

Freya finally found her voice. 'Verity. What happened to staying at the Eden Roc?'

Verity hesitated. 'I thought it would be much more fun to spend time here with family and friends,' She moved across to Effie to give her a kiss and a hug before turning to Freya and the two exchanged a somewhat awkward air kiss. Finally, Verity's glance travelled across to Clemmie and Angela. 'Hello, you two, long time no see,' she said quietly.

'Not long enough,' Clemmie muttered, standing up and gathering her things together. 'I'm going to bed. I'll see you all in the morning. Thanks for a lovely day, Freya. Night, everyone.' And a shaking Clemmie walked away.

Both Freya and Rebecca watched her go with sinking hearts. Freya because she hated seeing Clemmie upset and was furious with Verity for turning up without warning, whilst Rebecca worried that she'd inadvertently made a major mistake and Freya's wedding weekend was in danger of being ruined.

'Can I bring you anything else?' Rebecca asked. 'More pizzas? Another bottle of Prosecco?'

Freya shook her head. 'No thanks.'

'I'll leave you to it then. Enjoy the rest of the evening,' Rebecca said flatly.

'I'd love a G & T,' Verity said. 'I don't like Prosecco particularly,' she added, glancing at Freya, who glared at her before turning to follow Rebecca back up to the terrace.

'Rebecca, may I have a word?'

'Freya, I'm so sorry. I get the feeling you're unhappy about your surprise guest staying here. I can ask her to leave if you want me to.' They both spoke at once and stopped.

Rebecca gestured at Freya to go first, waiting for the inevitable angry words from an upset client. They didn't come.

'What story did Verity spin you?' Freya asked quietly.

'That she was your favourite cousin and you were upset she'd had to say no to the invitation originally, but things had changed and she could make it now, so she thought it would be fun to surprise you.'

Freya nodded as she listened. 'That sounds like a typical Verity story. I'm sorry she lied to you, but please don't blame yourself for being taken in by her. I'm sure she didn't give you much choice in the matter.'

'I do feel guilty though,' Rebecca said. 'The very least I should have done was to mention it to Marcus and checked you'd be okay with her surprising you. Like I said, I can tell her she's not welcome and ask her to leave if that's what you want.'

Freya shook her head. 'That would upset Effie – she's very protective of her only niece. No, now she's here, she'll have to stay. Hopefully Effie will keep her in line – she's about the only one who has a hope in hell of doing that. I just hope Clemmie will cope.'

Rebecca raised her eyebrows.

'Long story,' Freya said. 'Let's just say she's not Clemmie's favourite person. Thankfully, Clemmie's plus-one is arriving tomorrow so that should help. Right, let's get that G&T Verity demanded and I'll take it down to her.'

'I can do that,' Rebecca said.

'I know, but in this instance I'd rather like to do it,' Freya said, grinning at her wickedly. 'It will be heavy on tonic water, ice, lemon slices and very little gin. She'll hate it, especially when I tell her I personally made it for her because I know she's trying to be good, so don't worry, she won't complain to you.'

Rebecca looked at her, a questioning look on her face. 'Does she have a drink problem?'

Freya shook her head. 'No, but my aunt, Hyacinth – her mother – did, and I know my mother worries about Verity inheriting that particular gene.'

When Freya got back down to the pool, both Effie and Angela were sipping their drinks and listening to Verity extol the joy of eating at some London restaurant or other.

Freya held out the large glass she'd carried down carefully to Verity. 'The drink you ordered, mixed by my own fair hand.'

'Thank you.' Verity took the glass and took a long drink and, failing to conceal her dismay at the taste, stared at Freya, who stared back.

'Did I go too easy on the gin? Sorry,' Freya said, smiling at her cousin. 'Never mind, I'm sure it's refreshing. Besides we don't want you taking after aunt Hyacinth, do we?' Freya instantly felt guilty at her catty remark but she was determined Verity wasn't going to spoil the weekend for everyone by playing silly games.

16

'Marcus, would you ask Rebecca to bring a bottle of cognac and two glasses down to the pool when we get back please?' Rufus paused. 'And then disappear.'

The two of them had said goodbye to Hugo and the others after dinner at the restaurant and were walking along the ramparts towards where Marcus had suggested they met Rebecca. 'Need to walk dinner off and get some fresh air,' he'd explained when he rang to say they were ready.

Marcus glanced at Rufus. 'You went quiet on me today, but if I were to take a wild stab in the dark, I'd guess that Villa Sésame's owner is a certain Becky from years ago?'

Rufus nodded. 'Got it in one. Bit of a shock coming face to face with her again, but thinking about it, I'd quite like to talk to her in private. Renew our friendship.'

'Bit late in the day – by about a quarter of a century. What if she doesn't want to talk to you? She seemed uptight this evening when she drove us down. Not known her to be so silent before, she's usually quite a bubbly person.'

Rufus shrugged. 'I'd just like a drink with her for old times' sake. See where it goes, if anywhere.'

Marcus sighed. 'Okay. But...' He stopped and pointed to a parked car. 'There she is,' and the two of them crossed the road to where Rebecca was waiting.

'But what?' Rufus asked. 'I promise not to upset her or cause a problem over the weekend.'

'Just make sure you don't,' Marcus said. 'I don't want Freya upset. Or Rebecca for that matter. She's pulling out all the stops for our wedding.'

Before Rufus could reply, Marcus had opened the passenger door.

'Hi, Rebecca, sorry if we've kept you waiting,' and they both got in the car, Marcus in the front as before.

* * *

If Rebecca was surprised by Marcus's request for 'a bottle of cognac and two glasses down by the pool please' when they got back to the villa, she didn't show it.

'I'll put the car away and bring it down to you,' she said.

Walking carefully towards the pool with the requested drinks, Rebecca could see Rufus standing by one of the sun loungers where a figure was reclining. A female figure who was now sitting up and looking at Rufus with interest. There was no sign of Marcus.

Rebecca smiled to herself. *Nice try, Rufus.* He'd clearly tried to trick her into meeting him on her own – only the presence of a certain unwanted guest had thwarted that.

'Good evening again, Ms Stoppard,' Rebecca said frostily, moving forward and placing the tray on the nearest poolside table without looking at Rufus. She was a long way from even thinking about forgiving Verity for the surprise stunt she'd pulled and upsetting Freya, but her years of dealing with difficult guests on board the luxury yachts had taught her being professional and dignified was the only way to behave. Besides, Verity's presence down here was the perfect opportunity to postpone the meeting Rufus was clearly determined to have with her.

'What a delightful surprise. A nightcap with lovely company.' And Verity flashed a smile at Rufus. 'Long time no see, Rufus.

'Verity.'

Rebecca smothered a smile, knowing full well that Rufus hadn't anticipated anyone else being down by the pool. She'd sensed he'd greeted Verity through gritted teeth and was now completely wrong-footed and having to respond and be polite to a woman he clearly hadn't expected to see.

'Well, I'll leave the two of you together to enjoy a nightcap,' Rebecca said cheerfully. 'I would be grateful if you would please ensure to lock the French doors on the terrace when you both retire. Goodnight,' and Rebecca turned away.

Back in the villa, she checked the main door was locked, that the tall electronically controlled wrought-iron gates at the entrance drive to the villa were closed and secure before making her way upstairs to her apartment.

Standing in the shadows by the open balcony that overlooked the gardens and the pool, Rebecca noted that Rufus, still standing, was empty-handed, whilst Verity was now sipping a drink. Too far away to hear their voices, but Verity's tinkling laugh was clear.

Wearily, Rebecca got ready for bed. What a catastrophe of a day. Verity muscling her way in as an unwanted guest was bad enough from Freya's viewpoint, but while Rufus was a welcome and wanted guest of Marcus and Freya, for Rebecca he was definitely an unexpected and unwanted guest at Villa Sésame. She could only hope and pray that nothing else was going to upset the weekend.

One thing was clear though. Getting Marcus to order a nightcap for the two of them, Rufus had shown how cunning he could be in his determination to speak to her, to catch up on their past. She was definitely going to stay out of his way as much as she could for the next three days. Life was sure to get too complicated if she didn't.

* * *

Sitting down by the pool with a clearly disgruntled Rufus, who refused to engage in anything more than a monosyllabic conversation of 'Yes' and 'No', let alone reminisce about the few occasions they'd met in the past, was not Verity's idea of fun. In the end, she stood up, picked up the bottle of cognac and poured herself a smallish measure before looking at Rufus.

'I'm off to bed. I'll leave you to do the locking up as requested. Goodnight.'

As she turned on her heels and began to make her way indoors, she registered the barely concealed sigh of relief that Rufus breathed.

Once back in her room, Verity took off her make-up before wandering out onto the balcony, drink in hand. Standing there, breathing in the tang of salt in the night air, she sipped her cognac thoughtfully. What the hell had possessed her to come here this weekend? Some misguided sense of family loyalty? Of wanting to belong instead of feeling like an outsider every time they met up?

Verity smothered a wry smile. Freya might be her only cousin, but they'd not been close since the summer of the accident. She knew, like Clemmie, Freya had never forgiven her for the accident all those years ago. An accident she'd never apologised for. Instead, rather than face Clemmie, she'd stayed away from Dartmouth.

Down the years, both her mother and Effie had tried on numerous occasions to heal the rift between her and Freya, and whilst it was true the edges had become civilised, the animosity still lay buried just beneath the surface.

Verity, though, would never forget how kind Effie had been when her mother had sunk deeper into the depths of alcoholism and depression before it took its final toll. Telling her over and over again that the three of them were family and should always be there for each other, but whilst Verity had seen more of her aunt and enjoyed her company since then, she'd never been able to completely relax with Freya and consequently their relationship was still fraught with tensions every time they met.

As for this weekend, she should have stuck to her original plan and gone to Sussex for the society wedding of the year. At least there she'd have been rubbing shoulders with people who liked her, as well as with A-list celebrities, instead of being ostracised by her own family. Even Effie had seemed subdued with her welcome when she'd arrived out of the blue this evening.

Verity took a sip of her cognac. Freya giving her that insipid drink, insinuating that she needed to watch her drinking, had made her cross. She had no intention of following her mother down that particular path.

And Rufus's reaction when he'd come face to face with her by the pool had been less than flattering. Fleetingly, Verity wondered who he'd been hoping to meet there? Angela? Clemmie? She couldn't imagine either of them being his type.

Perhaps it had been a mistake to come and stay at the villa. She should have gone to the Eden Roc and simply turned up for the wedding on Saturday. Too late to change things now, she was here and would have to make the best of it. She'd not run a successful business for all those years without learning how to mask her true feelings from people. It was time to put that mask on and try to build bridges with her family. She'd spend time with Effie, chat with Freya and stay away from Clemmie.

17

Six-thirty, Friday morning, and Rebecca was sat out on her balcony with her first coffee of the day mentally trying to prepare herself for the busy weekend ahead, her phone and laptop on the table at her side.

The early-morning quiet was absolute. No traffic noise, a sea breeze wafting gently around the grounds, mingling with the perfume from the old-fashioned roses in the garden below and the cicadas still sleeping. Bliss.

This time of day had become a favourite of Rebecca's in her time as a stewardess. She'd lost count of the number of mornings she'd crept out on deck, made for the bow of whatever yacht she was currently working on and sat there hugging her knees, watching the dawn come up, listening to the rigging of nearby sailing yachts slapping against masts, the screeching of the gulls as they hovered and swooped in the air above. Those mornings were a large part of what she missed about that life.

Now, as she struggled to keep her thoughts on track for the weekend, she found herself wondering – did she miss it enough to sell up, buy her own boat and live a nomad's life along the

Mediterranean, like she'd suggested to Delphine? Her sister seemed happy at the prospect of solo travelling and Rebecca could only hope she wouldn't find it lonelier than she anticipated. Rebecca suspected that she personally, would find it difficult. No, thinking about it, she'd definitely prefer to be land-based.

She and Delphine had shared the villa's journey together from day one. Even when Delphine had been married to André, the two of them had remained close, looking out for each other and able to judge the other's mood and tell when they were worried about something. And they'd never ever lied to each other – always the truth between them. They each knew that whatever one of them told the other in confidence, that was the way it would remain – confidential. Except for that one crucial confidence that Rebecca had kept to herself even though she knew Delphine wouldn't judge her.

Rebecca's phone pinged with a text message, pulling her out of her reverie. Glancing at the caller ID, she quickly opened it.

Need to talk.

No time like the present, Rebecca thought and pressed the call button.

'You okay, Bart? What's up?' she asked when he answered.

'I'm not going to get back in time to help this weekend, like I promised, I'm sorry. There's a problem with the engine. The guys have ordered a new part and will be fitting it tomorrow and I should be able to begin to head home early Sunday morning.'

'No worries, darling, I always have a back-up plan.' And, for once, Rebecca couldn't help feeling grateful that Bart had been delayed. 'Frustrating for you though, hanging around. Will you be staying for a bit when you do get back or have you got another delivery lined up?'

'No deliveries booked in before the middle of July, so I'll be home for a while.'

'Good,' Rebecca said, her spirits lifting at the thought of Bart being home for a few weeks 'Your help will be needed for the fourth of July party. The three of us also need to have a family conference sometime.'

'What about?' he asked.

Rebecca hesitated. She didn't really want to tell Bart over the phone but thought it only fair to prepare him, give him time to think, maybe come up with a solution.

'Delphine wants to retire in October, which means I have to decide what I'm going to do with the Villa Sésame.'

'You'll carry on, won't you? Hire a chef and delegate more.' His voice was light but Rebecca heard the undertone of concern.

'You sound like Delphine,' Rebecca laughed. 'We'll talk about it when you get back. See you whenever you get here.' And Rebecca sighed inwardly as she ended the call. If only it was that easy to decide about the future.

Bart had asked one of the questions she didn't know the answer to. Would she carry on without Delphine? Right now, she had no real idea or desire other than wishing the weekend was over.

* * *

Clemmie, having tossed and turned the night away, felt shattered when she dragged herself out of bed. If Jonty hadn't been coming later, she'd have pleaded a migraine and stayed hidden away in her room all day. Forty-three years might have passed since she'd last seen Verity, but she still felt an intense dislike of the woman. It had been childish and immature of her to leave the others last evening when Verity arrived, but try as she might to be grown-up and accept her presence and push the childhood accident out of her mind, Clemmie hadn't been able to. In fact, it had all come flooding back in horrific detail the moment Verity appeared. The terror she'd felt as she'd fallen, the water closing over her as her body banged against the concrete landing steps, the days in hospital over fears of concussion. The frightened look on her parents' faces that day as they'd rushed to the small cottage hospital on the other side of the embankment, just metres away from where the accident happened. Verity had never personally apologised to her parents either. Clemmie knew that Effie had spoken to her mum and dad on Verity's behalf, but Verity had never ever mentioned the accident on her rare visits to Dartmouth afterwards.

But standing under the powerful shower in her en suite, with the water assaulting her senses and pounding her awake, Clemmie knew she had no option but to pull herself together for Freya's sake.

Once out of the shower and dry, she dressed quickly, pulling on a favourite summer sundress, and doing her make-up with extra care, before going downstairs with her fingers firmly crossed that she wouldn't bump into Verity.

After having breakfast with Angela out on the terrace and silently thanking the gods that there was no sign of Verity, Clemmie wondered about escaping to her room to do the last of the adjustments to Freya's hat before Jonty arrived. There was no sign of Freya – she and Marcus appeared to have skipped breakfast. Delphine had been a bit vague when Clemmie had asked her if she knew where they were.

'I think they had some last-minute things to do in town, I expect they'll turn up soon,' was all she'd said before hurrying away.

Angela had shrugged when Clemmie looked at her. 'I've no

idea either, but I think I'm going for a walk around the grounds. Freya did say Rebecca mentioned that there was a renovated old stone borie on the far edge of the villa land beyond the olive grove. I'd like to see if I can find it.'

'Is that some sort of stone-built hut?' Clemmie asked.

'Yes, a shepherd's hut left over from the time when the villa would have had much more land extending out to the back country. Paul had me traipsing all over Dartmoor one year looking for long-lost huts and I've been interested in their history ever since. I'd quite like to see if these French ones are similar.'

'Want some company? I'd rather Freya tried the hat one more time before I put the final stitches in, but as she seems to have disappeared...' Clemmie hesitated. 'And to be honest, I'd rather not come face to face with Verity without at least one of you by my side.'

'Grab your sunglasses then and let's go.'

Clemmie burst out laughing.

'What?' Angela asked.

'At home in Devon, even in June, you'd probably have told me to grab my wellies or a coat.'

'True.'

Together, they walked across the wide crazy-paved terrace at the back of the villa and made their way down the shallow steps leading towards the paved area away from the swimming pool, where they could see Rufus swimming a powerful backstroke.

As they walked, Angela said, 'I love everything about this villa, don't you? These pale, almost golden stone walls that are everywhere here, holding up the terraces and creating secret little cosy niches, are wonderful.'

'Looks like they're erecting the bower of flowers for the wedding ceremony tomorrow,' Clemmie said, pointing in the direction of some workers busy attaching flowers and greenery to the arch under which Freya and Marcus would stand for the ceremony.

Leaving the immaculate lawn behind them, they wandered into the well-tended olive grove.

'What time is Jonty arriving?' Angela asked.

'Mid-morning, I think.' Clemmie looked at Angela. 'Do you think Freya would mind if he and I disappeared for a few hours after he's arrived and I've introduced him to everyone? I'm dreading having to be civil to Verity all day. The dinner tonight is going to be difficult enough, as for tomorrow...' Clemmie shrugged.

'Probably best if you do make yourself scarce for a few hours, rather than risk creating an atmosphere,' Angela said thoughtfully. 'You like Jonty, don't you?'

Clemmie nodded. 'Yes. I feel a connection between us, but I'm not sure he feels it too, although he must like me a little bit, agreeing to come here.' She sighed. 'I have to admit to being worried about how he's going to react to me being so anti-Verity. Having to explain why a teenage episode from so many years ago is still causing waves is difficult. Everything should have been forgotten, even forgiven, by now – we're all grown-ups for goodness' sake.' Clemmie shook her head. 'But Verity has never once said sorry to me for doing what she did, so I can hardly be expected to forgive her, can I? Or should I apologise first? I know saying what I did was unkind and provoked her.'

'I'm not sure you and Verity will ever be close friends, but if you feel you were unkind and provoked her action all those years ago, then you'd probably feel better if you said sorry, even if you can't forgive her. If you want my opinion, I think she was jealous of the three of us growing up, especially Freya, and she's never got over that jealousy. We all knew her home life wasn't brilliant, particularly after her dad and mum split.'

Clemmie nodded thoughtfully. 'Think you may be right.'

'Sometimes, even when you know you should do the right thing and admit you're in the wrong so you can be forgiven, it's impossible to imagine ever being forgiven.' Angela's voice was barely above a whisper and Clemmie, glancing at her, quickly saw her eyes filling with tears.

'Are you all right?'

Angela nodded shakily as she searched in a pocket for a tissue. 'Sorry. My emotions are all over the place since Paul died.' Locating a tissue, she wiped her eyes and blew her nose.

'Do you want to talk about it?' Clemmie asked gently.

'No thanks, I'm fine now. Let's walk.' And the two of them wandered on through the olive grove, each lost in their own thoughts, before Angela pointed ahead. 'That pile of stones looks like it might be the borie.'

'It's smaller than I expected,' Clemmie said a few moments later as they stood alongside the shelter and she bent down to look in through the open archway. 'Looks like it was a question of sitting rather than standing inside. Bit claustrophobic for me,' and Clemmie straightened up. 'Still, I suppose in bad weather, one would be grateful to simply have somewhere to shelter. Nice view though,' and she gestured at the countryside rolling away into the distance, dotted with several small villages and a bigger town in the distance.

Angela glanced at her watch. 'Better turn back now. I quite fancy another coffee. Not to mention that you want to be there when Jonty arrives.'

18

When Clemmie and Angela reached the terrace, Delphine had cleared the breakfast table and was busy placing champagne flutes, a jug of freshly squeezed orange juice and an ice bucket with a bottle of champagne nestling in it.

'Any particular reason for the Buck's Fizz?' Clemmie asked. 'Not complaining, just wondering.'

'I'm sure Freya and Marcus will explain when they return,' Delphine said with a smile. 'Ah, here they are now.'

Clemmie and Angela turned to see a smiling Freya and Marcus walking hand in hand towards them, followed by Effie.

'You two are looking very happy,' Angela said.

'That's because we are,' Marcus replied. 'We did the official French civil wedding ceremony this morning. Freya is, once again, officially Mrs Jackman.'

'But what about the wedding here tomorrow? And what about us being witnesses? And why did you sneak off without telling us?' Clemmie demanded.

'Have a glass of Buck's Fizz and we'll explain,' Freya said. 'Here in France, marriages have to be conducted and registered by the *maire* at the local *mairie*. It's impossible to get married legally here at Villa Sésame – or anywhere else – without first obtaining the all-important legal piece of paper with the *maire's* signature and the obligatory rubber stamp. The marriage simply wouldn't be recognised. We did try to do the deed last week, but this morning was the only time they could fit us in.'

Freya paused and started to hand around the glasses of Buck's Fizz that Marcus had poured. Verity and Rufus joined them at that moment and Freya handed them both a glass.

'We deliberately didn't tell anyone about this morning because as far as we are concerned tomorrow is our real wedding day when we'll be in this wonderful place surrounded by our family and friends. And tomorrow is the day we'll celebrate in the future as our anniversary, but we can't let this morning go without a little celebratory toast.'

'Freya and Marcus,' Rufus said, holding up his glass. '*Félicitations,* as they say here. Let the wedding weekend begin.'

As everyone raised their glasses in a toast, Rebecca showed a couple out onto the terrace.

'Madeleine, darling, you're here,' Freya said, putting her glass down and rushing to pick up and hug her granddaughter, Lily, before turning to her daughter and husband. 'You're both looking really well.'

Madeleine pulled a face. 'Could live without the morning sickness this time round.'

'Come and sit down and have a glass of orange juice,' Freya said.

Effie moved closer to Angela. 'About our wander around Antibes today, do you mind if I bail out on you? I didn't realise Madeleine would be arriving so early and I'd quite like to stay and spend some time with her and Lily.'

'Of course,' Angela said, her heart sinking. With Clemmie

planning on spending time away from the villa with Jonty once he'd arrived, she'd be left to her own devices.

'If you'd like some company, I wouldn't mind a trip into Antibes.' Verity smiled diffidently at Angela. 'Unless you and Clemmie have plans?' and she gave a quick glance in Clemmie's direction.

Angela shook her head, trying to think of an excuse as to why the two of them joining forces was not a good idea, and failed to find one. 'No, Clemmie has her own plans. If you're sure, I was thinking of asking Rebecca if she'd mind running me down to the *bord de mer* and I'd walk in from there.'

'Sounds like a plan,' Verity said. 'Shall we leave in say, quarter of an hour?'

Angela nodded, even as she wondered how Clemmie would react to hearing who her companion was for the day, but as she moved across to talk to her, Clemmie was on her way across the terrace to greet a new arrival.

'Jonty, you've made it,' and Clemmie happily returned the kiss that Jonty placed on her cheek. 'Come and meet everyone.'

* * *

Standing at Jonty's side as she introduced him to her friends, Clemmie relaxed as she sensed everyone warming to him. She even managed to introduce him briefly to Verity without stumbling over her words. Watching him being effortlessly charming to her friends, Clemmie smiled. The despair that had descended on her with Verity's appearance last night had lifted now Jonty had arrived. With him at her side, she'd cope and she was once again looking forward to the weekend.

As Marcus and Rufus claimed Jonty's attention for a few moments with some typical male banter, Angela nudged her arm.

'Nice. Really nice,' she whispered in Clemmie's ear. 'Are you still planning on the two of you spending a few hours away from the villa?'

Clemmie nodded. 'Why?'

'Effie wants to stay here with Madeleine and Lily rather than showing me the sights of Antibes and I've agreed to Verity taking her place.' Angela looked at Clemmie anxiously. 'That's not a problem for you, is it?'

'No, of course not. I think she knows down here quite well, so she'll be able to show you the best places.'

'I'll see you later then.'

Clemmie watched as Angela made her way over to Verity and the two of them said their goodbyes before leaving together.

It was another half an hour before Clemmie and Jonty managed to say their goodbyes and leave Freya and her family to enjoy some time together.

Clemmie smiled when she saw Jonty's hire car – a sleek convertible, with the roof already folded away. 'Very south of France,' she said as he opened the passenger door for her and she gave Freya a happy wave.

Jonty drove down to the *bord de mer*, before turning right to go west along the coast. 'I thought we'd visit the castle at Mandelieu-la-Napoule. Have you ever been there?'

Clemmie shook her head. 'No.'

'We'll have lunch first at a restaurant my friends have recommended near Bocca and then head along the coast. Okay?'

'Sounds great,' Clemmie said, settling back in her seat to enjoy the drive.

Twenty minutes later, they were sitting at a table on the terrace of a restaurant overlooking the sea, and Clemmie raised her glass of rosé towards Jonty and his non-alcoholic lager.

'*Bonne santé*. It's so lovely to have you here. Thanks for coming. I definitely owe you one.'

Jonty shook his head. 'No you don't. I like spending time with you and being here knowing I can't be dragged away by a phone call gives us a chance to talk properly and for me to try to explain some important things without the danger of interruption.' He glanced at her. 'But, first, Verity did turn up then.'

Clemmie nodded ruefully. 'Last night and I'm afraid I ran to my room rather than spend any time with her.'

'What happened between you two?'

'She nearly killed me when I was fourteen,' Clemmie said briefly. 'I know I should be over something that happened forty-three years ago but...' she shrugged. 'It's the fact that she's never said sorry in all that time. Although, to be fair, I've avoided coming face to face with her as much as she's avoided me. But she could have written me a short note. Told my parents she was sorry.' Clemmie took a drink of her wine before turning the subject away from herself. 'What important things do you want to tell me?'

'Things that I need and want you to know about me, my past and my marriage,' Jonty said, recognising that Clemmie wanted the conversation changed.

'Sounds ominous.'

Jonty shook his head. 'More complicated than ominous.'

There was a brief pause before he continued.

'Victoria is the major complication. I've already told Emma about you and she's looking forward to meeting you, but Victoria...' He shook his head. 'I told you she's my ex-wife, which isn't strictly true. She will be very soon, the decree nisi is due on the first of July, but right now she is still arguing about the business we run together, which has been kept separate from the divorce. My preference is for Victoria to keep the business and run it herself – it's far more hers than mine anyway – involve Emma more and I move on and out. It's not as if I want buying out, I just want out. She, on the other hand, wants us to keep working together because she says we make a good team.'

The waiter arrived at that moment with their food – a salad Niçoise for Clemmie, grilled fish for Jonty and a bowl of frites for them to share.

As the waiter left them, Clemmie looked at Jonty.

'Are you a good team?'

'We were once upon a time. Not now. I find it difficult to get past the fact that she cheated on me.' He indicated she should help herself to some frites.

'Having been cheated on, I know how hard that is to forgive. And after the fourth or fifth time, it becomes totally impossible,' Clemmie said.

Jonty looked at her. 'Your husband seriously cheated on you like that?'

Clemmie nodded. 'He did and tried to say I drove him to it. Anyway, it's all in the past for me, thankfully. What sort of business is it you have?'

'A café bookshop. Victoria's grandfather opened the bookshop back in the 1950s. When he died, her father ran it and then Victoria inherited it about ten years ago. Together we turned it into the shop it is today.'

'So it's a real family business,' Clemmie said thoughtfully. 'Is Emma keen to follow in her mother's footsteps one day and run it?'

Jonty nodded. 'Yes, eventually, but she's got her own family now, and besides, well let's say she doesn't find working with Victoria at the moment easy. I can smooth things over when I'm around, so she's not keen either for me to take a back seat.' He let out a deep sigh. 'But I have to for my own sake – and yours.'

Clemmie stared at him and waited.

'I like you, Clemmie, and I get the feeling you aren't indifferent to me?' He paused as she smiled at him. 'Good. But before I can even think about you and me, I have to untangle myself as much as possible from Victoria. There will always be some involvement because of Emma and the grandkids, but I can't carry on being at Victoria's beck and call all the time. She has to accept that we aren't the team we were in the past and never will be again.' He placed his cutlery on his now empty plate. 'All this has been going on for two years now. So, I've asked my solicitor to send Victoria an official letter telling her that from the thirtieth of June I will no longer be a part of the business. In other words, I'm walking away and she needs to make alternative arrangements before then.'

'Do you think she is going to accept that?'

'When I don't drop everything the next time she rings and rush to her aid, she will have to. Plus, as a last resort, I intend to block her.' And Jonty flashed Clemmie a wicked smile. 'Come on, time for some culture,' and he stood up and held out his hand. 'Château Mandelieu-la-Napoule, here we come.'

Driving the short distance along the coast, Jonty told Clemmie a little of the chequered history of the château. 'It dates from the fourteenth century but these days it's more of a pseudo-medieval fantasy castle thanks to the sculptor, Henry Clews, who bought the place with his wife after the First World War.'

Ten minutes later and they were wandering hand in hand around the beautiful grounds of the château and admiring the current exhibition of statues.

'I love this place,' Clemmie said, looking around her in wonder. 'It's magical. Thank you for bringing me here. Can you imagine the things this place has seen?'

Jonty laughed. 'This place is full of legends. Apparently there were some wild fancy dress parties back in the nineteen thirties before Henry died.'

'Oh look, there's a concert this weekend. What a pity we're not free,' Clemmie said.

'I'll put it on the to do list for the next time we're down here.'

Clemmie turned to look at Jonty. 'We're coming down here together?'

'Definitely. I want you to meet my friends and there isn't time today, so we have to come back.'

'Okay,' Clemmie said, smiling at him. 'It's a plan.'

19

Rebecca dropped Verity and Angela near the town end of the Juan-les-Pins long esplanade and Verity immediately took charge and suggested they make for one of the beach cafes.

'It's almost lunchtime, so we may as well eat, build up our energy and see how we feel about walking afterwards. Or not bother if we're too full or too hot,' she added with a smile. 'Come on, this is one of my favourite places to eat.'

And within minutes, Angela found herself sitting at a table on the beach with the gentle Mediterranean waves slipping and sliding up and down on the sand barely two metres away. She reached into her bag and took out her phone.

'I'm not one for taking selfies usually,' she said. 'But I have to take a picture of where we're having lunch and send it to Will.' Angela carefully framed a shot of the table, the sand and the sea before pressing the button and quickly typed the caption, 'Wish you were here?' before sending it to Will and sitting down.

'Shall we go for the house speciality – moules and frites?' Verity asked, looking at the menu. 'And share a bottle of Sauvignon Blanc as neither of us are driving. Or would you prefer something else?'

'Moules and frites sound lovely,' Angela answered. 'And a dry white wine sounds the perfect accompaniment.' She looked around. 'The last time I had lunch on a beach, it was a case of sitting on a blanket, trying to keep the sand out of the sandwiches, and drinking warm lager. This is so much more civilised.'

Verity nodded. 'Juan-les-Pins is one of my favourite places for lunch. Actually, it's one of my favourite places for anything. Years ago, I almost opened a branch of my business here, but...' she shrugged. 'It never happened. French bureaucracy was just too much.'

A waiter appeared at her side and Angela watched and listened in admiration as Verity gave him their lunch and drinks order in what sounded to her ears like flawless French.

'I can't imagine what it's like to be a successful businesswoman like you and Clemmie. Freya has made a success of her painting too,' Angela said quietly. 'I was never ambitious in that way. All I ever wanted was to be a mum and have a family. Big mistake now, I realise. You've retired early, Clemmie has her hats, Freya has her painting and I have... I have nothing now Paul is dead.'

'I was sorry to hear about Paul's accident,' Verity said softly. 'But we all have regrets of one kind or another.' She hesitated for a second or two. 'Mine are the opposite of yours. I sacrificed getting married and having a family for building the business. So please don't think I did everything right, because at the end of the day, I go home alone to an empty house. And I doubt that is ever likely to change now. You have a son, don't you?'

Angela nodded. 'Yes, Will, whom I adore, but he has to live his own life and I can't live the rest of mine through him. Besides, if he knew the truth—' She stopped and shook her head when Verity looked at her curiously.

How would Verity react if she was to tell her the truth? Angela gave herself a mental shake. Now was not the time or the place to break her silence over the accident, but she determined to make a definite effort to talk to Clemmie and Freya before the weekend was over.

'It's not fair to burden a child with one's mistakes,' Angela said, relieved to see their waiter approaching with their wine and the ubiquitous bread basket.

He poured them both a glass of wine before placing the bottle in the terracotta cooler and leaving them with the promise their food would be another five minutes.

Angela picked a piece of bread out of the basket and began to break it into bite-sized morsels, chewing each one thoughtfully as she watched a couple waterskiing out in the bay and a paraglider having fun in the sky.

'If I ever visit Freya and Marcus, I might have to try water-skiing – it looks exhilarating. Though I think I'll give the paragliding a miss,' she said. 'I do love speed... Or rather I did before the accident. Now I'm not so sure.'

'Have you been to Freya and Marcus's house yet?' Verity asked.

Angela shook her head. 'No. I'm hoping there will perhaps be time before Clemmie and I leave on Monday. Have you?'

'No. I haven't seen Effie's apartment yet either, although I could have stayed there this weekend.' She glanced at Angela. 'I very nearly didn't come to this wedding.'

'That makes two of us then. What would your excuse have been? Mine was I wasn't sure I was ready to cope with the emotion of everything on my own. Clemmie convinced me to try. So far it's been good, but tomorrow is sure to be an emotional day. Your turn,' Angela said, looking at Verity expectantly.

'I'm the guest that rubs family, and certain of their friends, the wrong way. Well, one person in particular anyway, and I'm sure you know who that is and the reason for it. Ah, here comes our lunch.' Verity gave Angela a rueful look before turning to smile at the waiter.

As they tucked into their delicious bowls of moules and frites, Angela gave Verity several surreptitious glances. She was surprised just how easy she was to talk to and what good company she was.

'So why did you decide to come?' she asked.

Verity sighed. 'Honestly? I get on with most people, except my family, but that's probably my fault. My jealous streak takes over and I make sarcastic comments and push them away. This weekend, I vowed I wouldn't do that. I would make an effort and try to heal the rift. Arriving as a surprise wasn't my greatest idea though.'

'You're jealous of Freya and Effie?' Angela was taken aback to hear Verity confess so easily to what she had suspected.

'Ashamed to admit it, but yes. Always have been. Freya's childhood always seemed so idyllic to me. My parents weren't happy and that had a knock-on effect for me. My mum, bless her, did her best, but she was no match for my waste-of-space father. She gave up in the end and found her solace in a bottle, which was desperately sad to see.' Verity took a drink of her wine. 'Whereas Freya and Effie have always been close. Uncle Tom was nice too.'

'I'm sorry,' Angela said.

Verity shrugged. 'I'm not the first to have a difficult childhood and sadly I won't be the last, but I have to admit it put me off relationships and marriage. I would have loved a family, but I'd probably have been a rubbish parent.'

Angela shook her head, feeling desperately sorry for Verity. At least she herself had Will in her life. 'No, I don't think that's necessarily true. You'd probably have been determined to make sure your children had the kind of childhood you wished you'd had. And gone overboard in your attempt to give it to them.'

Verity laughed. 'Perhaps. We'll never know now though.'

Angela, determining to try and reach out in friendship to Verity, leant towards her as she indicated the bread basket. 'Would it be considered bad etiquette to soak up this wonderful creamy sauce?' she whispered.

'Definitely not – on the beach anything goes,' and Verity took a piece of bread and did the same as she grinned at Angela conspiratorially and they both wiped their plates clean.

* * *

Rufus joined Freya and the family for lunch around the pool before excusing himself and leaving them to enjoy some family time. He could see two women up on the terrace preparing the table for the evening's pre-wedding dinner and decided to wander up and see if Rebecca was around. Maybe he could persuade her to spend some time with him, if she wasn't too busy with the wedding preparations. The feeling of disappointment over the failure of his plan to talk to Rebecca last night was acute.

Delphine was one of the women busy organising the terrace and she glanced at him as he appeared.

'Can I help you?'

Rufus hesitated. He was pretty certain that Rebecca would have told Delphine that she'd known him in the past, but he wasn't sure how close she was to her sister or how much she would have shared with her.

'I was wondering whether Rebecca was around this afternoon?'

'Sorry, no, she isn't.'

'Any chance she will be later?'

Delphine shrugged. 'We've got a busy time ahead of us, so yes, Rebecca will be around later, but I doubt she'll have time to stop and chat with you – even if she was inclined to do so.' And Delphine gave him a look that told Rufus the chances of him having a heart-to-heart about the past with Rebecca were currently lower than zero.

If Delphine hadn't been so busy and if he hadn't promised Marcus that he wouldn't make waves over the weekend, he might have pushed a bit more.

'Okay, thanks,' he said and, deep in thought, he left the terrace and wandered down through the grounds in the direction of the olive grove.

Why was Rebecca deliberately avoiding him? Usually when he met up with a good friend after an absence of years, it was a case of grabbing a couple of bottles and spending an hour or two reminiscing, catching up with all the news and promising not to lose touch again. Granted, twenty-five years was longer than average to be out of touch, but why relinquish the chance of connecting again? Or even rekindling what had seemed to be the beginning of a wonderful relationship.

If there was one thing he was determined on now that Rebecca had turned up unexpectedly in his life all these years later, it was to get answers from her about the past and he was damned if he was going to leave Villa Sésame without them.

20

Rebecca, waiting in the foyer of the villa, greeted the wedding guests who'd been invited to the pre-wedding dinner and led them out to the terrace, pointing out the steps leading down to the pool area where aperitifs were being served.

As she showed the last couple to arrive out to the terrace, Rufus, chatting away to Jonty and Clemmie, turned his head and looked directly at her. She quickly ushered the couple forward and stepped back out of sight before returning to the sanctuary of the villa.

Delphine was in charge of the kitchen, as usual, and Rebecca had asked Christine to work front of house for the evening. Three of their most experienced waiters were on duty tonight, so everything was covered and Rebecca intended to stay well out of the way behind the scenes, ready to give a hand if necessary but praying she wouldn't have to show her face to the guests.

Once everyone had finished their aperitifs and were making their way to the terrace, where tables had been brought together in a horseshoe shape, Delphine and the kitchen staff were swiftly into their choreographed routine of plating and serving food –

beginning with a lobster and celeriac rémoulade – and sending the waiters out to the tables. As the dinner progressed on through its several courses and the wine flowed, people relaxed, conversation got louder, laughter more uninhibited until it was time for the coffee, petit fours and chocolate to be served.

Hidden in a corner of the kitchen out of sight, doing her last job of the evening, Rebecca placed a selection of the handmade dark chocolates and petit fours on small plates. She could feel herself relaxing. She knew the evening had gone well. Just the big day to get through tomorrow with the marriage ceremony, the wedding breakfast and then the party in the evening.

Sunday would be quieter, with only the villa guests to cater for, and then by Monday afternoon, everyone, including Rufus Whelan, would have left, life would return to normal and she would be able to breathe easier again.

* * *

The full moon was high in a cloudless sky as a church clock in the distance struck eleven and the evening drew to a close with people preparing to leave. Jonty took Clemmie's hand in his as she walked with him to his car.

'It's been such a lovely day,' she said. 'And now there is tomorrow to look forward to. I'm so happy you came.'

Jonty squeezed her hand. 'I wouldn't have missed it for the world.'

'Even though I saw Freya and Marcus giving you the third degree earlier?' Clemmie teased.

'They're looking out for you, like good friends do. When you meet my friends, not to mention Emma, you can expect the same kind of grilling.' Jonty pressed the key fob and the lights on his hire car flashed before he turned to Clemmie. 'I'll see you tomorrow, you are going to be a beautiful bridesmaid,' and he leant in and gave her a gentle kiss before moving away and getting in the car.

'See you tomorrow, drive carefully,' Clemmie echoed and blew him a kiss. She watched as the car tail lights disappeared down the drive, before turning to wander back to the villa in the moonlight. She'd learnt more about Jonty and his past in the last few hours than in the months since she'd met him. Did his past bother her? No. Nobody went through life without collecting baggage, herself included.

At fifty-seven years of age, she'd never expected to be attracted to anyone ever again, but Jonty had broken through her defences. She'd enjoyed his company today and at dinner this evening and found herself wishing that he'd agreed to stay here at the villa rather than return to his friends in Cannes. She hoped the growing closeness between them that she'd sensed today would continue when they were both back in the UK and prove to be the beginning of... of what, Clemmie wasn't sure, but having Jonty in her life felt right.

'Can we talk?' Clemmie jumped as a voice interrupted her thoughts and she saw someone standing in the shadows of the terrace steps. Verity. Clemmie's first instinct was to shake her head and keep walking, but then a little voice inside her said, *You wanted to apologise for saying what you did all those years ago, maybe this is your opportunity.*

Clemmie took a deep breath, managing to swallow the words, *As long as you don't plan on pushing me down the steps or into the pool*, and saying instead, 'Depends.'

'I wanted to say sorry for nearly drowning you,' Verity said quietly. 'I know it's years too late but...' she shrugged. 'Better late than never.'

Clemmie caught her breath in surprise, maybe it wasn't just

her feeling that it was time for past wrongs to be forgotten and forgiven after all.

'Thank you. It has been a long time coming, but it is appreciated.' She looked at Verity for several seconds. 'My turn. I'm sorry for the way I provoked you, saying no one liked you and you should stay in London. No excuse, but I suspect I was a horrible teenage girl that year.'

She watched as Verity closed her eyes and exhaled a deep sigh of relief.

'I feel as though a weight has finally been lifted,' Verity said. 'Thank you.'

'Me too,' Clemmie said with a smile. 'Thank you. Come on, lights are being switched off on the terrace. It's time for bed. Big day tomorrow.'

21

Both Rebecca and Delphine were up in time to hear the dawn chorus the next morning, while everyone else slept in. Their routine was always the same on wedding days. They were unlikely to have time to eat until after the marriage ceremony had taken place, so Rebecca always joined Delphine in the kitchen, where they would eat a substantial breakfast – usually scrambled eggs with smoked salmon, toast and coffee – before going through a lengthy checklist of what still needed doing to ensure the smooth running of the day.

'Florist is bringing Freya's bouquet, posies for the bridesmaids and buttonhole flowers at twelve o'clock,' Rebecca said, looking at her ever-present clipboard. 'She'll check on the bower and the table decorations whilst she's here.'

'Pierre is organised to set up the chairs, place the cushions and wedding programmes ready, and roll out the red carpet towards the bower,' Delphine added. 'Christine and he will start to set the table after that. Using the same horseshoe layout as for the dinner last night means there aren't any tables and chairs to move around, which is a great help. As is the two o'clock ceremony. Gives us plenty of time. Kitchen staff will be in as usual at eight o'clock, so we'll get breakfasts done and then get organised for the wedding meal – most of the prep is done already. The waiters will be here from midday ready to hand the champagne around.'

'It's all so different from the early days,' Rebecca commented, glancing at the list on her clipboard. 'Finding and affording staff for events was a nightmare at times. Not sure how we did it all, to be honest.'

Delphine smiled. 'There were a couple of times when we almost didn't if I remember correctly.'

Rebecca nodded. 'Hairdresser and beautician are due at ten. I've checked the Butterfly Room and everything is ready there. Everyone's outfit is up there ready to be put on once Hailey and Beth have finished hair and make-up.'

'Photographer?' Delphine asked.

'Freya didn't want any photos until after everyone had make-up and hair done, so he's coming about one o'clock and will wander around taking pictures of everything and everyone.'

'It's not on the list, but Freya has asked Rufus as best man to take Marcus down to the house for the morning,' Delphine said. 'His outfit is there, so the plan is for Rufus to take his suit and get ready down there as well, bring Marcus back in good time but keep him out of everyone's hair.'

Delphine pretended not to notice her sister's sharp intake of breath at the mention of Rufus, followed by a quiet sigh of relief at the news he was not going to be around for the morning.

'I can't help wonder why you're so intent on avoiding Rufus. He seems like a gentleman, and nice with it. Surely it would be easier to see him and put the past to bed, so to speak,' she added, giving Rebecca a direct look.

Rebecca glanced at her sister suspiciously. Had she guessed

who he was? Probably, she wasn't stupid. Rebecca gave a determined shake of her head.

'Easier in one way to see and to talk to him, but in every other way it would be a huge disaster and the knock-on effects are unimaginable.' She shrugged. 'I'm sorry I haven't confided in you, but I promise once the Jackmans' wedding party have all left on Monday, we will sit down together and I will tell you everything, okay?'

'I have a shrewd idea what it is about already,' Delphine said, giving Rebecca a sharp glance. 'It will be interesting to have you confirm it. Just be sure you're not making another major mistake by not taking the opportunity of talking to Rufus and facing up to things.'

* * *

'The gods are shining on you today, mate,' Rufus said as he took the last parking space on the Ramparts near Marcus's townhouse. Taking his suit hanging on its hanger in its protective bag out of the car, he followed Marcus the short distance to the house.

'You can shower and change later in the en suite on the second floor,' Marcus said. 'But first coffee and a couple of Delphine's croissants, I think, up on the terrace.'

While Marcus organised the coffee, Rufus had a look at some of Freya's paintings stacked against a wall.

'Are these going into the exhibition?'

'A couple are, but I think Freya wants to have some prints made first and then the rest will go up here. There's still some empty wall space on the two upper floors.'

'Hugo was telling me last night he has high hopes of Freya making a breakthrough with this exhibition,' Rufus said as he carefully moved the paintings to look at a couple at the back of the stack, and caught his breath as he looked at them. 'Any chance of Freya selling me one or both of these?' he said, placing them side by side against a wall. 'Market price of course.'

Marcus turned and smiled. 'Ah, the good old Gunfield Hotel and the castle as seen from the river Dart. Freya's done several of that view, so I guess she'd happily sell you one or two. You can ask her later.' He glanced curiously at his friend. 'Why do you want them? I mean, Freya and I feel sentimental about the place because she grew up in Dartmouth and we got married there but I didn't realise you felt so strongly about the place.'

Rufus still staring at the paintings glanced briefly up at Marcus and said simply, 'Becky.'

'Ah, I'd forgotten it was Dartmouth where you two met.'

The machine finished hissing coffee into the jug Marcus had placed ready and he turned it off before picking it up.

'Come on up to the terrace. Bring the croissants.'

The two men headed up to the terrace and Rufus stared out to the horizon, deep in thought, while Marcus busied himself pouring the coffee into two mugs.

'Right, we've got a couple of hours to kill, so is there anything you want to talk about? Ask my opinion?' Marcus said as he handed Rufus a coffee and helped himself to a croissant.

Rufus sighed. 'Since I arrived on Thursday and discovered my Becky was one of the women who owns Villa Sésame, apart from the silent treatment in the car driving us down to Antibes, followed by the fiasco by the pool with Verity, I've barely had even a fleeting glance of her. She seems determined to avoid me. And, so far, she's been very successful. I don't know why she is avoiding me, or how to break through the barrier she's put up between us – any ideas?'

'You just called her "my Becky",' Marcus said quietly. 'Is that how you still think of her after all these years?'

Rufus went to protest that it was a slip of his tongue but stopped as he realised that was how he had always thought of her.

He shrugged the question away. 'I just want to talk to her and learn how her life has been. If she tells me to my face she doesn't want to renew our friendship, then...' Rufus took a deep breath. 'Then at least I'll have proper closure after all these years.'

Staring out over the terrace and watching a container ship on the horizon making its way westwards across the Mediterranean, he sipped his coffee thoughtfully as doubt flooded into his mind. Was that true? Did he really want closure and to bring to an end all those years of speculation wondering about what might have been? Wasn't he still hoping that he and Becky would somehow reunite and the loss he'd felt so acutely for the past twenty-five years would fade away? How could he explain that to Marcus? His friend would think he was stupid clinging to such a long-lost dream.

'There is the possibility, of course, that Rebecca doesn't want to create an atmosphere – or worse – that could affect our wedding,' Marcus said, interrupting his thoughts. 'So, how about you try to suppress your feelings, let the heat die out of the situation and enjoy today and the rest of our time at the villa. Then, when we all leave Villa Sésame late Monday morning, you come and stay here with us for a couple of days, during which time you can go back up to the villa and try to get Rebecca to see you and talk. She'll probably be less busy and stressed, although not necessarily more receptive to talking to you, but you'll have more of a chance of having a conversation with her.'

Rufus turned his attention away from the view and looked at Marcus. 'That sounds like a plan, if you think Freya will be okay with it, thank you.'

Driving Marcus back up to Villa Sésame, Rufus smothered a

sigh. Whether he could stick to such a simple plan as he'd agreed with Marcus was debatable. Deep down he knew that if the opportunity presented itself for him to speak to Becky over the weekend, he was likely to grab it with both hands, whatever the cost.

* * *

By midday, Villa Sésame was basking under a sun shining from a cloudless Côte d'Azur sky and humming with activity everywhere.

Up in the bespoke Butterfly Room – the specially dedicated place in the villa where brides and their attendants prepared for their special day, being pampered with massages, facials, nail polishing, hairstyling – everyone was relaxed and happy. Little Lily was toddling around showing everyone her glittery nails that Hailey had painted and enjoying being the centre of attention.

As Rebecca appeared with a tray of glasses and a bottle of champagne, newly washed hair was being brushed into flattering styles.

'How's it all going? The photographer is taking some scenic shots outside, he's ready to come up here when you say the word,' Rebecca said, looking at Freya. 'I know you said you didn't want any before photos, but you all look amazing.'

'Maybe give us another twenty minutes and then send him up? Everyone all right with that? Good.'

Freya didn't add that the atmosphere in the room for the last few hours had, to her amazement, been friendly and she wanted that to last as long as possible. When Clemmie had whispered to her at breakfast that she and Verity were speaking to each other and maybe she ought to be included in the hair and make-up sessions she'd agreed reluctantly and had invited Verity to join them in the Butterfly Room as they all got ready for the wedding. She'd braced herself for the inevitable backlash from Verity, only none had come. Effie had given her a wordless look, clearly nonplussed at what was going on. Freya had smiled back and shrugged, equally at a loss but happy nonetheless at the lack of tension.

The whole morning, so far, had been filled with fun and laughter and currently there was a lively discussion going on about the merits of living in London as opposed to anywhere else.

'I loved my time in London,' Clemmie said. 'I have to admit there's a lot more going on there than there is in Devon, but when I divorced Sam and moved back to Dartmouth, it was like taking a deep breath and beginning to live properly again. I can't imagine living anywhere else now. Although somewhere like this could tempt me.'

'As a Londoner through and through, I've always thought that Samuel Johnson was right with his *"When a man is tired of London, he is tired of life,"'* Verity said. 'But these days I'm not so sure. I remembered how much I love Juan-les-Pins the other day when Angela and I had lunch there and I could happily live there. In fact, when I get back, I'm going to seriously consider it.'

'You'd be close to family then,' Effie said quietly. 'If that's what you want.'

Verity smiled at her pensively but didn't say anything.

Freya, listening to the conversation, gave Verity a quick glance. This quieter, gentler version of her cousin, reminded her of the friendship they'd once shared long before the accident had changed things between them.

Rebecca stayed for a few more moments, pouring the champagne and handing glasses around, thankful that Verity's unexpected presence had somehow been accepted and the past seemed to have been put firmly in its place.

She'd turned to leave the women to their final preparations when Freya stopped her. 'I should have given this to Marcus earlier, ready for the ceremony. Please could you make sure to give it to Rufus before everything starts? As best man, it's probably best if he has it in his pocket,' and she quickly slipped her original wedding ring off her right hand and held it out to Rebecca.

'Of course, I'll make sure he gets it. I'll send the photographer up too,' and Rebecca left the room with the ring held tightly in her hand.

There was no way she was going to seek Rufus out and give him the ring directly. She'd find Delphine or Christine and ask them to do it.

* * *

Rebecca took her time going downstairs to find Delphine or Christine. The photographer was on the terrace busy snapping the table settings with their sparkling cut glassware, silver cutlery, tablecloths with their delicately embroidered flower motifs and crystal centres, while miniature golden flower pots had been placed down the length of the table holding yellow and white roses alternately. Freya had specifically asked for nothing too showy and had been thrilled with the table design Rebecca had come up with. 'It's different and has a hint of luxury but it's not over the top,' she'd said.

Once she'd told the photographer he could go on up and the women would be ready for him, Rebecca made her way to the office. Hopefully Christine would be in there and she could give her the ring to pass to Rufus for safekeeping. But the office was empty and she closed the door behind her, intending to find Delphine in the kitchen, at the exact moment Rufus walked into the foyer and she came to a sudden stop. As did Rufus.

Rebecca was the first to recover and she held out the ring to him. 'Freya has forgotten to give Marcus her wedding ring ready for the ceremony. She asked me to make sure the best man had it safe before the ceremony begins,' and she dropped the ring into Rufus's outstretched hand.

Before she could move away, his other hand caught her arm.

'Becky, please talk to me.'

Rebecca held up her hand in protest to silence him. 'No. Not now. This weekend is all about Marcus and Freya. I have no time to think about anything else. Now, please excuse me, guests will be arriving soon.'

And she walked away from him, leaving the words 'not now' ringing in his ears, leaving him hopeful that maybe Marcus was right and once the celebrations were over she would talk to him.

As slight a hope as it was, it was one he was going to cling to for the rest of the weekend.

22

A quarter of an hour before the wedding was due to start, Rebecca made her way back upstairs to the Butterfly Room. This was the part of hosting wedding days that she enjoyed, seeing a beautiful bride surrounded by her bridesmaids ready for her special day. Although, since she'd seen Rufus and handed him Freya's ring, her normal upbeat mood had dipped somewhat. It had suddenly struck her as ironic that she was good at organising wedding days for others, but she'd never experienced one herself. There had been a time, particularly when Bart was small, when she'd dreamt of what life would be like married to his father. She pushed the thought away. Now was not the time to drag those subconscious memories up or to start speculating about how different things would have been if only the two of them had married.

Rebecca stifled a sigh. There had been too many 'if onlys' in her life to bear thinking about. For a simple two-letter word, 'if' wielded the power to throw her thoughts into instant disarray. Today was not an 'if only' day for her. Today was all about Freya and Marcus. She pulled her shoulders back. Smiling, she opened the door of the Butterfly Room.

'How are we doing, ladies? The countdown is about to begin. Freya, you look wonderful. Your dress is spectacular.'

'Thank you,' Freya said. 'It does feel pretty special,' and she glanced at herself in the long mirror. The dress, made from two layers of the palest champagne-coloured chiffon material, with pearl embellishment swirling down and around the dress, suited her tall figure and fitted her perfectly as it finished above her ankles, showing off her silver Jimmy Choo shoes with their ankle strap and stiletto heel and a large pearl sitting on the top of the peep-toe style. 'It couldn't be more different to the traditional white dress I wore the first time,' she added. 'And I love what Hailey has done to my hair with a flower or two.' She turned to Clemmie. 'I promise you I love the hat you made me, which would have complemented the silk trouser suit I bought and intended to wear, until I fell in love with this dress.'

'You look absolutely as a bride should,' Clemmie said. 'Any hat would have been totally wrong with that dress. Keep it to wear to someone else's wedding. Or a day at the races!'

Rebecca glanced across at Effie, Madeleine holding Lily by the hand and Verity. She smiled at Lily. 'You look very pretty. If you three would like to take Lily and make your way out to where everyone is waiting and find your seats, I'll bring the bride and the others down in...' she glanced at her watch, 'another six minutes so that Freya is fashionably late.'

Effie was the first to give Freya a careful hug. 'I'm glad you and Marcus are back together, my darling. Lily, are you going to hold my hand?' And the little girl happily took hold of her great-grandmother's hand while Madeleine and Verity both gave Freya gentle hugs and wished her 'every happiness' before they all left the Butterfly Room.

When they went downstairs a few moments later, Rebecca stopped in the foyer and handed Freya her bouquet: a beautiful mixture of roses, lilies, freesias, dahlias, with eucalyptus leaves, ferns and a sprig or two of olive leaves. She handed Clemmie and Angela simpler posies containing the same flowers.

'The celebrant and Marcus are ready and waiting for you. Just follow the red carpet.' Rebecca opened the door and ushered them out onto the terrace. 'Enjoy your wedding day, Freya.'

* * *

As they walked a few paces behind Freya, Clemmie gave Angela a quick look. 'You okay?'

Angela smiled. 'Yes, I'm fine. I'm looking forward to the ceremony in this beautiful setting.'

A few moments later, Angela, standing next to Clemmie to the side of Freya and Marcus, began to realise that she was not fine. Keeping her emotions in check as she listened to the words of the celebrant as he joyfully married Freya and Marcus was hard – so hard. The humanist ceremony they'd chosen meant they had been able to personalise it to suit themselves and there were several references to their younger selves. It was the mention of their first wedding in St Petrox out on the headland at Dartmouth that jogged Angela's memory and caused her tears.

Her mum and dad had offered to have one-year-old Will on the Saturday and Sunday so she and Paul had had a rare child-free weekend. Paul had been an usher and once her bridesmaid duties were completed, they'd enjoyed the reception and the evening dance as much as the newly married Freya and Marcus.

Angela swallowed hard. Paul would have loved to been here today to celebrate this second marriage and to spend the evening dancing with her.

She sensed Clemmie edging closer and pressing a tissue into her hand with a whispered, 'Everyone cries at weddings, so don't worry. I'm not far off blubbing myself.'

'Thank you,' Angela mouthed,

As the short service finished with the very traditional instruction to Marcus 'You may kiss the bride', Angela forced a smile on her face and prayed nobody would guess how difficult it was.

'Come on, time for a glass of champagne, let's find Jonty,' Clemmie said to a subdued Angela and turned, hoping that Jonty had remembered about Angela maybe needing some support. To her relief, she saw him talking to Rufus and the two of them making their way towards them.

'Angela, as best man it is my duty to escort the chief brides-maid for the rest of the day,' Rufus said, taking hold of her hand.

'Oh, but I don't think I'm technically the chief bridesmaid, or even matron of honour,' Angela protested, looking at Clemmie.

'Well, I'm certainly not,' Clemmie said. 'Besides, Jonty is officially my plus-one,' and emphasising the point she moved closer to Jonty.

'Settled, come on, we need to join the bride and groom,' and Rufus led Angela towards the terrace.

'Did you put him up to that?' Clemmie asked.

Jonty shrugged. 'Guilty as charged. I saw you pass her a tissue earlier and I thought neither of them had a partner, so best man, chief bridesmaid, a natural pairing.'

'Thank you, you're a star,' and Clemmie stood on tiptoe to kiss his cheek. 'You're looking very smart today.'

'And you are looking beautiful,' Jonty said, bending to return the kiss. 'Come on. I think you might be needed for the photographs.'

* * *

The wedding afternoon passed in a whirl of photographs, food, champagne, and lots of laughter. Toddler Lily enchanted everyone, especially when she saw the cake for the first time. As Freya and Marcus stood there smiling for the photographer, poised ready to cut the highly decorated five tier sponge cake, Lily escaped from Madeleine's grasp and ran over.

'Cake. I want cake, Granny.'

As friends of Marcus and Freya began to arrive for the evening party and the sun started to set, the red Esterel mountains appeared to be once again surrounded by a fiery sea of lava. Freya and Marcus walked hand in hand down to the small lantern-lit terrace for their first dance as a newly married couple. Freya smiled as she recognised the tune.

'I couldn't resist asking for the same music as we had all those years ago,' Marcus whispered, taking her in his arms. 'Because like the song says "I will always love you". Always have, always will.'

Once their special dance was over, Clemmie and Jonty, Rufus and Angela, as well as other couples, joined them on the small terrace to dance the night away.

Clemmie, dancing with Jonty, realised she was the happiest she'd been for years. She really liked Jonty and since his words yesterday in Bocca, she had no doubt that he really liked her too. She snuggled in closer and felt his arms tighten around her as he whispered in her ear, 'Clemmie, my love, I have to go soon. Tomorrow, my friends have plans for me, so I'll leave you to have a final day here with everyone, but if you'd like me to, I'll come back, Monday morning, to drive you and Angela to the airport.'

Sleepily, Clemmie murmured, 'Sounds good, thank you,' when in truth what she really wanted was for him to stay here at the villa with her tonight. But she obviously couldn't say that, could she?

* * *

Nearly midnight, and the band were slowing the tempo down with some classic end-of-the-party music. 'The Way We Were' lyrics of the old Barbra Streisand song were currently being softly sung and drifted on the air to where Rebecca was standing hidden in the shadows of the top terrace watching the romantic scene below. Several couples, including the bride and groom and Clemmie and Jonty, were wrapped in each other's arms gently swaying together, enjoying the romance of the moment.

She was happy that there had been no hitches to spoil the day and relieved everything had gone well. She hoped that Freya and Marcus would agree that they'd had the perfect wedding day. Rebecca gave a startled jump as Rufus appeared at her side holding two full champagne flutes.

'I get the feeling you have once more been avoiding me this evening, so now I've tracked you down – dance or drink?'

Rebecca shook her head. 'Neither. You're a guest and I don't drink or dance with the guests, it would look and be unprofessional.'

Rufus inclined his head. 'I understand that, so no to a dance then, but standing here in the shadows no one would see you enjoying a glass of champagne and toasting the happy couple.'

Rebecca didn't answer and Rufus sighed.

'How about making an exception just this once because I'm more than just a guest, I'm an old friend. Please, Becky,' and he held out a glass.

Rebecca studied Rufus thoughtfully, her heart pounding. Should she risk just one drink with him? The weekend would soon be over and once again they would go their separate ways. It would be good to make one more happy memory with him to add to the others.

'Thank you.' She smiled as she took the glass he was holding out for her. The jolt through her hand as his fingers brushed hers made her regret the decision instantly. This was not a good idea. From the look Rufus gave her, she knew he'd felt it too.

'Freya and Marcus,' Rebecca said and they clicked glasses before they both took a sip. 'And here's to old friends.' Rufus held his glass out again, waiting for her to respond as he held her gaze.

'To ships that pass in the night.' Rebecca went to clink her glass against his as she said the words quietly but firmly. It was far too late to rekindle their friendship. But Rufus had moved his glass out of reach.

'Were we just ships that passed in the night? It didn't feel like that to me at the time,' he said, staring at her. 'And it still doesn't.'

Rebecca swallowed, her throat constricting, making speech impossible for several seconds as Rufus continued to stare.

'Whatever we were to each other, it was a long time ago and things are different now,' Rebecca finally managed. She took a deep breath. 'It's impossible to turn the clock back without hurting people, us, so please, Rufus, if you still feel anything for me, let it go. Leave Villa Sésame on Monday and forget about me.'

She thrust her glass back at him, spilling the champagne over his fingers with the violence of her action before turning and leaving him standing there, shock on his face, as she disappeared into the villa.

23

After a night where she'd tossed and turned for hours, Rebecca finally fell asleep at around five o'clock on Sunday morning. Less than two hours later, she was awake again. Sighing and knowing that any more sleep would be impossible, she dragged herself out of bed and pulled on her silk kimono. In the kitchen, stifling a yawn, she made herself a coffee and took it out to the balcony and sat watching the dawn break.

What a monumental mess. A mess of her own making maybe, but it was one she'd come to terms with and reluctantly accepted, never expecting the very foundation of the long-ago event to rear up and taunt her like this. However she reacted, whatever she did to rectify the situation, there would be consequences to be faced. Other people would want their say; other people would try to influence her one way or the other; other people would be disappointed in her. Other people would...

Rebecca took a sip of her coffee and closed off the end of the next thought. There was only one person who should have any say in all this and it was impossible to talk to him right now. And she needed to have a contingency plan in place before that happened. She had to show everybody that, although it might not look like it, she had known what she was doing when she had made her original decision all those years ago. She twisted her mouth into a grimace. Not strictly true. She'd not had any real choice in the matter at the time. But she definitely had difficult decisions to make now.

She glanced at her watch. Almost 7 a.m. The whole day stretched before her – a day of presenting a happy face to both guests and staff, of being polite, whilst at the same time making sure she avoided Rufus, when all she wanted to do was to run away. Disappear somewhere and try to form a plan of action before returning to do whatever she decided she needed to do.

Freya and Marcus had planned a quiet day lazing around the pool for everyone, a buffet-type lunch of salads and meats, with a barbecue in the evening. Delphine and the staff who were on duty that day would cope without her being around, would barely notice her absence, in fact, as the routine of the day's work went on.

Rebecca finished her coffee and stood up. That's what she'd do. Disappear for a few hours and really concentrate on searching for answers to her problems. A quick shower, write a note for Delphine – asking her to cover for her, not to worry, she'd be back this evening, explain she just needed some time and space away from the villa to think – and then she'd get in the car and spend the day alone thinking.

Twenty minutes later, while everyone in the villa was still asleep, Rebecca was in her car going down the driveway, determined to escape before anyone could stop her.

* * *

A relaxing Sunday around the pool was just what everyone needed for their final day and was the perfect antidote to the excitement of Saturday.

'I could get used to this life,' Angela murmured from her sunbed as she reached for her glass of ice-cold lemonade. 'I really, really, don't want to go home tomorrow. Imagine having enough money to own a place like this and live here full-time.'

'I bet it eats money,' Verity noted. 'Hence the need to do functions.'

'Which they do terribly well,' Freya said. 'Rebecca is an amazing organiser and Delphine's food is worthy of five stars in anyone's book.'

'Hard work though, like anything catering-related,' Angela said. 'I know it's not the same, but Paul and I thought about running a gastro pub once.' She shook her head. 'When we started to examine what it entailed, we backed off. It wouldn't have been an easy life, that's for sure.' A niggling voice in her head whispered, *And there would have been no time to ride a motorbike.*

She glanced around. Madeleine had fallen asleep on her sun lounger under the large colourful parasol. Effie, too, had her eyes closed and looked as though she was enjoying a little nap. The men were in the pool playing some sort of noisy, crazy volleyball game. Clemmie was smoothing factor 30 sun lotion over her body, while Verity was idly flicking through a glossy magazine and Freya was cuddling Lily, who had fallen asleep on her lap sucking her thumb. Remembering her determination on the beach to talk to her friends and tell them the truth before the weekend was over, Angela took a deep breath and sat up.

'I need to talk to you all. Ask your advice.' Her voice faltered as Clemmie closed the lid on her lotion, Freya gave her a quick glance as she settled Lily into a more comfortable position, Effie's eyelids flickered but remained closed and Verity stopped turning the pages of the magazine. 'You remember I told you I'd met someone who brought the memory of the accident flooding back? Well, I've remembered who he was. He was the first person on the scene of the accident. In fact, I'm sure he saved my life.'

'A hero then,' Clemmie said. 'Why did seeing him again upset you so much?'

Angela closed her eyes and chewed her bottom lip, trying to summon up the strength to continue. When she opened her eyes a few seconds later, tears forced their way out. 'That afternoon was the first time I had persuaded Paul to let me ride the bike. Paul was the pillion passenger. I was the cause of Paul's death that afternoon.'

Her words hung in the silent air for a moment as the others stared at her and she forced herself to continue.

'I was enjoying the ride before it all went horribly wrong. The road had been clean, clear and free of traffic for miles. I'd throttled back for the bend coming up because I was aware it had a certain reputation as a black spot for accidents, but before we reached it, the bike hit a wide strip of muck left by a tractor and I lost control. I remember hurtling towards the drystone wall at the back of the verge and the impact throwing both of us off as the bike crashed into it.'

While she was speaking, Clemmie had moved across to sit next to her and put her arms around her in a tight hug.

'Oh, Angie,' Clemmie murmured. 'I'm so, so sorry.'

'I understand your guilty feelings and I'm sorry for you. But why are you so upset by meeting the man who helped you?' Verity asked, for once putting into words what they were all thinking.

Angela took a deep breath. 'I think this man might know that I was driving. The air ambulance whisked me away to hospital and the police, when they arrived, assumed that Paul was driving because, well, with a motorbike it's usually the man, isn't it?'

'You said earlier you wanted our advice?' Freya said.

Angela nodded. 'I don't know what to do. I'm worried that this man might tell them. Should I go to the police and confess? But I'm scared that they'll prosecute me for withholding information, perhaps charge me with dangerous driving. The other thing, which for me, is as big a dilemma is...' and Angela took a deep breath. 'Do I tell Will the truth and risk him never forgiving me for killing his father?'

It was Effie who broke the long, thoughtful silence that descended as the others sought to get their heads around Angela's questions and give her some advice that would help her overcome both of her fears.

'My advice as an old woman, regarding your first question, is to leave well alone. Whoever the man is, as the first on the scene, the police will already have spoken to him. It's been several months since the accident and they haven't questioned you, so even if he did suspect or even know, it's highly unlikely that he's mentioned it to them. The second question is harder to advise on,' and Effie gave Angela a serious look. 'Ask yourself what purpose will telling Will the truth about the accident serve? His father is dead, nothing is going to bring him back. You're both going through a grieving period where you and he can support each other. If you tell him what happened and he rejects you, he will in essence have lost both parents. And you, you will have lost your son as well as your husband. So it might be kinder to both of you, not to tell him. Just remember that whatever you decide you have to live with it.'

Effie stood up. 'I'm sure you are going to find the next few months difficult, but please don't let the guilt take over and consume you. You need to remember and accept that Paul's death was a tragic accident and give yourself permission to forgive yourself so that in time you can move on.'

Angela stared at Effie, speechless, the words ringing in her ears. She wiped her tear stained eyes with the back of her hand and took a deep breath. Sharing her guilty secret and her worries with her friends had been difficult but their reaction had buoyed her up and given her hope.

24

Once she was on the coast road, Rebecca automatically drove in the direction of Antibes but without giving any real thought to where she was going. Still early morning, the road was quiet and there were few people about. Through Golfe-Juan, she was stopped by a red light as she witnessed the pompiers rushing out of the station, klaxon blaring, into the morning. At Juan-les-Pins, she passed three or four lone joggers on the esplanade and a few dog walkers making for the entrance to the nearby section of the forest that spread for nine hectares on the Cap d'Antibes.

As she drove past the iconic Hôtel Le Provençal, she remembered, years ago, visiting the Notre-Dame de la Garoupe chapel high on the peninsula in the shadow of the lighthouse. An unexpected desire to see the panoramic view again and to sit on a pew in the unpretentious chapel spilled into her mind. Some silent contemplation might help her to sort things out. She'd walk up rather than drive, she decided. If nothing else, the walk along the Chemin du Calvaire to the top of the peninsula would do her good.

Five minutes later, Rebecca had found some unrestricted

parking on one of the roads leading away from the *bord de mer* and she set off to find the footpath she needed. It was quiet in the forest and she walked contentedly with the aroma of the Mediterranean pines all around. The path was gentle when she joined it and began the climb to the top.

An hour later and the path had become steeper until, to the relief of her leg muscles, she reached the plateau.

The view was as breathtaking in its scope as she remembered – Italy to the east and Cap Camarat to the west – and she stood there for some time drinking it all in. It wasn't until the sound of shutters being banged back against walls broke into her reverie that she turned away and took in her immediate surroundings. The chapel with the lighthouse towering over it was as she remembered too, but she saw there was a cafe with a courtyard to the side, which she didn't recall from her last visit. Best of all, they were opening for business and she wandered over to sit at one of the tables.

A few moments later, along with her coffee and pain au raisin, the young waiter delivered the information that the chapel would be open in twenty minutes. Rebecca took her time drinking and eating, listening to the noises coming from the cafe as the staff prepared for the day ahead and delicious smells started to filter out from the kitchen. Holidaymakers were starting to arrive, some on foot, panting with the exertion, others, less brave, parking to the side of the cafe. Wanting to have some time alone in the chapel, Rebecca left some euros in the small dish with the bill and made her way across to the now open chapel door.

Even though it had been renovated, the chapel had clearly retained the allegiance of the local seafaring community as a place of pilgrimage for mariners. Model ships hung from the ceiling, a ship's wheel had been placed high up near the altar, photographs of old fishermen and sailors decorated the walls, requests to keep loved ones safe, prayers for those lost at sea, framed pictures of stricken boats sunk at sea. It should have been a depressing place with all these reminders of how many men lost their lives at sea, but somehow it wasn't. It was uplifting in a way. A peaceful place thanking and honouring all these men and their families. Lots of candles were burning on the metal tables and Rebecca vowed to light one herself before she left.

Sinking down onto one of the many wooden pews, Rebecca forced herself to try to think positively about Rufus and what to do. He was a good man, an honourable man, and he deserved to know the truth, but how could she possibly tell him something of such monumental importance after all these years? He was unlikely to say, 'Hey, Rebecca, no worries. I completely understand. I know now and that's all that matters.' Because knowing wouldn't be the end of it. There was all the stuff he didn't know that would drift along in its wake. All the questions, the whys and the what ifs, the answers which would be different to those that would have been given at the very beginning, simply because they were both older and life experience had changed their opinions on so many things.

If she was totally honest with herself, and being here in this place of homage surrounded by the spirits of all these brave souls there was no question of being anything but honest, there was only one option available to her. She had to talk to Rufus. Tell him the truth. But even as she accepted the inevitable, Rebecca felt herself shrink both mentally and physically at the thought.

Delphine's comment on the morning of the wedding about having a shrewd idea of the truth had hit home. If she'd put two and two together and guessed who Rufus was then there was also the chance that Rufus would realise that she didn't want to talk to him because she had a secret she'd never told him. And then the recriminations would follow.

Swallowing a sigh, Rebecca rose to leave the chapel. Slowly, she walked over to the table full of candles and lit a red one. Standing there, watching the flickering wicks of a dozen or so candles lit in honour and remembrance, Rebecca hoped silently that she would be strong enough to cope with the fallout that would follow when she told Rufus the truth. Because whatever the consequences were, she knew had to tell him.

She turned away and made for the exit. She'd have lunch at the cafe, spend the afternoon wandering around Antibes and then it would be time to go home and prepare for the ordeal of facing Rufus.

25

As the others drifted away from the pool in the late afternoon to shower and prepare for their last evening at the villa, Angela felt a deep need for some time away from everyone to try to find a way through the turmoil in her mind. And the tranquility of the olive grove was calling to her. Taking her phone out of her pocket as she wandered down through the grounds, she snapped several pictures of the villa, the pool and finally, as she turned away from the villa getting closer towards the olive grove, she took a panoramic shot of the nearest group of the ancient trees. Memories to take home with her.

She'd been relieved when the others hadn't condemned her when she'd told them her terrible secret, offering instead love and support. She should have known that was the way they'd react and talked to them before. Effie pointing out that it was unlikely the police would be in touch after all these months was reassuring.

Effie's other words regarding Will's possible reaction to learning the truth were swirling around in her head as she walked. Would telling him serve a purpose for either of them? It wouldn't make her guilty conscience disappear. That was something she knew she was going to live with for the rest of her life. But Effie pointing out how badly Will might react made her heart skip a beat. She'd already lost Paul, and she'd briefly considered that Will might hate her for a while, but the thought of him turning against her forever if she told him the truth about that dreadful afternoon was unbearable. It would be another burden for both of them to bear.

There was a peacefulness here in this ancient olive grove, as though time stood still whilst one wandered around. Angela stopped, reaching out to touch the thick gnarled trunk of the nearest olive tree. The olive sapling she'd planted for Paul in the Remembrance Garden came into her mind. Chosen because Paul had loved olive trees, it would take years to reach this size in southern England, but hopefully it would survive and live up to its reputation as the tree of life and live for hundreds of years.

Angela took a deep breath and placed her arms around its trunk as far as she could reach, pressing her forehead against the rough bark and closing her eyes. She stood there for several moments without conscious thought before opening her eyes and letting her arms fall to her side as she moved away.

Could Effie possibly be right saying there was no point in burdening Will with his mother's guilt? It did belong to her and to her alone. She could only pray that it would fade as the years went by and she would be able to forgive herself and move on, as Effie had insisted she should.

* * *

The final barbecue of the weekend was fired up on Sunday evening and a thoughtful Delphine was skilfully cooking the steaks, fish and sausages. A variety of salads, jacket potatoes and grilled asparagus had been laid out on a nearby table ready for everyone to help themselves.

So far, nobody had asked about Rebecca's whereabouts, for which she was thankful, but she couldn't help worry about her younger sister. She'd hoped she'd have returned by now. The couple of times Delphine had rung her mobile, it had gone straight to voicemail. She didn't bother to leave a message.

Although everybody was busy tucking into the food almost as fast as she could cook it, Delphine recognised the telltale subdued signs that always accompanied the final evening of a successful event. Nobody wanted the holiday to end but everybody accepted that end it would. Tomorrow morning, cases would be packed, goodbyes would be said and everyone would return to the reality of their own world with all its attendant problems. At least these particular guests were both family and old friends, so the memory of Freya and Marcus's wedding would be relived by them all from time to time.

'Rebecca not around this evening?' Rufus asked as she placed a steak on his plate.

'No. She's taken a day off,' Delphine said, sensing the despondency he was clearly trying to keep under wraps. She gave him a sympathetic smile. 'Would you like some fried onions and mushrooms with that?'

'Please.' Rufus nodded. 'Will she be around tomorrow when we all go our separate ways?' he asked, watching as she gave him a generous helping from the bowl keeping warm on the barbecue hotplate.

'We both usually make a point of saying goodbye to all our guests,' Delphine answered. 'But I suspect tomorrow you may have to make do without my sister. Sorry.'

Rufus sighed. 'Thanks. I guess you know why she is so determined to avoid me? Anything you can share with me?'

Delphine shook her head. 'Again, sorry. All she's told me is you and she knew each other a long time ago. Anything else is pure guesswork on my part.'

Rufus looked at her and waited but Delphine shook her head.

'Not my place to say anything. You'll have to keep hoping that Rebecca will eventually agree to talk to you.' As she started to turn the remaining beef burgers, she gave him a quick glance. 'Or give up and walk away.'

'I have no intention of walking away now that I've met up with Becky again,' Rufus said, leaving Delphine in no doubt that he was serious.

'If it's any consolation, I'm on your side. I think she should talk to you and I will try to put the pressure on for her to do so.'

'Thanks,' Rufus said.

There was a burst of laughter from the group around the table.

'I'd better get back to the others,' and Rufus turned to join his friends.

Delphine watched him walk away to join everyone around the large circular table, his shoulders slumped in dejection, his limp pronounced. Whatever reason her sister had for not talking to him, it was beyond cruel of her to treat Rufus like that – especially if what she suspected, turned out to be the truth.

Rebecca arrived back at the villa in time to stand unnoticed on the terrace for a few moments watching Delphine and Rufus talking. Sighing, she turned away and made for her apartment, where she planned to stay until Monday morning. She should have guessed that Delphine would see her car was back and come to find her after the barbecue finished.

It was almost ten o'clock when Delphine opened the apartment door and called out, 'Is it safe to come in?'

'Don't be silly, of course it's safe. I'm sorry I left you to deal with the day on your own. I hope there weren't any problems? I just needed to try to clear my head.'

'No problems, unless you count Rufus quizzing me about where you were and me not knowing what to say to him.'

'You and me both.' Rebecca bit her lip. 'I'm sorry.'

'Sorry is actually not good enough,' Delphine said. 'Are you going to talk to me now and tell me what is going on before I tell you what I suspect you're hiding.'

Rebecca eyed her sister. 'Go on then, tell me, what am I hiding?'

Delphine sighed in exasperation. 'You're hiding the fact that Rufus is Bart's father. Correct? Fast-forward twenty-five years and we have a father who has a son that he doesn't know exists and you have a son who, whilst knowing he does have a father out there somewhere, has never ever met him. And you don't want to talk about it. True or false?'

'Got it in one,' Rebecca said, fighting back the tears. 'A lucky guess or...'

'Bart looks like him,' Delphine said simply. 'And I'm his godmother, don't forget, so I know his middle name.'

Rebecca nodded. 'He does look like him. So as you're all-knowing, please tell me how I break that little gem of information to Rufus and...' Rebecca choked over her words. 'And how the hell do I tell Bart that his long-lost father has turned up?' The relief she'd felt when Bart had been unable to get home for the weekend had disappeared. Replaced by the knowledge there was no avoiding the truth now and she simply had to deal with it.

Delphine shook her head. 'I have no idea. I only know that you have to tell them.'

'I know that too,' Rebecca said. 'But it's going to be so difficult to find the right words for either of them.'

'You should have done it years ago. How could you be so selfish as to deny them a father-son relationship?' Delphine gave Rebecca a long, hard stare.

'I wasn't being selfish. I would have loved to have told Rufus I was pregnant, to have married him and had a proper family life, but I never got the chance. The thing I've never told you either is that Bart was the result of a one-night stand – well, one afternoon to give you the whole truth. The one and only time in my life I've ever done that and I fall pregnant.' Rebecca brushed tears away from her cheeks. 'Which was something I didn't find out until several weeks later by which time I was back here and had no way of contacting Rufus. I did try to find him.' She swallowed hard before continuing. 'I truly thought I'd found my soul mate that weekend and I sensed Rufus felt the same. Otherwise I would never have slept with him but there was such a connection between the two of us.' Rebecca's voice cracked. 'I couldn't believe something so lovely could turn so quickly into a major catastrophe of lost love. But I have no regrets over Bart.'

At her words, Delphine softened. 'Oh, Becky. You never said it was like that. I thought you were in a steady relationship with someone. A man on the yacht probably, who let you down. At least talk to Rufus now he's here and desperate to talk to you. Tell him the truth and see how he reacts.'

'What if he's got a wife – or a family already? How is that going to impact on everyone? Discovering you've got a twenty-four-year-old illegitimate son might come as a bit of a shock, don't you think?'

'He's here on his own,' Delphine said. 'I don't think he's married.'

'And what if he doesn't want to know Bart? Even if he does – is

Bart going to want to know him after all this time? He's always known he had a father out there somewhere and accepted that he wasn't in his life. He might be happy with the way things are and want to keep the status quo.' Rebecca pinched the bridge of her nose, closed her eyes and tried to breathe. 'I've spent the last two decades plus, putting Rufus out of my mind and my energy into this place while trying to raise a happy human being. And then it all begins to fall apart because Rufus turns up.'

It was Delphine's turn to sigh. 'You have to give both of them the opportunity of deciding for themselves the way forward.'

'You're right, of course you are. But as a mother, my first duty is to protect Bart, like it always has been, so I'll talk to Rufus first to see how he reacts. Find out if he wants to know about his son, have a belated relationship with him. If he walks away, I'll not tell Bart. If Rufus wants to meet him, I'll deal with it then. Does that sound like a plan?'

Delphine nodded. 'I think Rufus will insist on meeting Bart, even if he already has a family. It goes without saying that if you want me in on the conversation with Bart as moral support just say the word.'

'I will,' and Rebecca smiled at her sister. 'I'm just relieved that Bart hasn't been around this weekend. The thought of him and Rufus coming face to face without prior knowledge fills me with dread.'

PART III

AFTER THE WEDDING

26

Monday, mid-morning, and everyone was subdued taking their leave of Villa Sésame. Both Rebecca and Delphine were on the villa forecourt saying goodbye to the guests as cars were loaded and people prepared to set off.

To Verity's surprise, Effie had suggested she might like to stay with her for a few days, 'If you don't have anything to rush back for?'

'Nothing and no one to rush back for, so I'd love to stay with you,' Verity said. To her relief the weekend had gone well after her awkward surprise arrival and she'd enjoyed herself. 'I was going to see if I could stay at the Eden Roc for a few days. Staying with you will be much nicer. You can help me start to check out some properties – see if I find anything I like enough to move down here.' She'd meant what she'd said the other day about being tired of London but it was more than that she'd realised over the weekend. Something deep inside her had shifted, making her think seriously about living a different life to the one she'd created for herself. The life she envisaged living now was more family orientated. Put simply, she wanted to be closer to

Effie and Freya, her only family, and to have more contact with them.

Their suitcases were being loaded in the taxi she'd ordered for them both when Freya came over and gave her an unexpected hug.

'Marcus and I are so glad you came. I know things have been difficult between us for years, but hopefully this weekend has changed that a little?' and Freya smiled. 'How about a family supper for the six of us on Wednesday before Madeleine and co fly back? Mum will enjoy having you to herself for a day or two.'

'Family supper sounds good,' Verity said, hesitating. 'I finally managed to apologise to Clemmie, but I think I still owe you and Effie one for my behaviour down the years. I definitely need to apologise for my surprise appearance here.' Verity leant and kissed Freya on the cheek. 'Sorry. It was a wonderful wedding celebration by the way. I'm glad I didn't miss it.'

'I'm glad you came too,' Freya said, holding out her hand. 'Truce?'

'Truce,' Verity answered, shaking Freya's hand and smiling.

The taxi driver slammed the boot shut on the cases and opened the passenger door for Effie.

'Time to go, see you for the family supper in the week,' and Verity climbed in beside her aunt and the taxi drove away. Sitting there as the car made its way to Juan-les-Pins, Verity felt a wave of contentment sweep through her body. With Effie's oft repeated phrase 'family is family' going round and round in her head, she sensed everything after all these years was going to be all right.

* * *

Jonty, whose offer to chauffeur Clemmie and Angela to the airport had been gladly accepted by them, loaded their cases into his hire car and the three of them walked over to say their farewells to Rebecca and Delphine, then Freya and Marcus.

Freya hugged Clemmie and Angela. 'Promise me you'll both come and visit soon? We mustn't let time drift by again.'

'Oh, we're definitely visiting,' Clemmie said, glancing at Angela, who nodded in agreement.

'Thank you for letting a stranger gatecrash your wedding,' Jonty said.

'You might have arrived as a stranger, but you're leaving as a friend and I'm hoping that we will see more of you with Clemmie,' Freya said, smiling and giving him a hug too.

'Definitely,' Jonty replied, looking at Clemmie. 'Right, we'd better get going in case there are any hold-ups on the A8.'

As Jonty drove away, Rufus, placing his case in the car, waved in farewell. Remembering what Delphine had said to him, he'd been surprised to see Rebecca standing with her sister, laughing and joking as people said their goodbyes. Deciding he had nothing to lose, he made his way over to the two of them.

'Delphine, thank you for all of the wonderful food you've created this weekend.' He turned towards Rebecca and hesitated for a brief second or two. 'Becky, you and Delphine have created a wonderful venue here at Villa Sésame. I'm staying with Marcus and Freya for few days, any chance we could have that catch-up you've been avoiding ever since I arrived?'

Rebecca looked at him for several seconds before taking a deep breath and giving him a brief nod. 'We do need to talk and catch up with each other's lives. Would you like to have dinner with me in my apartment, Wednesday evening? It will be more private than meeting in a restaurant and... well, there is a lot of catching up to do. Eight o'clock okay for you?' She'd almost suggested tomorrow evening to get it over and done with, but forty-eight hours before facing him and telling him the truth would give her time to pull herself together. Decide how to phrase things to make them less hurtful for both of them.

Rufus stepped back, giving her an unfathomable look. 'I'll be here. See you then,' and he turned away, missing the look of consternation that crossed Rebecca's face as a car swept into the space on the forecourt vacated by Jonty and stopped close to where Rufus's car was parked.

Rebecca forced herself to stay calm, while she willed Rufus to reach his car without coming face to face with the new arrival who was opening his car door.

Deep in thought, Rufus barely noticed the young man getting out of the car next to his. He replied to his cheerful '*Bonjour*' with a quiet 'Hi' and a backward wave of acknowledgement, as he opened the driver's door and got in, trying to make sense of Rebecca's unexpected invitation to supper. Four days he'd been trying to talk to her. Four days she'd been avoiding him and now she wanted to have supper with him. And they had a lot of catching up to do? What the hell did that mean?

Starting the car, Rufus decided that dinner with Rebecca in her apartment at the villa promised to be interesting. But he promised himself he'd tell her how special their time together had been for him. He'd tell her too, how he'd tormented himself for months trying to find her.

Rebecca let out the breath she hadn't realised she was holding and watched as Rufus drove away.

'That was close,' Delphine murmured at her side.

Rebecca nodded and smiled as she was enveloped in a bear-like hug.

'Bart, darling. You're home.'

Freya, holding Lily by the hand, Marcus, Madeleine and Sean came over to say their farewells and Rebecca introduced Bart to them.

'This is my son. He's just returned from a delayed yacht delivery from Corsica, otherwise he would have been here helping over the weekend.'

'Corsica's not a bad place to be delayed though,' Marcus said as they shook hands. 'Had some good sailing over there.'

'Thank you so much for the goody box of wedding cake, chocolates and flowers. You gave us a wonderful and unforgettable weekend,' Freya said, before leaning down and speaking quietly to Lily. 'Can you give Rebecca the envelope I gave you to carry and remember the words I asked you to say?'

Lily nodded and held out a slightly screwed-up envelope to Rebecca.

'This is for you and...' Lily bit her lip before adding in a rush, 'everyone to have a treat. Granny and granddad loved getting married here. Thank you,' and Lily bobbed Rebecca a little curtsy.

Rebecca bent down and smiled. 'Thank you, Lily. It's been a pleasure having you all here.'

'Come on then, Lily, time to go.' And the family turned and made for their car. As they left, Lily could be seen waving frantically out of the window.

* * *

Freya, sitting next to Marcus as he drove, was quiet for a few moments before she glanced across at him.

'Did Bart remind you of anyone?'

Marcus gave a grim smile and nodded. 'Yep.'

'Are you thinking what I'm thinking then?'

'I'm thinking that it was a good job that he was unavoidably detained in Corsica, otherwise our wedding weekend could have become unforgettable for a different reason.'

'Do you think we should say something to Rufus?' Freya asked quietly.

'No.'

'But...' Freya sighed.

'I know he's planning to talk to Rebecca this week,' Marcus said. 'We'll just have to pray that he asks the right questions – and likes the answers he receives. And be there for him to help with the after-shocks.'

* * *

Jonty pulled to a stop in the 'Kiss and Fly' space outside Departures at Terminal 2 Nice Côte d'Azur airport and quickly got out of the car to hand the women their luggage. 'I'd come in with you, but I think I'd incur the wrath of a certain person, and probably a fine,' and he indicated an airport security man hovering nearby. 'I think it really had better be a case of kiss and fly today,' and he kissed Angela on her cheek before turning to get Clemmie's case.

Angela grasped the handle of her pull-along case. 'Thanks for the lift, Jonty, and for the company this weekend,' and she pulled her case nearer the entrance while Jonty pulled Clemmie's case out of the boot.

'I'm flying back Wednesday morning so have dinner with me that evening?' he asked. When Clemmie nodded, he smiled before giving her a kiss on the lips. 'I'll text you before then.'

Clemmie and Angela checked their luggage in and made sure they had their boarding passes and passports to hand, before making their way via security to duty-free, where they both spent more than they should on favourite perfumes and other things they couldn't resist, before carrying their posh carrier bags through to the departure lounge ready to board.

'I can't thank you enough for pushing me into coming with you this week,' Angela said, turning to look at Clemmie as the plane taxied along the runway, preparing for take-off, half an hour later. 'And I'm definitely going to take Freya up on her offer to visit. In fact, the last five days have been a bit of a wake-up call for me, especially Effie's forthright advice.'

'Are you going to do what she suggested?'

Angela looked thoughtful. 'I went for a walk in the olive grove and convinced myself that her advice was exactly what I needed to hear and act upon. I am going to try harder to accept the fact that Paul dying was a tragic accident and was down to the muck on the road, rather than my fault. And I'm going to let sleeping dogs lie, as they say, as far as the police are concerned but...' she hesitated. 'But I'm wavering again over the rest of what she said. I honestly do not know the best thing to do – to tell or not to tell Will.'

'I know you've found it hard keeping it to yourself since the accident and the guilt has been churning away inside,' Clemmie said gently. 'If it was me, I'm not sure I could live the rest of my life with a secret like that eating away at me.'

'I'm not sure I can either,' Angela confessed quietly. 'Part of me is convinced that my son will accept that it was a tragic accident that killed his father, one which would have happened whoever was driving the bike. But another part of me...' she shrugged. 'What if Effie is right, I tell him the truth and Will turns away from me?'

Clemmie was silent for several minutes. 'I don't think the Will I've known almost since the day he was born has grown into the kind of man who would be that hurtful to his mother.'

Angela turned and looked at Clemmie. 'You're right. As a boy, he was always comforting his friends when they were down, jollying them along and lifting them up to make them feel good. I've never known him to be deliberately unkind to anyone. Thanks for reminding me, Clemmie,' and Angela took the inflight magazine out of the seat pocket in front of her and began to flick through it, although her mind was elsewhere. She might have begun the long difficult process of forgiving herself for Paul's death but would Will forgive her once she told him the truth about the accident?

27

Clemmie insisted Angela stayed the night with her rather than drive home once they got back to Dartmouth on Monday evening. She treated Angela to a takeaway fish and chip supper as a small thank you for playing chauffeur and they took it out into the garden to enjoy with a glass of duty-free wine.

'Not quite the champagne we've been spoilt with, but we have to come back down to earth, ready for everyday life to start again tomorrow, after a wonderful time away,' Clemmie said, raising her glass. 'Cheers.'

'It was a surreal experience at times,' Angela said as they clinked glasses. 'I'm so pleased that Freya and Marcus got a second chance at their happy ever after. I loved the south of France too. It was the first time I'd been down there. Only ever been to Paris.'

'You said something on the plane earlier about having a wake-up call?' Clemmie said. 'Want to tell me about it?'

Angela smiled thoughtfully. 'Yes. Spending five days away from the sad routine that ruled my life at home, in the sublime tranquility of Villa Sésame, gave me some much-needed thinking space. I've realised nobody else is going to sort my life out, I'm the only one who can change things.'

'Any ideas how?'

'No idea, but clinging to things from the past is not healthy. I need to move forward, find something for me.' Angela finished her drink. 'May I ask you something?'

Clemmie nodded. 'Of course, anything.'

'Coming back here after your divorce, was that difficult? Or was it totally the right thing for you?'

'For me, coming back to my roots was the right thing to do,' Clemmie said without a second's hesitation. 'Neither you nor Freya were here, but other people who'd known me all my life were and that made it easier. There are a lot of incomers these days, but the real locals are still here too. The first day I moved back, I walked along the embankment and I met three people who knew me and were pleased to see me. I did think about going somewhere completely fresh, like the Cotswolds or Dorset, places where I don't know a soul, but I'm so glad I came home in the end.'

'Thanks, good to know. And now you've met Jonty,' Angela said, looking at Clemmie.

'Mm. I have.'

'And?'

'And nothing – yet,' and Clemmie smiled happily at her before switching the conversation back to Angela. 'Are you thinking of moving then?'

'It's only just dawning on me I'm free to go, live, wherever I want,' Angela admitted. 'Whether I've got enough courage to take a leap into the dark on my own...' she shrugged.

'Before you leave in the morning, we'll go for a walk around town,' Clemmie said. 'There's a couple of things thing I want to show you.'

Angela raised her eyebrows. 'What sort of things?'

'You'll see,' and Clemmie refused to be drawn on the subject.

* * *

Nine o'clock, Tuesday morning, the two of them walked down to the town's car park where Angela had left her car overnight and locked her case in the car boot.

'Come on, this way.' After crossing Mayor's Avenue, Clemmie led Angela towards Undercliffe, the narrow lane with its ancient fishermen's cottages that ran behind it.

'These have smartened up since I last saw them,' Angela commented as they walked past quirky cottages with hanging baskets and terracotta pots amassed with summer flowers guarding front doors.

'They're very desirable these days. A couple are currently up for sale,' Clemmie added, giving Angela an innocent look. 'I doubt they'll be on the market long.'

'Too small for me,' Angela said. 'And, to be honest, I'd prefer somewhere with a more open aspect.'

'In that case, you'll like the next one in Ford Valley. Come on.'

Angela did like the look of the next house Clemmie showed her, but it was the third one in South Town with its view out over the river that made her catch her breath. 'What a great position.'

Clemmie gave her a sly grin. 'I saved the best for last. Shall we pick up the details from the estate agent as we go through town?'

'Yes.' Angela didn't hesitate. Maybe a move back to Dartmouth would never happen but she found she was excited at the thought of living back in her home town. Being close to Clemmie as she began a new phase of her life without Paul in familiar surroundings would be a bonus.

* * *

Standing saying goodbye to her friend half an hour later, Clemmie gave her a hug.

'This morning was just a bit of fun, an exercise to show you what is available if you did decide to take a leap into the dark and come back home.'

'I've got some serious thinking to do,' Angie said. 'But, you know, the prospect of coming home to Dartmouth appeals enormously.'

'Sometimes, going back is the right thing to do, despite the soothsayers who will always yell, never go back. And don't forget you can always come and live with me for a bit while you're house hunting. We can do it together; I love looking at houses.'

'Aren't you going to be too busy keeping Jonty company to help me?' Angela said innocently.

Clemmie laughed. 'Always time for some house-hunting porn.'

After Angela had left, Clemmie wandered homewards back through town deep in thought about her friend. Angela had been more like her old self that morning, a different woman to the one Clemmie had accompanied to Villa Sésame a week ago. That woman wouldn't have been contemplating for a single moment the idea of selling up and moving. Spending time with old friends, talking to them about Paul's accident, had been good for Angela. Of course, in the end, Angela had to do what was right for her and Clemmie would support her whatever she decided to do but having her living back in Dartmouth would be good. Mentally, Clemmie crossed her fingers for that to happen. Climbing the steps from Fairfax Place towards The Cherub pub, Clemmie pushed thoughts of Angela to one side and began planning the rest of her day and hoping Jonty would text her soon as he'd promised.

She was sitting out in the garden eating a cheese sandwich for lunch when her phone pinged.

Looking forward to seeing you tomorrow night. 8 o'clock supper at my place? Will have a small surprise for you! Xx

See you then. Can I bring anything? Xx

Just yourself. Xx

Travel safe. xx

And Clemmie put her phone back down on the table, a happy smile on her face.

28

After leaving Clemmie, Angela had driven home on autopilot, so many things were swirling around in her brain. She knew she'd come home a different woman to the one she'd been just a week ago. Going to Freya's wedding, seeing her friends, talking about things, had finally pushed a switch in her brain after the months of torment and broken the barrier of grief she'd erected around herself. Of course, she'd continue to miss Paul and her love for him would never die, but she couldn't waste the rest of her own life wallowing in guilt. Paul would expect her to mourn, accept what had happened and then get on with her life. And that was exactly what she was determined to do now. Even though she knew it would be difficult, she had to take that first step.

Once she'd unloaded the car, opened the doors and windows to let some fresh air into the house, put the washing on, done all the routine things that needed to be done after a holiday, she began to make a list. Top of the list was talk to Will. She glanced at the clock – one o'clock – and picked up her phone and typed,

Are you free to talk? Xxx

and pressed send on WhatsApp.

Thirty seconds later her phone rang.

'You okay, Mum?' Will's anxious voice said as she answered.

'Everything is fine. I'm back home after a wonderful time and wanted to talk to you about a couple of things. Can you and Steph come down soon?'

'Possibly. I'll talk to Steph about it this evening and let you know.'

Angela could feel her buoyant mood sinking. She'd been silly expecting Will to drop everything and agree to a visit without consulting his partner.

'Can't you tell me now what it is you want to talk about?' Will asked.

'There's something I'd rather do face to face, although...' Angela hesitated. 'One of the things is – how would you feel about me selling this house and moving to Dartmouth?'

There was a second or two of silence and Angela pictured her son weighing up his words, which were a surprise to her when he did speak.

'I'm actually pleased that you have come up with that idea,' Will said. 'I think it would be good for you to sell the house and start afresh somewhere. Going back to Dartmouth though?'

'I can't think of anywhere else I'd rather live. I was happy growing up there and I'm sure I'd be happy living there now in my dotage,' she added, laughing, as an image of Bayards Cove with Freya, Clemmie and herself as teenagers sitting dangling their feet in the river, eating ice-creams, flashed into her mind. These days they'd probably eat their ice-creams decorously sitting on one of the benches.

'Fair enough, then go for it. Not that you're in your dotage – years to go yet. Put the house on the market. When it sells, Steph and I will definitely come and help with the move.'

'Thanks, I'd appreciate that,' Angela said. 'But please come for a weekend soon, even if Steph can't make it and you come alone. I do need to tell you something else, and no, I'm not doing it over the phone.'

'Okay. Right, I need to get back to work now. I'll ring you later. Love you, Mum,' and Will ended the call.

Angela heaved a sigh of relief. The wheels were in motion for a new beginning. She'd give the house and garden a good tidy-up and then next week she'd contact the local estate agent. After months of existing in a vacuum, she had a plan. For the first time since losing Paul she had a plan she felt excited about.

Tuesday afternoon and both Effie and Verity were sitting in the shade of a large parasol out on the small terrace at the back of Effie's ground-floor apartment. Verity sniffed appreciatively as the smell of orange blossom from the trees in pots by the back door drifted past her nostrils on the gentle breeze. Hearing the sound of splashing water and happy childish laughter coming from the large swimming pool in the grounds, Verity glanced across at her aunt.

'Fancy a swim later?'

'Perhaps,' Effie said. 'Once the children have been banished for the day. As much as I love children, I like to swim in peace.'

On the teak table in front of them were several property brochures Verity had picked up as she and Effie had walked home after lunch in Antibes. Verity started to thumb through the pages of a particularly glossy brochure extolling the many delights of an exclusive property situated on the Cap d'Antibes, whilst Effie became absorbed in the monthly property magazine published as a joint effort by all the local agents with the more down-market properties currently available.

Verity sighed as she threw the brochure she'd been looking at onto the table and picked up another one.

'You didn't fancy that one?' Effie said.

'Bit pricey. To be honest, Effie, I don't know what I'm looking for – or even why, really.'

Effie put her magazine down and looked at her niece.

'I'm so glad you decided to come to the wedding, although I admit I could have throttled you for turning up like you did,' Effie said. 'At least you and Freya have had a chance to get closer. Knowing you apologised to Clemmie meant a great deal to Freya.'

'It was something I should have had the courage to do years ago. Clemmie apologising to me was the last thing I expected,' Verity said. 'I'd never blamed her for saying what she did. The whole sorry incident was my fault.'

'Well, it may be selfish of me, but I can't help hoping that you do come and join the family down here. It would make your mum happy too, I know.'

'I've always loved it down here and I like the idea of being nearer you, Freya, and seeing little Lily and the new one growing up but...' Verity paused. 'I'm bored back home now that I don't have a regular job or a reason to get up in the morning. So, let's say I find somewhere I really like down here, I sell up and move. Once I'm in the new place and settled, six months down the line is life going to turn into the same boring routine I already have? Will I still be a lady "wot" lunches, only this time enjoying more sunshine? Maybe it's a case of the devil I know and staying put.' Verity shook her head. 'Moving itself is always such a hassle.'

'Personally, I find the extra sunshine uplifting and wonderful,' Effie said. 'And when it does rain, which it does, you know that it's unlikely to pour for more than a couple of days, rather than weeks. Although recently there's been a couple of devastating flash floods, so we're not immune to bad weather down here. But if you're worried about being bored, how about finding a job of some sort?'

'I've been my own boss for so long, I'd find that difficult,' Verity admitted. 'But I think I definitely need a challenge, wherever I decide to live.' She paused. 'If I get a chance to talk to Freya tomorrow night at supper, I'll ask her advice and see if she has any suggestions as to what I could usefully do down here.'

Effie nodded her agreement. 'Good idea. And tonight you can come with me and Cecily for a game of bridge. That'll be a challenge and a half and get your brain working!'

* * *

Rebecca, Delphine and Bart were having supper out on the small villa terrace on Tuesday evening, all signs of the past weekend's wedding activity having been cleared away, the terrace blown clear of leaves and litter before being pressure-washed. Bart, who loved cooking, had helped Delphine to rustle up a large pasta and ratatouille dish with grated parmesan cheese and a side salad.

'How far have you got with your travel plans, Delphine?' Bart asked.

'I've got the boots and the wet-weather gear and that's about it for now,' Delphine laughed. 'Haven't worked out an itinerary yet.'

'Boots and wet-weather gear sound like you're planning to climb a mountain,' Bart said.

'Definitely doing some hiking but no mountains – well, not tall ones anyway.'

'Have you thought any more about joining her, Mum, or selling up?'

Rebecca shook her head. 'Been too busy to give it much thought.' She smothered a yawn. 'Sorry, I'm a bit tired.'

Rebecca was finding it difficult to concentrate, not only on the food, but also on the conversation. Her thoughts kept zoning out from the other two, returning to Rufus and how he was likely to react when she told him the truth tomorrow evening. It didn't help that every time she looked at Bart, his face blurred and all she could see now was how much he resembled Rufus.

'Mum, I realise you've had a busy few days and you're probably tired, but you seem like you're miles away. Did you even hear what I just said?'

'Sorry. I'm listening now, so tell me again.' And Rebecca dragged her thoughts away from Rufus to concentrate on what her son was saying.

'I was telling you I have met someone special whom I really like. Her name is Kameela, she's from Martinique and she's a nurse at the Arnault Tzanck hospital in Mougins.' Bart took out his phone and scrolled through some photographs. 'Look, isn't she beautiful?' And he handed his phone to Rebecca. 'I want you and Delphine to meet her, so you're both invited to supper tomorrow evening at her apartment in Mougins,' Bart continued. 'I've checked your office diary and there are no parties or meetings scheduled in until the weekend, so no excuse,' and Bart gazed at her expectantly.

'She is beautiful,' Rebecca said as she gazed at the photo of Kameela for some time, hoping her face didn't show the shock she was feeling hearing his invitation. Her first thought, that she'd almost spoken aloud, was, *I can't meet her tomorrow evening because I'm having dinner with your father to tell him about your existence.* She handed the phone back and Bart smiled as he placed it on the table.

'I wanted to introduce you before I went away on that last

rush job, but there was no time,' Bart continued. 'Kameela is off duty tomorrow and it was her suggestion to invite you for supper.'

'How long have you known Kameela? You've never mentioned her before,' Rebecca said, delaying the moment of having to tell Bart she couldn't make it tomorrow, whilst her brain frantically tried to think of a legitimate excuse.

'Six months. So you'll come?'

Rebecca shook her head. 'I can't. I know there's nothing in the business diary, but I've agreed to have dinner with an old friend.' That was the truth. Bart didn't need to know the name of the friend for now but she wished she hadn't seen the look of disappointment on his face.

'Could you move it to another night? This is important for me, Mum. Or bring the friend with you – the more, the merrier. Do I know this friend?'

'No, you don't.' Rebecca's reply sounded sharper than she meant it to and Bart looked at her quizzically before shooting a quick glance at Delphine.

'While I was helping Delphine with supper earlier, she mentioned that an old boyfriend of yours had been a guest at the wedding last week,' Bart hesitated. 'Is it him you are having dinner with?'

'Yes. How about lunch on Thursday here? Could you both manage that?' Rebecca hoped she didn't sound as desperate as she felt. Why, oh why, had Delphine even mentioned to Bart that she'd known one of the wedding guests and why wouldn't Delphine look at her now?

'I could, but Kameela will be working. Can't you change to another evening?'

'I could try, I suppose,' Rebecca said. 'But I'm not sure how long Rufus is staying around for.' She immediately realised and regretted her mistake in mentioning his name, as Bart stiffened and narrowed his eyes.

'Rufus?'

Rebecca closed her eyes and nodded, sensing the sudden tension in the air and knowing exactly the direction the conversation was about to take. A conversation she'd intended to have after the painful one she was psyching herself up for tomorrow evening. When she would know Rufus's reaction to the news of his unknown son. The two conversations appeared to have swapped places and now she was having to have them the wrong way round, something she was unprepared for. Bart, on the other hand, was rapidly charging ahead and adding two and two together.

'Bartholomew Rufus West, my full name,' Bart said, emphasising each name. 'Interesting.'

The silence around the table deepened.

'Is there any significance in the fact that you gave me your old friend's name?' Bart asked, giving Rebecca a penetrating stare, which she tried to return without flinching, and failed. 'A man you lost touch with years ago? A man I have never met?' Bart gave her another sharp look. 'This Rufus guy isn't going to turn out to be my father is he?' Seeing her face, he stared at her and swore. '*Merde.* After all these years he deigns to turn up? Well, do me a favour and send him away. I'm too old to need a father figure in my life.'

'It isn't a question of him "deigning" to turn up. He has no idea about you. He was as surprised to see me as I was him,' Rebecca protested. Things were spiralling out of her control. This was not the reaction from Bart she'd hoped for. She wished he'd let her explain properly but right now he was clearly too upset to listen to reason. 'Dinner tomorrow is a chance for the two of us to catch up. For me to tell him about you. Afterwards, I'm looking forward...' she took a deep breath, 'to introducing the two of you to each other. I know it's not an ideal situation, but I'm sure the two of you will get on when you meet.' Rebecca glanced at Delphine, willing her to say something, but her sister simply grimaced at her and shook her head.

'If it's true he doesn't know about me, keep it that way because I'm not interested in meeting him.' Bart pushed his plate away and stood up. 'I'll tell Kameela tomorrow night is a no-go for you and that I have no idea now when she'll get to meet my mother. Delphine, you're still invited to come to supper if you would like to. Let me know. Right now, I'm going back to Antibes.' And he picked up his phone from the table where he'd placed it and left them.

'Well, that went well, didn't it?' Rebecca said to Delphine as she placed her elbows on the table and with a groan of despair covered her face with her hands. 'How can I explain if he won't even listen?'

'He'll come round,' Delphine said. 'Give him a day or two and once he's calmed down he'll want to know the truth.' She stood up and started to clear the supper things. 'For a start you can stop imagining the worst case scenario and think positive. To unexpectedly be told his birth father was actually here in Antibes must have been a huge shock for Bart and his instinct after all these years of not knowing anything about his father, was to lash out and deny it mattered to him.'

'I hope you're right,' Rebecca answered. 'Because if he doesn't I don't know what I'll do.'

Delphine stayed for another half-an-hour before leaving a calmer Rebecca to the rest of her evening. Walking back to her cottage, Delphine remembered Bart asking about her travel plans earlier. The last week had been too busy and stressful for her to even pull up the file grandly entitled 'My World Tour' she'd created on her laptop to keep track of everything. She did need to make a start on working out some sort of basic itinerary and begin to look into flights and accommodation. As she put her key in the front door of the cottage she resolved that this evening she would at least open the file and begin to think about the route she wanted to take. If nothing else, it would take her mind off the current crisis back at Villa Sésame.

Half an hour later, after a quick shower, putting her pyjamas on and pouring herself a glass of wine, Delphine sat in front of her open laptop staring at the list of the places she planned to visit. Australia, Mexico, Canada and America. They were all so far away from Europe. Maybe she should start with somewhere closer? Italy? She'd never been to Venice. André had promised to take her one day telling her, like Paris, it was a place for lovers. Not somewhere she wanted to go on her own then.

Delphine closed the laptop down. It was no good. She couldn't concentrate on planning her journey until Rebecca's unexpected time bomb from the past had been defused to everyone's satisfaction. And who knew how long that would take.

29

Clemmie hummed happily to herself as she walked to Jonty's on Wednesday evening. Despite him saying she wasn't to take anything, she couldn't go empty-handed so she'd slipped a box of Calissons de Provence she'd bought in duty-free at Nice airport into her tote. She hoped he liked the little diamond-shaped marzipan cakes with their iced tops that were a favourite of hers.

Dartmouth had been busy until five or six o'clock with day trippers, but now they'd left and the locals and the holiday-makers staying in the town were out enjoying the relative peace of the evening. The restaurants were busy. Walking past The Dartmouth Arms pub, Clemmie heard the sound of laughter and conversation drifting out and people were standing on Bayards Cove with drinks in their hands, happily chatting to friends.

Jonty's front door was a bright canary yellow with a brass anchor door knocker. As she gave a gentle tap, she heard a dog bark inside. Seconds later, as Jonty opened the door, Hamish, wearing a tartan scarf, was winding himself around her legs.

'Hamish, behave,' Jonty said as he leant in to give her a welcoming kiss.

'Victoria and Emma are back from Scotland then?' she asked.

'Yes. Glass of champagne awaits you in the sitting room.'

'Which is where?' Clemmie looked around.

'I'd forgotten you've not been here before. It's through here,' and Jonty took her by the hand and led her into a spacious open-plan room with the kitchen and a dining area where a glass-topped table was supper-ready, with cutlery, crockery and glasses placed on its surface. Further into the room, there were a couple of settees and a coffee table in front of a large double-glazed picture window overlooking the river. An ice bucket with a bottle of champagne and two glasses were on the low table.

'Wow. What a view – I thought mine was good, but this is spectacular. Does it get a bit hairy when we have a storm?'

'It's been fine so far, but if we get a strong southerly, I admit to crossing my fingers and praying.'

Jonty eased the cork out of the champagne bottle with a satisfactory pop and poured two glasses.

'*Santé*,' he said and they clinked glasses.

'Are we celebrating anything in particular?' Clemmie asked.

'A couple of things. One, it's the first of July, so my divorce is finally complete. Two, I have you in my life.' Jonty gave her an anxious look as he said this and smiled when she nodded and said: 'You do.' 'And thirdly, the surprise I mentioned to you is Hamish is now mine officially. I had to do a detour from the airport and pick him up instead of coming straight home.'

Clemmie looked at him, surprised.

'Emma has agreed to do more hours in the bookshop cafe and Victoria insists it isn't fair to leave him at home on his own for hours at a time – particularly when I, apparently, have nothing to do all day. So I agreed to have him, on the condition that he becomes my dog officially, but Emma has full visiting rights. Which I'm happy about actually, I'm fond of the little chap.'

'He's adorable,' Clemmie said, bending down to stroke Hamish.

'How was your flight home? Angela all right?'

'Yes, I'm so glad I persuaded her to go to France. She came home determined to get her life back on track. She's even thinking of selling up and moving back here, which would be lovely from my point of view.'

A buzzer pinged in the kitchen. 'Ah, that will be the garlic bread ready to go with our creamy chicken and mushroom pasta. And before you get the wrong idea, I'm no cook. The new delicatessen in town is highly recommended. Come on, time to eat.'

Clemmie reached into her tote. 'Before I forget, I brought you these. I hope you like them.' She held out the box of Calissons de Provence.

'A favourite treat. Thank you. We'll open them with coffee later.'

Both the main dish and the strawberry gateau for dessert were delicious. Over supper, conversation flowed, they talked about Freya and Marcus, the wedding, they made plans to go sailing and Clemmie sensed the time they'd spent together in France had moved their friendship up several notches. As the evening went on, she half expected Victoria to ring Jonty demanding his help on something or other.

Jonty saw her smother a smile and gave her a look. 'Penny for them?'

'I keep expecting your phone to ring with Victoria wanting something now that you're back from France,' she confessed.

Jonty shook his head. 'She knows I'm no longer available, except for real emergencies, and I've told her even then I am the last resort, not the first one. Would you like a coffee?'

Clemmie glanced at her watch. 'Gosh, it's eleven o'clock. I ought to think about going home.'

'Hamish and I will walk you back,' Jonty said.

Five minutes later and they were climbing the steps from Fairfax Place, past The Cherub and on up the next flight of steps into Above Town.

As she put her key in the front door lock, Clemmie looked at Jonty. 'I really enjoyed this evening, thank you. Would you like to come in for a coffee – or a nightcap?' She caught his glance downwards to Hamish and knew he'd realised the unspoken invitation behind her words and was worried about the dog. 'Hamish is welcome too. I have an old cushion he can sleep on.'

'In that case, yes, I would like to come in,' Jonty said, holding her gaze. 'For a nightcap.'

30

After Bart's outburst and him storming away the evening before, Rebecca found her thoughts going round and round in circles. Try as she might, she couldn't put Bart's unhappy reaction to the news that his unknown father had turned up out of her mind. She wished Bart's arrival had been delayed until later in the week when she would have had a chance to talk to Rufus. To discover how he felt about having an unknown grown-up son before she mentioned him to Bart. Now she had to face the possibility that even if Rufus was overjoyed to learn he had a son, it was a son who wanted nothing to do with him. Would it be kinder not to tell him about Bart after all?

In the early years after Bart had been born, she'd practised how she'd break the news to Rufus that he was a father, if he should happen to turn up in her life again. As the years wore on and the chances of her and him meeting up again became more and more remote, she'd pushed the need to be prepared into the depths of her brain. She'd also spent the last two decades plus, putting Rufus out of her mind, convincing herself she was over him. The last five days had proved how big a lie she'd been spinning herself all those years. The moment she'd heard his voice on Thursday morning, last week, she'd known she was in trouble – with no idea how to resolve things. Hiding away from him had solved nothing. In fact, every time she'd caught a sneaky glimpse of him, or the couple of occasions he'd approached her, had only served to bring those long-ago feelings hurtling to the front of her mind.

And now that the gods had decided to cause havoc by bringing Rufus back into her life, she couldn't find the right words to tell him about Bart. Casually drop it into the conversation over supper tonight? 'Oh, by the way you've got a twenty-four-year-old son, but don't worry, you don't have to play happy families because he doesn't want to meet you.'

Seeing Rufus this weekend had shown Rebecca how much Bart resembled his father. Every time she'd looked at him yesterday, she'd seen the young Rufus she'd known and fallen in love with. It was the way the corners of Bart's mouth turned up when he smiled, the way his eyes crinkled, the mole on his left cheek. It was like a mirror reflection of Rufus. Bart might have her brown hair and not Rufus's blond colouring, but nobody would ever doubt their connection if they saw them together in the same room.

Rebecca was riffling through her wardrobe desperately trying to decide what to wear when Delphine brought up the supper she'd asked her to prepare – lasagna and salad, followed by fresh raspberries from the kitchen garden and cream.

'Thanks for doing this,' Rebecca said. 'I'm so nervous about this evening, I doubt I could concentrate on getting a meal together.'

'Put the lasagna in the oven on 180°C for about thirty minutes when Rufus arrives,' Delphine said. 'No starter, but I've brought some nibbles up to go with this,' and Delphine held up a bottle of champagne before she deftly put everything in the fridge and turned to face her sister. 'It's bound to feel a bit strange at first, twenty-five years is a long time to be apart from someone without throwing the added complication of an unknown son into the mix, but I'm sure everything will work out in the end.'

'I'm not sure I'm going to tell Rufus about Bart this evening,' Rebecca said quietly.

'Why not?'

Rebecca shrugged. 'There's no guarantee he's going to want to acknowledge him after all this time. Besides, is there any point when Bart refuses to meet him?'

'Rufus still deserves to know he has a son,' Delphine said. 'Even if it does come as a shock.'

'We don't know that he hasn't already got a son, a family, somewhere. Telling him about Bart could perhaps create unwanted waves in his life.'

'Even so.' Delphine sighed.

'I'll treat this evening as a catch-up supper with an old friend,' Rebecca said decisively. 'Learn about how his life has been, ask about family and then decide whether or not to tell him about Bart.'

Delphine shook her head. 'I think you're wrong not to tell him tonight. Not being able to tell him from the beginning is one thing, but keeping the news a secret when you have the opportunity to talk to him is another thing altogether. I'll see you in the morning,' and Delphine shook her head in disbelief at her sister before she turned to leave. 'Nearly forgot. I've accepted Bart and Kameela's supper invitation for this evening. I'm looking forward to meeting her.'

Rebecca's mouth opened to protest, *You can't meet her before me*, as she looked at her sister, but before she could utter a word,

Delphine shrugged and left, closing the apartment door behind her.

Tiredly, Rebecca rubbed her eyes. Life was becoming impossibly complicated. She should have cancelled tonight's supper and spent the evening with Bart and his girlfriend, not hurt him like she had by refusing.

As for Rufus – what difference would an extra twenty-four hours' delay have made after so many years of no contact? There was no guarantee, though, that Rufus would have still been in Antibes tomorrow evening. But if he was truly desperate to talk to her he would have stayed for as long as necessary, wouldn't he? Or return on some date in the future? Which would leave her in a sword of Damocles situation, for who knew how long?

Taking a deep breath and deciding there was nothing she could do to change the current situation, she could only deal with the fallout tomorrow, Rebecca returned to searching through her wardrobe. She wanted to look good but not overdressed. In the end, she pulled on her favourite capri-type jeans, tucked a classic three-quarter-sleeved white cotton shirt in at the waist and slipped her feet into her favourite wedge sandals. There, she was ready for what was sure to be one of the most momentous evenings of her life, however it ended.

At five to eight, Rebecca went into the kitchen and set both the oven and the buzzer in case she forgot the time. Walking through the sitting room towards the apartment door, a framed photograph on the bookcase caught her eye. She and Bart were sitting at a table in a favourite restaurant down by the marina. Bart's birthday last year. Rebecca remembered Delphine insisting on recording the occasion with a photograph. Quickly, she placed a couple of books in front of it, pushing it out of sight.

Downstairs, waiting in the office for Rufus, she wondered about Delphine's reaction to her plan to delay telling him about his son. Surely it was better to wait, learn about his life, see how the evening went, before blurting out such a bombshell. Telling somebody such a huge piece of news that could throw their life into disarray after such a long absence could be mind-blowing.

No, telling Rufus about Bart was best put on the back-burner for the evening. Even if it did leave her with that flipping sword of Damocles hanging over her head.

* * *

Rufus was helping Freya set the table on the roof terrace ready for the family supper under the stars, before he left for his rendezvous with Becky. Lily was fast asleep in the travel cot and Madeleine had gone for a nap too in the cool of her bedroom. Marcus and Sean were due back soon after an afternoon sailing out in the bay.

'Freya, did Marcus mention to you I'd like to buy two of your paintings?' Rufus asked as he placed wine glasses on the table.

'The Gunfield Hotel ones? He did, and of course you can.'

'Thanks. I can give you a cheque or cash if you like tomorrow, but I'd like to take one with me this evening as a surprise for Becky, if that's okay with you.'

'Sure. We'll talk about payment tomorrow. Both the paintings are down in the hallway, take whichever one you want.' Freya hesitated, wondering whether she could somehow prepare him for the surprise he was likely to get this evening, if she and Marcus were correct in their assumption about Bart, and decided she couldn't. Only Rebecca had the right to break that kind of news to him. In the end, she kissed Rufus on the cheek and simply said. 'Good Luck for this evening. I really hope you get the answers you want and things work out.'

'You and me both.'

Rufus was about to leave for Villa Sésame when Freya opened the door to greet Effie and Verity.

'You're not joining us this evening?' Effie said as they exchanged cheek kisses. 'And don't give me any nonsense about not being family.'

'He knows he's more than welcome, but tonight he's got a prior engagement,' Freya answered. 'Mum, why don't make your way up to the terrace while I give Verity a quick guided tour of the house?'

'I'll see you all later,' Rufus said and, picking up the painting from where it was leaning against the wall now safely bubble-wrapped in some packaging Freya had found for him, he left.

He was apprehensive as he began the drive up to the villa. Becky had finally agreed to see him to catch up with each other, but why was she so keen on them meeting in private? Was she afraid of being seen out on the town with him for some reason? He was more than happy to talk about that long-ago weekend, but he also wanted to talk about the present and the future. To gently probe and see if that wonderful spark that had ignited between them all those years ago still existed. He knew without a doubt that it did for him.

The memory of the moment Marcus had called out to her on the Thursday he'd arrived at Villa Sésame would be etched on his mind forever. When the office door had opened and there she was, standing in front of him, coolly holding out her hand to greet him, he'd been taken back twenty-five years and thought he was dreaming. Within a minute though, as he'd stood there like an idiot, unable to string any words together, so surprised and unprepared for her to reappear back in his life after all this time, Becky had returned to her office and, metaphorically speaking, bolted the door against them renewing their friendship while he was staying at Villa Sésame.

Now, as he parked on the forecourt of the villa and got out of the car, he hesitated about taking the painting in. Perhaps Becky would feel it was a bit over the top as an 'I'm thrilled to be back in touch with you' type present. If the evening went well, he'd give it to her before he left. He reached instead for the luxury box of Jeff de Bruges chocolates he'd bought in Antibes that afternoon. He closed the car door and turned to see Becky waiting for him by the open door of the villa, a nervous smile on her face.

* * *

Delphine smiled at Bart as he threw open the door of Kameela's apartment and gave his aunt a tight hug. 'I wasn't sure that you would come,' he said. 'I thought maybe Mum would try to stop you.'

'You know better than that. Here, this is from both of us,' and Delphine held out a bottle of red wine she'd taken from the villa's stock. It wasn't from Rebecca as well, but that was her secret and Bart didn't need to know that.

'Come on through and meet Kameela, she's slaving away in the kitchen,' Bart said. Lowering his voice, he added, 'She's a bit nervous about meeting you. She's worried that her cooking won't be good enough for a famous chef.'

'Silly girl,' Delphine said. 'Does Kameela speak English?' Bart had been brought up speaking both French and English, but all three of them tended to lapse into English these days when they were at home together.

Bart shook his head. 'No. Just French. Come on through and meet her.'

'Kameela, it is a real pleasure to meet you,' Delphine said, slipping into French. 'And the photograph Bart showed us didn't do you justice. *Tu es belle.*'

Kameela smiled shyly. '*Enchanté*, Delphine.'

'Something smells delicious in here,' Delphine said, wrinkling her nose. 'Wouldn't be Chicken Colombo by any chance?'

Kameela nodded. 'My grandmother's recipe.'

'Family recipes are the best,' Delphine said.

'Please sit,' Kameela indicated the chairs round the kitchen table as she placed a plate of pâtés Créoles on the table. Bart poured them a glass of wine each from a bottle that was already open on the table, allowing it to breathe, to accompany the puff pastry starters.

'I feel guilty you've spent the day slaving away in the kitchen on your day off,' Delphine said.

'It's not a problem, I enjoy cooking. It relaxes me. Except cooking for someone who also cooks – well, that is stressful.' Kameela smiled nervously at Delphine.

'How's Mum?' Bart interrupted, before Delphine could reassure Kameela. 'Didn't surprise us and cancel her date to come here instead then.'

Delphine heard the bitter note in his voice and gave her nephew a severe look. 'This last week has been a difficult one for her. And you storming out the other day didn't help,' she said to Bart. 'Tonight isn't a date in the way you think. It's a chance for both of them, especially your mum, to come to terms with what happened twenty-five years ago.' Delphine took a sip of her wine. 'You have very little to blame your mother for. She did everything she could as a single mum, to give you the best childhood, to make sure you never went without, to try to ensure you grew up to be a decent human being. You need to talk to her, and listen to her explanation.'

'You sound like Kameela; she's had a go at me too.'

'Family is important,' Kameela said quietly. 'When they're just up the road, you can hug them every day. It's harder when they're in different countries. In my book, you don't fall out with family, they're too precious.'

Silence greeted her words as Delphine and Bart stared at her for several seconds before Delphine looked at Bart. 'Well, that's you told.'

Bart pushed his chair back and walked over to Kameela and took her in his arms.

'You're right. I will go and talk to Mum soon. I need to know the truth about my father – and decide whether I want to meet him.'

Later that evening, when Bart disappeared to take a phone call, Kameela asked Delphine about her travel plans.

'It sounds exciting. Which country are you going to first?

Delphine sighed. 'I haven't decided yet. Probably somewhere in Europe. Berlin maybe. I know I need to start organising a proper itinerary but with Rebecca being in such a state over things,' she shrugged. 'I can't concentrate – not even sure that I should be thinking of going right now.'

Kameela looked at her. 'Have you ever been to Martinique?' Delphine shook her head. 'No.'

'Why don't you start there? You speak the language and the people are friendly – my family would make you very welcome. We can skype and I can introduce you to my parents and Uncle Francois so you wouldn't be staying with strangers. I know Uncle Francois, in particular, would love to show you the sights. He's an official guide,' Kameela added.

'That sounds very tempting,' Delphine said as Bart reappeared.

'What does?' he asked.

'Delphine isn't sure where to go first on her travels so I've suggested she goes to Martinque and stays with my parents.'

Bart nodded and looked at Delphine. 'Good idea – so long as

you tell them how lucky their daughter is to have met me.' He saw the scandalised look on Kameela's face and laughed. 'Although, of course, I'm the lucky one and I love her to bits.' He gave Kameela a quick kiss as he sat down next to her.

Delphine, looking at the two of them, smiled, Kameela was good for Bart. Rebecca would be pleased about that.

If Bart did decide to meet his father after he'd spoken with Rebecca, Delphine hoped and prayed that Rufus would want to acknowledge him. And that, of course, depended on whether Rebecca went through with telling Rufus about his son this evening – and how he reacted to the news.

31

'I thought we'd have a glass of champagne on the balcony before supper. Celebrate, in the proper style, being back in touch,' Rebecca said, forcing herself to sound upbeat, as she led the way through the villa and upstairs to her apartment

'Thank you,' she said as Rufus handed her the chocolates. 'My favourite chocolatier. I'll open them with coffee later. How long have you known Marcus and Freya?' she asked as she took the champagne out of the fridge and they moved together out to the balcony.

'Marcus and I grew up together.' Rufus gave her a questioning glance. 'I was at his first wedding in Dartmouth when we met – remember?'

Rebecca turned and looked at him, stunned. 'That was Freya and Marcus's wedding, the weekend we met?'

Rufus nodded.

'I didn't make the connection. I never got the chance to meet them and I don't remember you ever mentioning their names,' Rebecca said, concentrating on easing the cork out of the bottle and pushing away the treacherous memories reminding her of just why she hadn't met them then. If she had, would it have made a difference to organising their wedding this time round?

'From what Marcus tells me, you've created one of the best venues on the Riviera, and having stayed here this weekend, I can believe it.'

'We do have a good reputation.' Rebecca smiled as she handed Rufus a glass of bubbling champagne.

'It's lovely to see you again, Becky,' Rufus said, a serious look on his face.

'You too.' And it was. Bittersweet, knowing what they'd missed out on in the intervening years, but Rebecca couldn't deny the smile that spread across her own face. 'Did you ever marry? I always imagined you married with a family.' Damn. That sounded as though she'd thought about him a lot, which, of course, she had down the years.

Rufus shook his head. 'No, I never married. Had a few girlfriends, one longish relationship... well, not that long really, six months.' He hesitated for a few seconds before continuing. 'I tried for a long time after that weekend in Dartmouth to find you but came up against a solid wall of indifference to my questions. *Sorry we are not at liberty to give personal details away.* That was from the owner of the yacht you were crew on. Took months for me to track him down in Monaco. He did give me the name of the agency you worked for in the end, but they gave me the same answer. It didn't help, of course, that I didn't know your surname.'

'I'm sorry. I tried to find you too. The hotel brushed me off with similar answers. I had to give up in the end.' Rebecca took a sip of her drink.

'How about you? Did you get married? Have a family?' Rufus stared at her intently.

'No, I never married. Too busy with Delphine making this place a success,' Rebecca said. Should she admit to having a son?

It was an ideal opening. No, she'd keep to her decision not to tell him tonight. 'When and how did you acquire the limp?' she asked, deciding a change of subject would be good.

'Would you believe a shark attack? No? You want the truth?' Rufus pulled a face. 'Okay. This is so embarrassing but I, um, I fell off a skateboard three years ago. I am living proof that men in their fifties should not try to keep up with their young nephews. Don't you dare laugh. It was very painful, still is occasionally.'

'I'm sorry,' Rebecca said, and she placed her hand across her mouth in a desperate attempt to hide the smile she could feel creeping across her face up into her eyes. In that instant, she pictured the young Rufus she had known and fallen in love with on that weekend.

'Twenty years as a pilot with The Royal Flying Doctor Service in Australia – not a scratch. Twenty minutes with a twelve-year-old boy in a skateboard park with ramps and jumps and I manage to permanently damage myself.' Rufus shrugged philosophically. 'It was good fun though – before I made a spectacular crash landing off a ramp.'

'You worked with the RFDS for twenty years? That was one place I would never have thought to search for you.'

'It was only intended to be five years at the max,' Rufus said. 'But it's not an easy career to walk away from, it's such a vital and necessary service. Besides, there was nothing to come back to Europe permanently for. I did come back regularly to the UK to see my parents and my sister, but life in Australia was good enough to keep me out there for the majority of the time.'

'How long are you over for now? Did you come over especially for Marcus and Freya's wedding?' Rebecca tried not to hold her breath waiting for the answer. Was he going to disappear out of her life again? Wasn't that what she'd wanted from the moment he'd arrived at Villa Sésame? So why did she suddenly feel apprehensive about what he was going to say? What else did she expect to happen?

'I'm back in Europe-full time now. My parents bought a place in Menton a year ago. They're both in their eighties and the plan is to at least be in the same country as them in case they need help in the future. Don't think I'm quite ready for a quiet life yet, so I'm looking for a business opportunity as well as a place to live.'

Rebecca looked at him as she absorbed the news that he was going to be living nearby – Menton was only the other side of Monaco. She jumped as the oven buzzer started to ping.

'Supper is ready,' she said. 'Would you like to eat out here or in the kitchen?'

'Out here. I'll give you a hand.'

Conversation as they sat out on the balcony, eating, drinking wine, talking and getting to know each other again, flowed between them. Both of them resolutely ignored the tension that seeped into the air as they studiously avoided the one subject neither were brave enough to raise. Their one and only weekend together.

The moon was high in the darkening sky when Rebecca stood up. 'Time for coffee, I think.'

'I left a present for you down in the car,' Rufus said. 'I'll run down and get it while the coffee brews.'

When he came back up, Rebecca had set the coffee and chocolates up on the small table in the sitting room. She watched him nervously as he took the packaging off the parcel. 'It's a painting?'

'Wait. Close your eyes.'

Rebecca did as she was told and she sensed him placing the object on the sofa, leaning it against the cushions, before he took her by the hand and walked her the two or three steps until she was standing in front of it.

Rufus was still holding her hand when he said. 'You can open your eyes now.'

Rebecca, not sure what she'd been expecting, gasped when she saw the painting and realised what it was.

'The old Gunfield Hotel, Dartmouth from the river. Thank you. I've dreamt of this place so often down the years. Did you paint it?' Rebecca asked, turning to look at him.

'No, it's one of Freya's. I saw two in her studio the other day and persuaded her to sell them to me – one for you and one for me. A reminder of a wonderful weekend I spent with the love of my life,' Rufus said quietly. 'And the reason I've never married.'

Rebecca caught her breath at his words and suddenly she couldn't hold the truth back any longer and the words started tumbling out of her mouth.

'Yes. It was the best weekend of my life too and I have a son who is a constant reminder of how wonderful it was...' Rebecca's voice trailed away as she saw the shocked look on Rufus's face and, realising what she'd said, she burst into tears.

Rufus caught hold of her hands and pulled her towards him before taking her in his arms and holding her in a tight hug. 'Becky, my love – let's talk about what this chance meeting really means to both of us. How about we start from the beginning...'

32

DARTMOUTH 25 YEARS AGO

Mooching around Dartmouth one Friday morning in April, Becky was not bored exactly but definitely restless. This season was meant to be her very last on the yachts and she'd been hoping to be on the way back to France by now for summer on the Med, but various things had put paid to that. First, the yacht's departure from Southampton had been delayed a week by the absence of its new Russian owner, Dmitri Firsova, due to business. Last week, the captain had received instructions to make for Dartmouth and Dimitri and his wife would join them there for the journey down to Gibraltar, into the Med and back to the yacht's new home port of Monaco.

The journey down the Channel had been uneventful and they'd berthed at Dartmouth's Dart Marina four days ago. Now they were waiting, not only for the owners but also for the Atlantic weather down the west coast of France to improve.

As chief stewardess, Becky was responsible for making sure everything ran smoothly on board the luxury boat. The captain was responsible for everyone's safety, but the welfare and comfort of the owners and their guests when on board was down to her. With nobody on board, once the general daily cleaning and polishing of already immac-

ulate surfaces was done and the chef had assured her that kitchen supplies were all topped up, there was nothing for her to do.

Which was why she was wandering down Foss Street, window shopping on a Friday morning. Becky paused outside The Kitchen Shop, one of the last shops in the street. She knew Delphine would have taken one look at the window display and insisted on going in. Kitchen shops were like siren calls to her sister. Becky smothered a laugh, pulled open the door and, as the bell tinkled above her head, walked in. If nothing else, she could tease Delphine about missing a shopping opportunity.

The woman behind the counter glanced at her. 'Good morning. If you need any help, please ask.'

'Thank you,' Becky said and wandered on past shelves and stands filled with a mixture of Le Creuset pots, candles, aprons, mugs, napkins, utensils, olive oil pourers, through to the back of the shop with its recipe books, cards, notebooks and kitchen wall decorations.

A tall fair-haired man, about her own age, standing in front of large shabby-chic kitchen clock with 'Home Sweet Home' written large across it glanced in her direction and smiled. Becky smiled back and time stood still as their eyes locked in a gaze. The man's voice brought her out of her reverie a few seconds later.

'If I was to give you this clock for a wedding present, would you be pleased?'

'Depends on the size of my kitchen,' Becky said, laughing. 'And whether I like clichés.'

The man sighed. 'I guess that's a no then?'

'From me, but perhaps the bride?'

He shook his head. 'No, you're right. It's too big, as well as clichéd.' He ran his hand through his hair. 'It's my own fault for leaving it to the last moment.'

'When's the wedding?'

'Tomorrow. Can you see anything here that you'd like to receive?'

Becky glanced around for a few moments. 'Do the couple like wine? How about that?' She pointed to a wall decoration on the far wall. 'It's a bit of kitsch, but it's fun. I'd quite like that – especially if you bought me a case of good wine to go with it.'

He followed her finger and saw the vintage-looking domed wooden wall plaque with its central two embossed bottles and wine glasses surrounded by slots ready to fill with wine corks from empty bottles.

'Genius,' the man said. 'It's perfect. I could hug you, but I will contain myself. Right, come on, let's pay for this and get to the vintners for some decent wine to go with it.'

'Oh, but...'

'And then I'm going to buy you lunch as a thank you. Please?' This as Becky shook her head. 'Unless you've got a husband or boyfriend lurking somewhere.' And he looked anxiously around before looking back at her.

Becky was about to say no she couldn't possibly, when the look in his eyes stopped her. She had no idea who this man was, but she liked him. It wasn't as if she made a habit of going for lunch with unknown men. If he wanted to buy her lunch, why not?

'No husband. No boyfriend. But I don't even know your name.'

'Rufus. And you're?'

'Becky.'

And that meeting had been the start of what the French term 'a coup de foudre', love at first sight, and a whirlwind weekend. Becky, who during her ten years on the boats, had turned down many overtures from men, determined not to be the female equivalent of sailors who had someone in every port, couldn't believe how happy Rufus made her feel. She'd had boyfriends, of course she had, usually when she was back home after the season finished, but none of them had filled her with happiness – or desire – like this unknown man called Rufus did.

Leaving the chosen case of red wine and the wall decoration with the vintner to collect later, they had lunch in one of the many fish restaurants the town possessed. Rufus had suggested the Dart Marina hotel or The Royal Castle, but Becky had opted for simple fish and chips instead.

'More relaxed than a hotel,' she'd said. Becky learnt that Rufus was a pilot and she told him about working on the yachts. Afterwards, they'd wandered through town and down on to Bayards Cove with its ancient fort. Rufus pointed out the Gunfield Hotel along the riverbank where he was staying and where the wedding reception was being held.

'I'm best man, for my sins, tomorrow, so I'll be busy all day, but if you're free, you could come to the evening party as my plus-one.' Rufus looked at her hopefully.

Becky shook her head. 'I'm sorry, that would be lovely, but I can't,' she said sadly. 'As much as I would like to spend more time with you, tomorrow is impossible. The other stewardess has asked for tomorrow off – her parents live locally and she's spending the day and evening with them, so I have to stay on board.'

'Can I see you on Sunday?' The disappointment on his face mirrored her own feelings.

'Possibly in the afternoon.' Becky glanced at her watch. 'I should be getting back now actually.'

'I'll walk you back to the marina,' Rufus said, catching hold of her hand. 'What time on Sunday do you think you could make?'

'If I can get away about three o'clock, where shall I meet you?'

'How about by the little ferry for the castle?' Rufus suggested. 'We can have a short boat ride, wander around the headland and then I'll take you back to The Gunfield for afternoon tea. I'm booked in there until Monday morning.'

'Sounds like a plan.' Becky said, already wishing that Sunday afternoon wasn't so far away.

Once back at the entrance to the marina, Becky removed her hand from his.

'I've loved today. Thank you for lunch. If I can't make Sunday, I'll ring The Gunfield and leave a message for you.'

Rufus leaned in and kissed her cheek. 'I've loved today too. Meeting you...' he shrugged. 'I have no words, other than to say I think you are a special person. Sunday can't come quick enough for me.'

Becky reached up and returned his cheek kiss. 'I'll do my best. Oh, and I do hope the happy couple like their present.' And she turned and began to hurry through the marina.

Rufus stood there watching her until she disappeared from sight before turning and making his way, deep in thought, slowly along the embankment back into town.

* * *

Becky spent the rest of Friday happily reliving the hours she'd spent with Rufus. She'd finally met a man to whom she truly felt connected. Thoughts and images of him had taken up residence in her mind, blotting out everything else, and she shivered every time she remembered the frisson that invaded her body when he'd kissed her cheek. She pushed the thought 'but you're leaving soon', away. She was confident now they'd met each other she and Rufus would keep in touch, whatever it took. Becky longed to talk to Delphine, to tell her that she knew, just knew, that she had met her soulmate.

Delphine, though, was currently working as a chef at a prestigious restaurant in the countryside between Cannes and Mougins, gaining extra experience and earning more money for their own dream venture. Becky glanced at her watch. Six o'clock, which meant it was seven o'clock in France. Becky knew that her sister would be frantically busy and wouldn't appreciate her phoning up and interrupting her routine, even if her phone was actually switched on. She'd have to wait and talk to her tomorrow.

Saturday morning, the other stewardess left early and Becky completed her usual routine of checking throughout the yacht. At mid-morning, she made a couple of coffees, put some biscuits on a plate and went up to the bridge, where the captain was sitting morosely looking at his various computer screens and satellite communication systems.

'Any news about... anything?' she asked, handing him a coffee. 'Weather improving? A date for the Firsovas arriving?'

The captain shook his head. 'The weather is set to improve in the next thirty-six hours, but there's not even an ETA from the Firsovas. We could be underway and on our way back to Monaco by midweek. On the other hand...' he shrugged. 'We could be stuck here for some time.' Becky's heart lifted at the possibility of being in port for a few more days, even though Rufus had said he was only here until Monday. Maybe he could stay longer.

'Is it all right if I have tomorrow afternoon off then?' Becky asked, quickly assuring him that her deputy would be back before she left. 'Only, I've got an invitation for afternoon tea in a posh hotel.'

He sighed. 'Okay. But please make sure you check with me before you leave and be back by seven at the latest.'

'Will do.' Becky left him to enjoy the rest of the biscuits. Sixteen hours before she saw Rufus again.

That evening, she made for the bow of the yacht in its outside berth at the marina which gave her a view downriver towards the mouth of the estuary and the Gunfield Hotel nestling in its riverside gardens.

Sitting there, she could see figures moving around in the grounds. Pulling the small pair of travelling binoculars that she always took on trips out of her pocket, she focused them and, ignoring the guilty 'you're turning into a stalker' thought, tried to see if she could recognise Rufus among the people who were mingling in the grounds. The answer turned out to be no; the binoculars weren't strong enough, she was too far away.

As the evening wore on and the moon cast its silvery light over the river, the embankment lights came on and house lights began to light up the town and the hillside behind, Becky sat there hugging her knees, listening to the lapping water, thinking about Rufus. She couldn't wait for tomorrow afternoon, but what would happen afterwards?

Getting ready for bed in her small cabin, she sighed. She knew how she felt about him and was pretty certain he felt the same way about her – but what if he didn't? Thinking she was 'a special person' didn't mean that he wanted to spend the rest of his life with her. Rufus would be leaving on Monday and the owners would arrive eventually and then the yacht would leave for France. She felt in her bones that she and Rufus were destined to be together, but where and when? She was based in France and had no idea where he lived, presumably it was somewhere in the UK.

Tomorrow, she resolved, she would try to remember to be sensible and ask some important questions. Before she got carried away with imagining her future with him, she had to discover if there could even be a future for them together. She liked him so much, there simply had to be.

The next afternoon, as she ran along the embankment towards the castle ferry landing steps, she saw Rufus standing there waiting for her and her heart missed a couple of beats.

'You made it,' he said, kissing her cheek.

'Yes, but I have to be back by seven.'

Rufus had already bought their tickets and he helped her into the small boat that was waiting in position alongside the steps with several passengers on board already and they sat close together on the wooden seating fixed to the port side. Four more passengers clambered on before mooring ropes were untied, the inboard engine was put into gear and they were underway, making for the castle.

Fifteen minutes later, they'd disembarked and were walking hand in hand up the riverside pathway leading to Dartmouth Castle.

'I can't give you the cream tea I promised you at the hotel, I'm *afraid. All the staff have been given the afternoon off after the wedding, but I can buy you an ice cream with clotted cream on top and a flake.'*

'*Sounds wonderfully decadent,' Becky laughed.*

Ice creams in hand and, in an attempt to escape the Sunday-afternoon crowds surrounding the castle environments, they wandered into the ancient graveyard of St. Petrox Church. Dried rose petal confetti littered the pathways whilst ancient lichen-covered gravestones, their carved dedications faint, worn away by centuries of wind and rain, stood at drunken angles guarding simple grassy mounds.

Once the ice creams were finished, Rufus took her hand. 'Shall we walk down to the hotel? Sit in the garden there for a while? Celebrate our meeting with a drink?'

Becky nodded. 'Sounds good.'

Strolling along the narrow tree-lined road with woods on one side that led to the hotel, her hand in Rufus's, Becky had never felt happier.

The hotel was quiet when they walked in, no receptionist, no reception desk. In fact, no one was around at all. It felt more like walking into a private house than a hotel.

'*The bar is this way,' Rufus said.*

Becky watched in amazement as Rufus went into the tiny bar area and took a bottle of champagne out of the fridge.

'*What are you doing?'*

'*It's okay, there's an Honesty Book,' and Rufus picked up a pen and opened a notebook that was on the bar. On the latest page, he put the date, his room number followed by 'one bottle of champagne'.*

Becky looked at him in amazement. 'I've never seen that in any hotel before.'

'*This is a hotel like no other, trust me,' Rufus said. 'The owner is a real laid-back guy, likes people to feel at home here and trusts them to do the right thing. Apparently, guests have been known to help out waitressing and clearing tables when it's busy and they're short-staffed.'*

Becky, used to the formality of the yachts where guests would no more help the staff than stop asking for room service at midnight when the crew were off duty, shook her head in amazement.

'Come on, let's sit in the garden and watch the river for a while. My room has a wonderful view too if...?' Rufus looked at her questioningly.

Becky smiled and, realising what would happen if she agreed, didn't hesitate. 'I'd love to see the view from your room.'

A few moments later, they were both standing in front of the window watching the river traffic toing and froing, a glass of champagne in their hands. Below them, the hotel garden ran down to the river's edge.

'How did it all go yesterday?' Becky asked. 'Did your best man duties go to plan? Last night I could see people in the garden from the yacht. It looked a very romantic setting with the moon and the lights.'

'The wedding was fine. I'm afraid I was a bit of a party pooper in the evening though. I missed you. I wanted you to be there,' Rufus said.

'I would have loved to have been there with you,' Becky said, turning to face him.

Rufus took the glass of champagne from her and placed it with his own on the occasional table standing in front of the window. 'Becky, I've never felt the way you make me feel about anyone before. The fact that we've only known each other for hours doesn't seem to matter. I meant it when I said you are special. You are. Very special. I think – I'm sure, I've fallen in love with you.'

'And me with you,' Becky whispered.

As he took her in his arms and kissed her, all the questions she wanted to ask him fled her mind and she lost herself in the arms of the man who thought he was sure he loved her and time stood still.

* * *

Snuggled into Rufus with his arm around her holding her tight, Becky gave a happy sigh. She wanted to stay in this moment for ever, to hold *onto the love she felt for Rufus. Right now, she had no desire to be, or to go, anywhere else. Lazily, she raised her hand to gently run her fingers through Rufus's hair – and froze as she saw the time on her watch. Six fifteen.*

She struggled out from under Rufus's arm and sat up. 'I've got to go. I'm going to be late back. Will the little ferry still be running?' Frantically, she began to gather her clothes together and started to get dressed. Silently, Rufus found his own clothes.

Becky was thankful the hotel was still quiet, with no sign of either guests or staff as they ran downstairs and out through the main entrance. They could see the ferry beginning to make its approach, ready to come alongside the landing place, and they increased their pace to run down the path. To Becky's dismay, there was already a group of people waiting.

'There weren't this many on board when we came out. How many does the boat carry? Are we going to get on? Or should we start running round by road?'

'Let's wait and worry about it when its current passengers disembark and we can start boarding,' Rufus said.

Becky could hardly contain her anxiety as she waited. One of the yacht's strict rules was that you were never late on board without a cast-iron excuse.

'It's going to be okay, I think,' Rufus said as they watched the couple in front of them climb onto the ferry and prepared to follow them.

'Sorry, only one more person allowed,' the driver held up his hand. 'Regulations. I'll be back in about half an hour.'

'You go,' Rufus said. 'I'll come to the marina and see you tomorrow before I leave.' He gave her a quick kiss, a whispered 'love you', and stepped back while Becky took the hand of the boatman and stepped onto the boat.

'About eleven o'clock is usually a good time,' she said. 'I'll see you then.' She mouthed 'love you too' at him.

Once back in Dartmouth, Becky stepped off the boat on to the pavement and began to run along the embankment towards the Dart Marina. She slowed down once she reached the Higher Ferry slipway in an effort to catch her breath. That was close, she'd made it with five minutes to spare. Making her way along the pontoon, she frowned. There was an air of activity aboard the yacht that she hadn't been expecting. It looked as if the boat was being prepared to leave port. The captain was up on the bridge.

As she hurried up the gangway, she saw one of the deckhands pulling in fenders.

'Has the owner arrived?'

The deckhand shook his head. 'No.'

That was a relief. For a moment there, she'd thought the yacht was being prepared to leave port, but now it seemed more likely they'd probably just been asked to move moorings.

'The captain wants to see you,' the deckhand continued.

Becky hurried up to the bridge. 'You wanted to see me?'

The captain turned from the instrument panel he was studying.

'Weather forecast is finally good enough, but the Firsovas are detained yet again. New instructions an hour ago are to make for Gibraltar now and they'll join us there in about a week for the trip through the Med. Typical owners. Keep us hanging around for weeks and probably won't even make it to Gib. Never mind, we should be back in Monaco in a week or two. By the way, three more minutes and we would have sailed without you.'

'We're leaving right now?' Becky could barely ask the question as she felt her heart breaking.

'Yes, the tide is on the turn, which will help us leave the river and head for the Channel,' and the captain turned back to his computer.

Becky bit her bottom lip hard as she left the bridge, determined not to let the tears fall until she was in the safety of her own cabin.

As the yacht motored downriver away from the marina towards the Channel, all Becky was conscious of, looking out through the port-hole in her cabin was her last sighting of the Gunfield Hotel. Then later, as they passed the headland, with its church and castle, the image of the solitary figure of Rufus standing on the pontoon tomorrow morning wondering where the hell the yacht was popped into her mind. And wouldn't go away.

In the whirlwind that had swept them along since they'd met, they'd never got around to exchanging contact details so what were the chances of them ever meeting up again? Less than zero, she estimated as the tears fell silently down her cheeks. It had all been too perfect to be true. All she would ever have were the memories of a wonderful man called Rufus.

33

'And the rest, as they say, is history. Sadly, not the history we both wanted and definitely not the one I dreamt of,' Rebecca added, giving Rufus a bleak smile. 'I can't tell you how bereft I felt as the boat made its way downriver that Sunday evening. My heart was breaking. I even thought about jumping into the Dart and swimming ashore – even though I couldn't swim more than five metres at the time.' Rebecca closed her eyes and took a deep breath before she opened them again. 'Those feelings were overshadowed by the ones I had six weeks later when I realised I was pregnant.'

She couldn't tell him about the despair of those first weeks when she realised she was carrying his baby. Despair that was mixed in with elation that she was having Rufus's baby. Having a termination had never ever come into the equation. Without thinking about it, she'd known she wouldn't be able to live with herself if she did away with the child of the man she'd loved, however briefly they'd known each other. There was a lot of sadness too at not being able to tell Rufus the news, and knowing they would never be the happy family she dreamt of. Thankfully,

Delphine and André had been there for her and they'd formed their own little family unit.

Rebecca reached across and pulled the photograph she'd pushed out of sight earlier behind the books and held it out to him. 'You may have seen him yesterday. He arrived just as you were leaving.'

'He was the guy who parked next to me?' Rufus asked, studying the photo.

Rebecca nodded. 'That was taken last year on his birthday.'

'Which is?'

'December first. Rufus,' she said and he looked up at her sharply, 'I'm sorry, but now he knows you are here, he doesn't want any contact with you. And given he's currently not speaking to me, I haven't had a chance to explain things to him.'

'Why isn't he speaking to you?'

'Because, ironically, he's met someone who he says is "special" and wanted to introduce the two of us tonight. I had to say I couldn't as I had already arranged to have dinner with an old friend.' Rebecca sighed. 'And then when he put a bit of pressure on for me to try to change the arrangement, I inadvertently said your name. It didn't take Bart more than a minute to work out that I was meeting his unknown father.'

'How?'

'His middle name is Rufus,' she answered softly, holding his gaze.

'Thank you for that.'

'I've always stressed to him how much I loved his father and that I wished things could have been different, that we could have been a proper family.'

It was Rebecca who broke the lingering silence that developed between them after she stopped speaking.

'Any idea what we are going to do from here on?'

Rufus shook his head. 'To be honest, I have no idea. I need to do some serious thinking, but right this moment I feel shell-shocked. There are two things though, I am determined on.'

Rebecca held her breath as he took her in his arms.

'It's too late for you and I to have a lifetime together like we planned that Sunday afternoon all those years ago, but now I've found my soulmate again, nothing – *nothing* – is going to separate me from her for the rest of our lives. As for Bart, I will meet my son, Becky, have no doubt of that. Whether he wants to meet me or not.'

Standing there secure in Rufus's arms listening to his words 'soulmate' and 'nothing is going to separate us', Rebecca knew without a doubt that they would be together forever now. The only cloud putting a damper on her happiness was Bart and his attitude to the unexpected arrival of his father in his life.

* * *

Rufus drove back down to Antibes in a daze. He parked near the port and slowly walked up through the bottom of town to the ramparts. Lights in Marcus and Freya's house were still on and he could hear quiet voices up on the terrace as he let himself in and made his way upstairs.

'Please tell me you weren't waiting up for me?' he said, as he got to the terrace, where Freya and Marcus were sat enjoying the balmy night air.

Freya hastened to reassure him. 'No, we were just chilling after Effie and Verity left. It's great up here at this time of night. How did this evening go? Would you like a glass of wine?'

'Got anything stronger? Whisky?'

'That bad, eh?' Marcus said, moving across to a shelf and picking up a bottle of whisky and two clean glasses. 'I'll join you.'

And he poured them both a good measure and handed a glass to Rufus. 'Santé'.

Rufus took a swig of his drink. 'I knew she was avoiding me for a reason, but I was totally unprepared for the possibility of there being a child involved – now a grown man – it didn't occur to me. Naive of me, I suppose.'

His words were greeted with silence. Rufus gave them both a suspicious look. 'You both knew, didn't you?'

'Not until yesterday,' Marcus said. 'When Rebecca introduced us to her son, who is the spitting image of you, mate, I have to say, we both jumped to that conclusion.'

'To think I didn't register the guy in the car next to me,' Rufus said, shaking his head. 'You didn't think to warn me tonight before I left?'

'I nearly did when we were talking earlier,' Freya admitted quietly. 'I do feel bad about it, but really it wasn't our news to tell, was it?'

'So you were waiting up.'

'Guilty as charged,' Freya said with a smile. 'We wanted to make sure you were all right.'

'I feel like a teenage kid having to confess to my parents that I've been a naughty boy and got some girl in trouble.' Miserably, Rufus shook his head. 'I keep thinking about Mum and Dad's reaction. For years they've wanted me to marry and have kids and I kept having to tell them I hadn't met the right woman, when all the time, unknown to me, the woman I'd wanted to marry had given birth to my child. I really have no idea how they will react when I tell them they've got an unknown grown-up grandson.' Rufus gave a shallow laugh. 'It's a funny old life sometimes.'

'Knowing your mum and dad, they'll take it in their stride and welcome Bart into the family,' Freya said. 'Have you made arrangements with Rebecca to meet Bart?'

'Cue the first problem.' Rufus shook his head. 'Rebecca told me that Bart stormed out of the villa when he heard the news and doesn't want anything to do with me.'

'Knee-jerk reaction,' Marcus said. 'He will when he calms down. Wait and see.'

Rufus looked at him. 'I sure as hell hope you're right there. Because there is no way now that I know I have a son that I will allow him to be a stranger to either me or to my family.'

34

The next morning, after a restless night, where sleep had evaded her for some hours, Rebecca was busy in the office with Christine, sorting out the never-ending paperwork, and it was lunchtime before she saw her sister. Delphine had insisted they had lunch as usual, although Rebecca had protested she wasn't hungry. Food was the last thing on her mind. Worry about Bart's negative reaction to learning about Rufus had shoe-horned itself into her mind, making it impossible to think about anything else.

Sitting out on the terrace, she was systematically breaking the Spanish omelette Delphine had placed in front of her into small pieces and pushing them around her plate.

'You are supposed to fork that up and eat it, not play with it,' Delphine sighed. 'We've got a fourth of July party to organise for this Saturday, you need to keep your strength up for that if nothing else.'

'Christine is on the case. I'll eat something later.' Rebecca glanced at her sister. 'So how did last night go? How was Bart? Is Kameela as lovely as I hope she is?'

'Kameela is beautiful – inside as well as outside. She's a great cook and very family-orientated too. She agreed with me when I told Bart he had to talk to you, so fingers crossed he will – sooner rather than later.'

'I thought Rufus would be back this morning, ready to form a plan of action,' Rebecca admitted.

'Maybe he's finding the news hard to deal with? Wants time to let it all sink in?'

'What do I tell Bart if he shows up before Rufus?' No way was she going to put into words the worry whirling around in her head that Rufus might have had second thoughts about meeting a son who said he didn't want to know or meet him? And where would that leave her?

'Until he calms down and comes to see you, you can't tell Bart anything anyway. And then you tell him the truth, like you planned.'

'I thought... hoped that Rufus and I would do that together.' Rebecca stood up. 'I'm sorry, I really can't eat anything. I'm going up to the apartment. I need some space and to think. See you later.'

Back in the apartment, Rebecca lay down on her bed and closed her eyes, wanting to blot everything out. Within minutes, the sleep that had evaded her in the night overtook her and she drifted off.

The opening and closing of the apartment door woke her sometime later.

'Delphine, I'm in the bedroom,' she called out drowsily.

'It's me.'

Rebecca sat up. Bart. 'I'll be right out.'

Bart eyed her warily as she opened the bedroom door.

'Delphine and Kameela tell me I can't ignore my father now

he knows about me,' Bart said. 'So I've come to ask you to tell me about him. And are you sure it's Rufus?'

Rebecca stared at him in shock. 'I'll ignore that unbelievably rude and hurtful remark and forget you ever uttered it.'

She marched past Bart to open the sitting room French doors and went out onto the balcony and sat at the table, gesturing to Bart to join her.

Bart mouthed an apologetic 'Sorry' at her as she continued.

'There has never been any doubt about who your father is. And, I can tell you, you look just like him.'

'So he's tall and good-looking too?' Bart said, trying to crack a weak joke to lighten the situation.

Rebecca gave a brief nod. 'You're very alike. I know I've never talked to you about him, but you've never asked me about your father since, oh, since you were about seven. Before then, you were always asking why you didn't have a dad and why couldn't you have one living at home like everyone else. I remember trying to explain to you that although both Mummy and Daddy loved you, it wasn't possible for reasons you'd understand when you were bigger, and I promised to explain them when you were older. Then you just stopped asking and seemed to accept that it was me and you. Even as a teenager you didn't remind me of my promise and demand answers. And I, I'm sorry to say, took the easy route and remained silent.'

Bart shrugged. 'You're right. I did stop asking about my father when I was seven. Remember my friend Dan?'

'Yes, of course I do. I was friends with his mum. You were inseparable until they moved away.' Rebecca looked at him curiously.

'Dan told me his dad used to take his belt to him if he was naughty or even if he just got in the way and annoyed him. Showed me the welts on his back one day. That was when I decided I was better off without a dad in my life. So I stopped asking questions in case you suddenly produced one for me. Besides, I was lucky, I had Uncle André and I reckoned he was better than any substitute father. I do miss him.'

Rebecca was silent. She'd known, of course, that her friend's husband had abused her but hadn't realised little Dan had been a victim too. No wonder the two of them had simply vanished one night, gone back to her parents in England and safety. 'Poor Dan,' she said.

Bart brought the conversation back on track with his next words. 'Why didn't Rufus try to contact us down the years? Visit you? Want to see me?'

'I told you, he didn't know about you,' Rebecca said quietly. 'You've always known you had a father out there somewhere, but Rufus didn't know about you until I told him last night.'

'Why didn't you tell him you were pregnant?'

Rebecca took a deep breath. 'I never got the chance. We'd lost contact by the time I realised.'

'And his reaction last night?' Bart's eyes fixed on her face, looking for any change in emotion.

'Shocked was one reaction. Sadness. Acceptance. Followed by determination to meet you.' Rebecca, grateful that Bart was at least asking questions about his father, waited for his reaction to her words.

But Bart ignored her last words, asking instead. 'Is he married? Do I have any brothers or sisters?'

Rebecca shook her head. 'He's never married and you are his only child. But you do have grandparents and a couple of cousins.'

Bart took a couple of seconds to digest this information before asking, 'How long were you together?'

'Part of a weekend,' Rebecca said quietly. 'And before you say anything, it was a *coup de foudre* that neither of us anticipated. I also didn't anticipate becoming pregnant.' She stood up. 'I'm having a glass of wine and then I'll tell you about Rufus and I. Would you like a beer?'

'Please.'

Rebecca took the wine and beer out of the fridge and put them on the table while she fetched the glasses. She poured herself a glass of wine, while Bart took the cap off his bottle.

'So where did you two meet?'

'I met Rufus in the UK, Dartmouth in Devon on the south coast...' And taking a deep breath, Rebecca told him the truth about how his parents had met and fallen in love, only for it to all fall apart when they lost contact almost as quickly as they'd met.

As Rebecca finished speaking, Bart wiped away a tear. 'Mum, I'm so sorry. I don't know what to say.'

'There's not a lot anyone can say. I'm sad it happened the way it did and if I could change things, I would. But I would never want to change meeting Rufus and having you. Yes, it was hard, but I hope you can look back on a happy childhood and know that you've always been loved. Not just by me, but Delphine and André too. You were right when you said earlier about André being like a substitute father to you, he was. As far as he was concerned, he thought of you as his son.'

'I know.' Bart was quiet for several seconds before taking a deep breath, looking at Rebecca and asking quietly. 'When can I meet Rufus?'

Rebecca shook her head. 'At the moment I'm waiting to hear from him, but I hope it will be soon. And I need to meet Kameela. Delphine loved her last night so I know I will too. And you? Do you love her? Is she the one for you?'

Bart nodded. 'Yes. I can't imagine not having her in my life now.'

Rebecca gave him a rueful smile. She remembered having those same feelings about Rufus twenty-five years ago, only to have her dreams snatched away by circumstances. Yesterday they'd been rekindled but where was Rufus today? Why hadn't he returned so they could start making plans?

35

After Bart left, Rebecca had a quick shower to freshen herself up before going to find Delphine and something to eat to curb her sudden hunger. As she ran downstairs, the phone in her pocket buzzed. She gave the caller ID a quick glance – Rufus.

'Can I please take you out to dinner this evening?' he asked when she answered. 'We need to talk.'

'Yes,' Rebecca said instantly. 'But somewhere simple?'

'You choose, anywhere you like. I'll pick you up at seven, okay?'

'See you then,' and Rebecca smiled as the call ended.

Delphine was in the kitchen talking with Christine, who glanced up as Rebecca pushed the door open. 'The Americans have cancelled Saturday night.'

Rebecca sighed. At least they'd had the decency to cancel rather than just be 'no shows'. 'The reason?'

'Several of their members are ill with some sort of virus and they feel it's better to cancel now rather than wait.'

'Fair enough,' Rebecca said. 'Usual cancellation routine

applies then. Refund their deposit, minus the usual ten per cent for incurred expenses. I'll leave you to do that while I talk to Delphine.'

As the kitchen door swung closed behind Christine, Delphine looked at Rebecca.

'Bart came to see you earlier?'

'Yes. He knows everything now and thankfully has decided he wants to meet Rufus,' Rebecca answered as she moved towards the bread bin and slotted two slices into the toaster. 'Rufus rang me. I'm having supper with him tonight.' She turned to look at her sister. 'It's almost too much to take in after all these years. I never expected to see him again, or to feel giddy about him, like I did back then, but I do.'

Delphine smiled. 'It's lovely to see you happy and looking forward to whatever the future holds.' She watched as Rebecca slathered butter on the first piece of toast. 'Don't eat too much now or you won't want your supper.'

'Says the person who was urging me to eat at lunchtime.'

'I'm off to see the girls and collect any late eggs. Enjoy this evening if I don't see you before you leave,' Delphine said, taking her willow basket off the kitchen door and leaving Rebecca to her toast.

Several of the chickens were busy enjoying dust baths, whilst others were wandering around in a desultory fashion, rather like the holidaymakers down on the coast who were too hot and bothered to do anything energetic. Delphine checked their food and water before opening the lid on the nesting box, where she found five eggs in amongst the straw bed.

Standing there watching the chickens, Delphine thought about the life changes that were ahead for them all in the next couple of months. When she'd told Rebecca that she wanted to become a sleeping partner and go travelling, she'd assumed that in her absence, life would go on as normal at the villa. Rebecca suggesting that now was perhaps the time to sell had thrown her a little, but while she understood her sister's reaction, she hadn't truly been able to picture her away from the villa. Maybe now though, with Rufus back in her life, it really was the right time for a complete change for both of them. A shift of priorities.

Bart, too, was moving into a new phase of his life with Kameela. Helping out at the villa as well as working as a yacht deliverer would curtail the time he could spend with her. Something would have to give.

So many changes happening in the coming months. She and Rebecca would have to sit down and make some decisions soon. Delphine mentally crossed her fingers and prayed they would be the right ones and work out for everyone.

* * *

Thursday evening, and Verity enjoyed a leisurely swim in the pool at the complex where Effie lived. Effie had declined to join her, saying their day out on St Honorat had exhausted her and she planned to do nothing more than sit on the terrace and check out the bottle of liquor she'd purchased in the monastery shop. When Verity joined her on the terrace after her swim, Effie handed a glass to her. 'Nightcap. It's rather good. I'm off to bed. I'll see you in the morning.'

'You are still coming with me tomorrow to check out that villa again, aren't you?' Verity asked.

'Of course,' Effie answered.

Verity stayed out on the terrace sipping her drink and thinking about her future. On Wednesday, she and Freya had talked about her coming to live down here and Verity had mentioned how frightened she was of not having anything to do and turning into a lady wot lunches, much as she was in London. Freya had made several suggestions and Verity had been sifting them through her mind ever since.

Freya had talked of her being a consultant to newcomers in the area, helping them find their feet, telling them the best places to shop, the tradespeople to use, how to register with a doctor, collecting people from the airport, the list was endless. Verity had been sceptical in the beginning, not believing that people would pay for a service like that but Freya had assured her that there were lots of people who'd willingly pay for help.

'And it's not as if you need a full time job is it? If you only get one or two people needing your help a month, it will be enough to stop you being bored. You could get involved with the various charities down here too. They are always crying out for help with administration.' She'd leant in and whispered. 'Otherwise it will be bridge every afternoon and somehow I don't see you going down that road, although Mum says you're not a bad partner.'

Finishing her drink, Verity smiled to herself. She'd enjoyed the game of bridge Effie had taken her to but she definitely didn't want to play on a regular basis. And if things worked out, she wouldn't have time.

Yesterday she and Effie had had three appointments with an estate agent to check out a couple of apartments and a villa in need of renovation. To be honest, she hadn't held out much hope of finding something she liked on this visit and she'd already asked Effie if she could come back down in September for a more concentrated search when it wasn't so hot and the tourist season was over. Her flight home was booked for this Sunday afternoon so she still had a few days to enjoy being around family and to visit again the ramshackle villa the agent had shown them yesterday.

Neither of the apartments had appealed, Verity simply couldn't see herself living in either of them, although one had a decent enough view of the sea. Ten minutes later, when the estate agent parked in front of a pair of rusty green metal gates on a suburban road set back from the bord de mer, Verity had glimpsed the faded pink paint of a provençal villa and caught her breath. She'd waited impatiently while the agent pushed one of the metal gates open and then followed him across the overgrown drive towards the small flight of steps that led up to the front door. The agent's phone buzzed as he opened the front door and he glanced apologetically at Verity and Effie.

'Please go in. I need to answer this.'

The inside of the villa was dark as the shutters were closed and it had clearly been vandalised as there was rubbish strewn over the ground floor everywhere. Verity wrestled with the bar on long shutters and managed to lift it off to reveal a pair of french doors. Peering through the dirty glass she'd seen an overgrown garden and a pool that nobody had swum in for years, given its current state. Empty of furniture, their footsteps echoed as the two of them wandered around before climbing the wooden uncarpeted stairs to the next floor.

Three good sized bedrooms, an antiquated bathroom and another small room, all with wonderful views of the Mediterranean. Verity looked at Effie. 'Seen enough?'

'More than enough. Why haven't the sellers at least cleaned the place to make it look respectable?'

Verity shook her head. 'No idea. But I quite like it. Definitely got potential. I mean, it's not a belle epoque villa but I think it has a certain charm and could be wonderful. Come on, let's go back downstairs and talk to the agent. Find out more about it.'

'Are you serious?' Effie said. 'When I think about your beautiful house in London and compare it to this,' she held up her hands in horror.

'That was a challenge too. Oh, nothing on this scale but I enjoyed sorting it out and I think I'd enjoy living down here and bringing this villa back to life,' Verity said. 'It would certainly give me something to do.'

36

Rebecca took Rufus at his word when he said it was her choice where they ate that evening and booked a table at a simple beach restaurant where she knew the food was good.

She was ready and waiting for Rufus when he arrived and responded happily to his greeting kiss before getting in his car.

'Where are we going?' Rufus asked, starting the car.

'Villeneuve-Loubet. A beach restaurant – well, more of a shack really off the tourist trail. What have you been up to today?'

'I went to Menton to see my parents,' Rufus said. 'I needed to tell them about us and the fact that they have an unknown grandson.'

'How did they react?' Rebecca asked, being told you had a twenty-four year old grandson must have been something of a shock to people in their eighties.

'Well, let's just say I was given strict instructions to take you to Menton sooner rather than later – they can't wait to meet you both.' He glanced across at her. 'Has the situation improved at all with Bart? I know you and I can go at any time to see my parents, but I'm desperate to meet Bart first.'

'Delphine and his girlfriend, Kameela, both gave him strict instructions that he had to talk to me. He came to see me this afternoon,' Rebecca said. 'We had a long talk and I told him the truth about why you were never in his life and he's now curious to meet you.' Rebecca sensed the lessening of tension in Rufus's body at her words.

'That's a relief. I don't think I could have coped with a son who was reluctant to meet me, because I can't tell you how much I want to meet up with him. Marcus and Freya know our secret by the way. And, before you ask, no, I didn't tell them, they guessed apparently, the moment you introduced Bart to them as they were leaving.'

'I'm not surprised. They've known you a long time and Bart does look like you.'

'So he's tall and good-looking too?'

Rebecca burst out laughing. 'That is, word for word, what Bart said when I told him how much he looked like you.'

'Great. I have a son who has the same sense of humour as me. We're going to get on just fine,' and he turned to give her a quick look, the beam on his face telling Rebecca how happy he was at the thought.

'You need to take a left turn at the next traffic lights,' Rebecca said. 'And then the first left down a narrow lane. The restaurant is about five hundred metres down there.'

Five minutes later, Rufus parked the car on a designated patch of shingle behind a wooden building that had seen better days and made for the beach. Rebecca slipped her shoes off as they reached the sand and, hand in hand, they made their way round the side of the building on the beach. The front of the building was currently wide open with its wooden shutters folded back on either side. A thatched roof reached out over a terrace where there were several wooden tables and chairs. There was a small bar and a blackboard against the wall described the menu for the evening. An open doorway next to the bar, partially covered by a beaded hanging curtain, led to the kitchen.

'This really is a shack,' Rufus whispered.

'Mm, but the food is great. I hope you like seafood. You do, don't you? Because there's no choice – you get what the chef has decided to cook for the evening.' She glanced at the board. 'And tonight the main course is Mediterranean seafood pasta with prawns and calamari and other delightful things.'

Rufus nodded. 'Sounds delicious. I didn't know places like this existed round here.'

'I much prefer somewhere like this to the trendy places,' Rebecca said.

With no one to show them where to sit, Rebecca chose a table for two on the edge of the terrace with a view of the Mediterranean. They'd been there barely three minutes, admiring the view, when a lanky teenage boy appeared and wished them '*Bonne soirée*' before asking what they would like to drink. 'Food will be about ten minutes.'

Rebecca asked for a glass of sparkling Crémant wine while Rufus said he'd stick to non-alcoholic beer as he was driving.

'So when and where can I meet Bart?' he asked.

'Tomorrow sometime?' Rebecca suggested. 'How about you come up to the villa about midday and I'll make sure Bart is there too.'

'Great. I'll do that. Now, what does the future hold for the two of us?' Rufus said, a serious edge to his voice. 'I know the future I would like – I need to hear your thoughts.'

The waiter arrived at that moment and Rebecca thought about her answer while he placed their drinks on the table before disappearing again.

'Delphine intends to retire on the first of October and I'm not sure about carrying on without her, so I've been thinking about selling up but not made any real decision yet,' Rebecca said quietly. 'If we do sell up, it does mean that both Delphine and I will have lost our homes and we will have to find something suitable for both of us. You do realise it's a case of love me, love my sister, don't you? Bart and I are all she's got.'

Rufus reached out a reassuring hand across the table and held her hand that was fiddling nervously with the cutlery. 'I understand that completely.'

'How about you?' Rebecca asked. 'Do you have any set plans for the future, other than being there for your parents?'

'Until this week that was my only goal. Now I have you and a son to take into the equation, so we definitely need to live near my parents, but it has to be convenient too, for you and Bart.'

Rebecca smiled as she picked up the emphasis on one of the words. 'We?'

'Yes, of course. You don't think we're going to live separate lives in separate houses now we've found each other again, do you? Because that is definitely not happening.'

Rebecca shook her head at his words. What had been the stuff of fantasies all those years ago now seemed to be about to come true in real life. 'No, it's going to be difficult sorting everything out though. The other night you said you were looking for a business opportunity, what sort of business?'

Rufus shrugged. 'No idea. Something suitable will turn up. Marcus has a few contacts. To be honest, I've rather put it on the back-burner for now. I have other things on my mind,' and Rebecca blushed as he stared at her with a naughty grin.

The waiter returned at that moment with their starters – a dish each of hot crabmeat dip, with slices of garlic bread and a small side salad. '*Bon appétit*,' he said before moving to greet another two couples as the shack slowly filled with customers.

After a couple of mouthfuls, Rufus looked at Rebecca. 'I can't believe what I'm eating. It's delicious.'

'Told you the food was good here,' Rebecca said.

'They'd make a fortune if they found a place somewhere along the beach, in Juan-les-Pin, say.'

Rebecca shook her head. 'The chef's not interested. He just wants to cook good food. He's happy with this set-up. He's not trying to prove anything.'

'Fair enough.' Rufus scooped the final mouthful of dip on to a piece of garlic bread before saying. 'If I'm meeting Bart tomorrow, how do you feel about Sunday lunch in Menton with my parents?'

'Just me or Bart too?'

'If you say yes, then I'll ask Bart if he's free. I rather like the idea of taking the two of you. My family unit.'

'Sounds like a plan.' Rebecca hesitated. 'I'm a bit worried about meeting your parents, if I'm honest. Are you sure they're not just saying all the right things, the things you want to hear, about me? They don't think it was scandalous of me becoming a single mother all those years ago?' she added quietly.

'My parents aren't like that,' Rufus said. 'When you meet them, you're going to love them as much as I do and they'll love you too. Stop worrying.'

As the waiter cleared their empty starter plates, another waiter placed the main course on the table.

The seafood pasta with its prawns and calamari, capers, sun-dried tomatoes all tossed in a wine sauce was pronounced 'Sublime' by Rufus a few moments later.

'I think you're a bit of a foody on the quiet, aren't you?' Rebecca said, laughing. 'I've got so much to learn about you. Anyway, I hope you're full once you finish this because there is rarely a dessert, other than home-made ice cream, in this place.'

'Couldn't force even ice cream down,' Rufus said. 'Thank you for bringing me here.'

They lingered over coffee for a while before paying and reluctantly leaving. Walking back to the car, Rufus put his arm around Rebecca's shoulders and squeezed.

'I'm so lucky to have found you again,' he said. 'But there is one thing I'd like to change about you,' and he turned her to face him. 'The morning I arrived at the villa you told me in a definite voice that you were Rebecca now. I'm sorry, but you are and always will be Becky to me. Please can I revert back to using that name?'

'I loved being Becky,' she said. 'I've never allowed anyone to use it since you.'

'Welcome back to my Becky,' Rufus said, before kissing her in a way that Rebecca definitely remembered Becky enjoying.

37

Friday morning, and Rebecca was nervous. There was no reason to think that the two most important men in her life wouldn't get on, but there was always the chance they wouldn't for some reason or other. And how should she introduce them? She really couldn't face saying, Rufus, this is your son, Bart, this is your father, when they both knew that was who they were meeting. But to simply say Rufus, Bart and wait for them to shake hands wasn't right either for such a momentous occasion.

In the end, she let the problem solve itself. Standing in the foyer, she heard a car arriving. Rufus was early. As she went to go out and greet him, Bart drove up and parked alongside. Berating herself for being a coward, Rebecca stayed where she was, watching and listening as both men got out of their cars and looked at each other.

Rufus was the first to react and moved towards Bart, his hand outstretched.

'You must be Bart. I have to tell you that you look remarkably like my father does in photographs of when he was young.'

'Great. First, Mum tells me I look like my dad and now my father tells me I look like my grandfather,' but Bart was smiling as he spoke and took Rufus's proffered hand in his.

'Want to walk round the grounds with me and chat? I have so many questions to ask you, and I guess you might have a fair few to ask me?' Rufus said.

'Just a few.'

As father and son walked off together to chat and to start to learn about each other, Rebecca gave a huge sigh of relief and went in search of Delphine, who, as always, was in the kitchen.

'Coffee?' Delphine asked as she walked in. 'I thought you were doing introductions?'

'They did it without any help from me and have gone for a wander around the grounds together. I thought maybe now would be a good time for us to have a chat about the future?'

'Of course.'

Sitting out on the terrace with coffee and biscuits in front of them, Rebecca said, 'You're still going travelling at the end of the season?'

'Yes. And, as Kameela suggested, I'm making Martinique my first port of call. I'm guessing you've changed your mind about coming with me?' Delphine said with a smile.

'Definitely not coming, but I seriously think the time to sell Villa Sésame has come. Shall we start to put the wheels in motion over summer? It will take time to sell, but hopefully by this time next year, we will have found a buyer. We'll not take any more bookings for this year, but we'll honour the ones we have. I'll need to find a freelance chef too, for while you're away.'

'Any idea what you'll do afterwards?' Delphine asked quietly. 'Where you and Rufus are likely to live?'

Rebecca shrugged. 'No, but wherever we are, you have to like it too. You made it clear to André that I was part of your life and Rufus knows that the three of us are not inseparable but we do come as a package. So don't start worrying about that. I can see that look in your eyes.'

'I'll tell you something that does worry me about going travelling and selling this place,' Delphine said. 'My girls. They need looking after.' She picked up a biscuit and broke a bit off. 'You know what – I think I'll ask Bart and Kameela if they would like to live in the cottage whilst I'm away and in return look after the hens? That would be good. They could save some money that way too.'

'It would be a shorter commute for Kameela to the hospital too,' Rebecca said thoughtfully. 'No harm in asking.'

'Father and son are on their way back,' Delphine said, looking down towards the olive grove. 'They look quite happy.'

Watching them make their way up to the villa, Rebecca wanted to pinch herself to check she wasn't dreaming. That after all these years she really was seeing Bart laughing as he walked with his father.

As they climbed the steps onto the terrace, Delphine got up to fetch another pot of coffee and Bart looked at his mum.

'Quiet here today. I thought you'd be busy with the American party stuff for tomorrow.'

'They cancelled yesterday,' Rebecca said. 'Is Kameela working tomorrow night? No? In that case, why don't you both come for dinner.' She turned to Rufus. 'We could meet her together then, like proper parents.' She grinned at him. 'Actually, I've just had a thought. Would your parents like to come as well? You could bring them over during the day, Bart and I can meet them and the three of you can stay overnight, plenty of room. We could have our first celebration as a family. What do you think?'

'That I like the sound of a family party. I'll phone them and ask them right now,' Rufus said. 'And I'd quite like to invite Marcus and Freya. They're my oldest friends and they're the reason we can even talk about having a family celebration. Without them, we wouldn't have met up again.' Pulling his phone out of his pocket, he stood up and wandered along the terrace to phone both his parents and Marcus.

Rebecca glanced across at Bart, willing him to say something about his first chat with Rufus. When Bart just smiled knowingly at her, she was driven to ask, 'So?'

'So what?' was his infuriating reply.

'How did you and Rufus get on?'

Bart gave a nonchalant shrug. 'Okay.'

'Bart! It's important to me to know that you and he will get on.'

'Well, on the basis of one meeting, I'd say we're in with a fair chance of that happening,' Bart said, finally taking pity on his mother and grinning at her as Rufus returned to the table.

Rufus sat back down with a smile. 'Saturday night is party night. And Mum and Dad would very much like to accept your offer of staying. I've promised to pick them up and bring them over tomorrow afternoon.'

As Delphine arrived back with the coffee, Rebecca was busy making notes on her phone for their own fourth of July family party the next day. A party that she was determined would stand out in the history of parties held at Villa Sésame – and one that would be remembered as the beginning of her new family life with Rufus.

* * *

Since arriving home at the beginning of the week, Angela's new sense of purpose had carried her along on a wave of optimism. When Will had rung to say that both he and Steph would come and stay overnight on Saturday and catch the afternoon train back to London on Sunday, she'd been galvanised into action.

The first thing she did was to ring a local estate agent and arrange for someone to come on Monday morning to give her a valuation and put the house on the market. Pleased that she'd at least taken all the black bags from the bedroom to the charity shop before she left for France, she'd started in the master bedroom and given the house a mammoth cleaning blitz from top to bottom over the last two days.

Friday evening, she poured herself a glass of wine and, wandering from the kitchen to the sitting room sipping it, she congratulated herself on a job well done. The whole place was sparkling, ready not only for Will and Steph tomorrow but also for the agent to photograph on Monday. This house had been her home for so long it would feel strange leaving it behind and Angela knew that if Paul was still alive, they would have stayed living in it for many more years. Paul had adored Dartmoor and it had been his idea to base themselves on the edge of it all those years ago when Will was young.

When they'd found this house they'd both realised what a perfect family home it would make and so it had proved. But Angela had always secretly missed Dartmouth with its river running down to the sea. The thought of living back there lifted her spirits even though she'd give anything to have Paul back at her side. Living on Dartmoor had been Paul's dream, now, returning to Dartmouth had become hers. A dream she hoped and prayed was realistic enough to deal with any problems that might arise and come to fruition. The fact that Will had said it was a good idea for her to move back gave her added hope that everything would work out.

Angela was in Totnes the next morning with time to do a quick supermarket shop for lunch, picking up a roasted chicken, salad and a couple of bottles of wine, before heading to the station to meet Will and Steph. Standing on the platform, watching the train advancing down the track towards the station, Angela took a deep breath. In a few hours Will would know the truth about his father's death. Her peace of mind in the future depended so much on his reaction to the news of her involvement. As the train pulled in alongside the platform, Angela scanned the passengers alighting and waved as soon as she spotted Will and Steph. As soon as they joined her, she enveloped both of them in a hug, Steph first and then Will.

'I'm so pleased you could both make it. I've got lots to tell you but it can wait until we're home. I've organised lunch and I thought tonight we could eat in the village pub's garden restaurant, the weather is so nice, if that's okay with you both.' Angela told them as they walked to the car.

'Sounds like a plan,' Will said as they all settled themselves in the car and Angela started to drive home.

'Have you done anything about selling the house yet?' Will asked.

'Estate agent is coming Monday.'

'Have you started to—'

'Yes,' Angela interrupted him, knowing what he was going to say. 'I took everything I could to the charity shops before I went to France. And since I've been back I've been busy making the house presentable.'

'That's good. What was it you wanted to tell me?'

Angela gripped the steering wheel tightly. She wanted a glass of wine in her hand or at least nearby when she talked to Will. 'Not while I'm driving. I need to concentrate on these lanes.'

Once back at the house, Angela quickly put the lunch things on the table while Will and Steph took their overnight case upstairs and freshened up.

Will was the first to come down. 'The house is looking great, Mum. You must have worked like a trojan.'

Angela gave him a rueful smile. 'I'm ashamed I let it get so bad.' She handed him a bottle of wine and the corkscrew. 'Would you, please? And then pour us both a glass.'

Will gave her a concerned look as he twisted the corkscrew into place and pulled the cork out.

'I've been in a bad place for the last few months since your dad...' her voice trailed away and she gave a slight shrug. 'Certain things about the accident have been hard to accept.'

'Is this to do with what you want to talk to me about?' Will poured two glasses of wine and handed her one.

Angela nodded. 'Yes.' She clinked her glass against Will's before taking a drink. 'You need to know the truth but I'm frightened of your reaction.'

'Well, until you tell me neither of us will know how I react, so?' Will watched her as he took a sip of his own wine. Angela took a deep breath.

'You know I grew up surrounded by bikes because Uncle Tony and Alex were obsessed with them. They both had off road bikes before they were old enough to have a license for the road. I was a bit of a tomboy in those days and they taught me to ride the trials bikes but my mum refused to let me have a proper motorbike – even though the boys said I was a good rider and knew what I was doing.' She took another drink before continuing.

'I'd been badgering Paul for a few weeks to let me have a go on the Yamaha and he finally agreed that afternoon.' Angela took a deep breath. The moment of truth.

'Paul was riding pillion when we, I, had the accident.' As Will's face registered shock, Angela couldn't hold back the tears. 'I'm so, so sorry.'

'You were riding the bike, not Dad?'

Angela nodded. 'The guilt has been eating away at me ever since.'

Will put his glass on the table and put his arms around her. 'Oh, Mum. No wonder you were in such a state.' He held her for ten or fifteen seconds before speaking again.

'Mum, you need to accept that Dad's death was a tragic accident. One that you couldn't have done anything to avoid. The real culprit was the person who left the muck on the road by a dangerous bend.'

Angela could feel the tension leaving her body as she heard Will's words. But there was a question she had to ask. 'Are you sure you won't blame me for the rest of your life for the accident?'

Will sighed and shook his head.

'Like I said, it was a tragic accident waiting to happen on that particular stretch of road. And I know for a fact Dad would want you to live and enjoy the rest of your life. Not beat yourself up about the accident.'

'I miss him so much,' Angela said quietly.

'So do I,' Will confessed. 'Can I ask you something?'

'Anything.'

'I realise now why, whenever I've been home since the funeral, you've rarely brought Dad up in conversation. Can we talk about him sometimes? Remember the things we all did together. I know it will be difficult for you but I suspect it will be healing too.'

Angela nodded. 'Yes. We must do that.' She heard the

bedroom door upstairs closing and Steph starting to come downstairs.

'Thank you for coming down this weekend. I couldn't tell you something so important over the phone. Confessing to you has taken a weight off my mind. Steph is coming, better pour her a glass of wine and then I've got some Dartmouth property details you might like to look at over lunch.'

38

Freya was tired. It had been lovely having Madeleine and the family staying for a few days after the wedding week, but there had been so much to do. Between them, this week she and Marcus had carried all the paintings down to Hugo's gallery and left them there for him to hang ready for the exhibition. The family supper with Effie and Verity had been fun too. She'd been surprised to discover that her cousin could be the life and soul of the party when she wanted to be.

It was hard to believe that it was only Saturday last week, when she and Marcus had remarried and partied not quite the whole night away but a lot of it. And later today they were returning to Villa Sésame for a fourth of July party that Rufus had been insistent they attended. 'It's a little thank you for putting up with me for the past five days.'

Freya smiled at the thought of Rufus. She'd never seen him as happy as he was now with Rebecca and Bart in his life.

This morning, as he'd thanked her for having him to stay, he'd told her that he wouldn't be back that night. He and his parents were staying at the villa for the night after the party and then he would drive them back on Sunday and use their place as a base while he and Becky sorted things out.

Freya was about to take a coffee up to the terrace for a quiet five or ten minutes before starting to get ready for the party, when her phone rang. Clemmie.

'How are you?' Freya asked. 'Still "friends" with Jonty?'

'My friend and I are both well, thank you,' Clemmie answered primly, before bursting into laughter. 'And I absolutely adore Hamish. I'm meeting Jonty's daughter and children tomorrow,' she added quietly. 'I'm cooking lunch for us all.'

'You feeling stressed about that?'

'A bit. I know it's important for Jonty that Emma and I get on.'

'Which you will, I know,' Freya said. 'Stop worrying. Jonty is a lovely man, I'm sure his daughter will be equally lovely. And your roasts are always delicious.'

'Thanks for the morale boost. Anyway, part of the reason I rang was to congratulate you on your first week's anniversary,' Clemmie continued. 'I hope you are celebrating.'

'We're going to a party at the villa this evening, would you believe,' Freya said. 'Rufus and Rebecca are celebrating.'

'Hang on, Rufus and Rebecca? What have I missed?'

'It's a long story, but basically...' And Freya gave Clemmie a quick rundown on the events at the villa over the past week and reminded her the part their first wedding had played in the story. 'You remember our evening reception at the Gunfield when we all teased Rufus for being miserable, a real party pooper?'

'Yes, so unlike him. Hadn't he met some girl he'd wanted to invite but she couldn't make it – oh,' Clemmie let out a squeal. 'Was that Rebecca? Small world.'

'Yes. And there's more,' Freya said. 'But I'll fill you in on the details when you and Jonty visit next month. Have you heard from Angela?'

'Will and Steph are down this weekend. She was planning to talk to Will and promised she'd phone me on Sunday evening after they'd left to let me know how it had gone. The house is going up for sale and she's coming back to Dartmouth. That's basically all I know.'

'Sounds as though she's starting to think a bit more positively about living without Paul,' Freya said. 'Returning to Dartmouth will be good for her.'

'I'd better go,' Clemmie said. 'Jonty's arrived with fish and chips. Give Rufus my love tonight. I'm glad he's finally got someone in his life. Always thought he should be married. Would have made a wonderful dad. Enjoy the party this evening, speak soon.'

Freya smiled as the call ended. Rufus being a dad was one of the things she hadn't got round to mentioning to Clemmie. But she had to agree, she already knew Rufus was going to make a wonderful dad.

39

Saturday was a day that Rebecca knew she would remember for a whole host of different reasons. Meeting Rufus's parents was one reason. Rufus had been so right about loving his parents. Brenda Whelan had given her a hug so tight that she almost couldn't breathe before she'd released her slightly and held her away to give her a serious look.

'For years I've wished for Rufus to meet someone, to have a family, and all this time he never mentioned loving and losing you. I'm, the only word I can use, is ecstatic. I'm ecstatic that you and he have found each other again. I am ecstatic at the news he has a son. I'm only sorry that you and he have lost so much time together. And I'm ecstatic at the thought of meeting my newest but oldest grandson.'

Lionel, Rufus's father, had smiled at his wife. 'Overuse of the word ecstatic, Brenda. Becky, I too am very happy to welcome you and your son into our lives,' and he'd given her a gentle hug. 'My son, I have to say, is happier than I ever remember seeing him and that is down to the welcome presence of you and your son in his life. Thank you.'

Their kindness was overwhelming and Brenda hugging her so hard brought back memories of similar hugs from her own mum. Rebecca had smiled and blinked back the tears as she realised how much their acceptance meant to her.

Bart, arriving in time for afternoon tea, had been given the same enthusiastic greeting by Brenda, who'd taken one look at him and declared him to be a Whelan through and through. Bart had spent an hour or so with his new grandparents before leaving to collect Kameela to return for the party.

After Bart had left, Brenda and Lionel decided they'd like to have a quick nap in their room so that they'd be 'ready to party the night away', according to Brenda. Rufus fetched their overnight case from the car and took them upstairs. His own overnight case he left at the foot of the stairs. Afterwards, Delphine, Rebecca and Rufus set to work preparing the food and the terrace for the party.

A white linen tablecloth was thrown over the large rectangular table, nine chairs were placed around it, plates, glasses and cutlery were laid and plates of food were ready in the kitchen to be arranged down the centre. Delphine and Rebecca had decided a cold buffet was easiest: no one would need to slave away in the kitchen or over the barbecue. The fridge was full of charcuterie meats – ham, chicken, salami, sausages – cheeses, smoked salmon, pasta salad, mozzarella and tomato salad. Crusty baguettes, crisps and sourdough bread were on the kitchen table, along with the tin of meringues Delphine always had ready to accompany the home-made raspberry ice cream in the freezer in case anyone wanted a sweet dessert to finish. The drinks fridge had champagne, rosé, white wine and bottles of beer.

The three of them had decided that they could do no more until closer to party time when they heard a car. Bart was back with Kameela.

Rebecca looked at Rufus. 'More introductions – and a first for us as parents.'

Rufus took her hand as they went outside to greet Bart and his girlfriend.

'Kameela, this is...' Bart hesitated, clearly not sure how to introduce them. 'These are apparently my parents,' he joked in the end. 'Mum and Rufus. Even though I've only just met my dad, I think he'll turn out to be good in the end,' and he grinned at Rufus.

'Less of your cheek, my boy,' Rufus growled in mock anger, before he returned Bart's smile with his own. Rebecca shook her head in despair at the two of them before turning to greet Kameela.

'It's lovely to meet you, Kameela. Can I give you a hug?' Rebecca said, holding out her arms.

Kameela smiled and hugged Rebecca back. Rufus gave her a kiss on the cheek as he said '*Enchanté.*'

'Rufus and I were just about to go and change, ready for the party. Your aunt, as usual, has to simply discard her overall to be party-ready. Me, I've got to go and change and Rufus managed to spill something down his shirt. Go on through and find yourselves a drink. Delphine is in the kitchen. We'll be about ten minutes.'

At the foot of the stairs, Rebecca saw Rufus's overnight bag. 'If you'd like to pick that up, I'll show you to your room,' and she started to go upstairs. Past the bedroom Brenda and Lionel were in, past the Butterfly Room, until she stopped to open the door marked 'Private' at the bottom of the staircase that led to her apartment.

'I thought you might like to stay in the private penthouse apartment,' she said, opening the door and heading up the stairs. 'Only if you want to, of course. No pressure. There are other rooms available.' She turned as she reached the top landing and grinned at Rufus as he joined her.

'Is it only available for tonight?' Rufus asked quietly as he took her in his arms.

'It's available for a permanent stay, if that's what you want,' Rebecca managed to say before he kissed her. When he released her, she shook her head. 'We don't have time for this right now. We have a party to get ready for. Freya and Marcus will be here soon and I think I can hear Brenda and Lionel making their way downstairs.'

'I'm tempted to say I don't care, but you're right. We need to get back downstairs. But we can squeeze one more kiss in, can't we?'

Rebecca didn't hesitate.

Rebecca and Rufus got downstairs in time to help Delphine, Kameela and Bart put the food on the table, open a bottle of champagne and to start the sound system playing some bistro-type background music before anyone appeared. Brenda and Lionel wandered downstairs soon afterwards and happily accepted a glass of champagne. By the time Freya and Marcus arrived, Bart and Kameela were talking to Delphine about the cottage and chickens.

When Rebecca called, 'À table, it's time to eat,' conversation, like the wine, was flowing. Leaving everyone tucking into the food, Rebecca went into the kitchen to get extra bottles of red and white wine for the table. She stood for a few moments watching the sun set and the sky becoming its customary scarlet over the Esterel mountains. As she watched, the pool and garden lights came on and Rebecca smiled at the scene in front of her. She was going to miss Villa Sésame.

Rufus made her jump as he put his arms around her and said quietly, 'Shall we get married here before you sell Villa Sésame?'

Rebecca's heart skipped a beat. 'Is that a proposal, Mr Whelan?'

'I do believe it is.'

'Having our wedding here would be wonderful,' Rebecca said.

'That's what we'll do then.'

'Thank you,' Rebecca whispered. 'I can't wait to marry you.'

As they sat back down at the table, they heard Bart say, 'There's usually fireworks somewhere along the coast for Independence Day. Doubt they'll be starting any time soon though, they're usually quite late.'

They were all still sitting there languidly putting the world to rights at almost midnight when they heard the first loud bang of a firework rocket being set off, a warning the real display would begin in a few moments.

When it did begin, with a deafening bang, they all stood on the top terrace and watched as fireworks creating a sparkling shimmering tableau depicting the American flag exploded into the night sky to signify this fireworks display, celebrating the fourth of July, was underway. For twenty minutes, loud bangs were followed by a frenzy of shimmering bright colours lighting up the Côte d'Azur sky in various designs. A row of exploding silver formed the words *Bonne Nuit* high in the sky and suddenly it was all over.

Rebecca, standing happily in the circle of Rufus's arms on the terrace, sighed contentedly. The fireworks were a perfect end to what had been a red-letter day here at the villa, but this day also marked the beginning of the rest of her life. A life she'd given up dreaming about years ago, which had unexpectedly materialised. Rufus was back in her life and this time he was back for good.

EPILOGUE

A YEAR LATER

ANGELA. The house on the edge of Dartmoor sold far quicker than Angela expected and she took up Clemmie's offer of staying with her while she house-hunted. Two months before Christmas this year, she moved into the South Town house Clemmie had shown her. Will and Steph came down and helped her move in and promised to come for Christmas. She still misses Paul but her new life is keeping her busy. In the New Year, Angela has lots of decorating to do and will also start work as a teaching assistant in the local primary school at the top of the town. In the New Year too, she will become a grandmother when Will and Steph's baby arrives.

* * *

VERITY has also sold up and moved to Antibes. She bought the delapidated villa in Juan-les-Pins and is having fun doing it up. She took Freya's advice and started to let it be known that she was available to help ex-pats. She was amazed at the response she got and has earnt the nick name Jill of all trades locally as she helps fill in forms, set up bank accounts, picks people up from the airport and is regarded as being worth every penny of her fee. Recently, she has been asked to manage a small complex of holiday lets and is considering it. Her diary is full and she laughs when she remembers those days when she was just a lady 'wot' lunches. She doesn't miss her old life at all. Living in the south of France with family close to hand is something she never dreamt would happen for her but she couldn't be happier.

* * *

CLEMMIE and **JONTY (and Hamish of course)** are a still a couple and enjoying life together. They sail a lot, walk Hamish, and have lunch at the Yacht Club quite often. Victoria no longer rings Jonty on a whim. Emma and the children visit often and get on well with Clemmie. Jonty is hoping to surprise Clemmie with a visit in the very near future to Australia to see her daughter, Lucy. He's also hoping to persuade her to marry him in the not too distant future.

* * *

FREYA and MARCUS are blissfully happy second time around. Marcus couldn't be prouder of his wife. Freya's art exhibition was hugely successful and she was the talk of the town for several weeks. There is another exhibition of her work planned soon and once again she spends most of her days painting. Madeleine and Sean visit as often as they can, bringing their new little boy, Alex. Lily absolutely dotes on her baby brother and is all set to be a very bossy big sister as he grows. Clemmie and Jonty have visited once since the wedding and Freya loves seeing her old friend happy again. She's hoping that Angela will visit them soon.

* * *

EFFIE continues to enjoy her retirement in Antibes and is busier than ever now that Verity often involves her in things. And, of course, her friend Cecily still drags her off to yoga, shopping, the bridge club and now there is talk of tea dances being held in Juan-les-Pins at one of the larger hotels. She also enjoyed her fifteen minutes of fame being known as the mother of Freya Jackman, the new, highly acclaimed artist recently arrived in town.

* * *

DELPHINE enjoyed her months of travelling. The highlight of her trip was the time she spent in Martinique with Kameela's family, and especially Uncle Francois. As she promised André, she's been to all the places he wanted to see: Australia, Mexico, Canada and America. But now she is back in France and looking forward to settling down into a life that revolves around her close family. In time, she hopes to become a great-aunty to Bart and Kameela's future children. Now that Villa Sésame has been sold she has moved into a cottage in the grounds of Rebecca and Rufus's new home.

* * *

BART is still operating his yacht delivery business but on a smaller scale, concentrating instead on organising rather than actually going away on deliveries. Rufus has made him a partner in a small boatyard he's bought on the outskirts of Cannes La Bocca that is ripe for expansion and will eventually take him away from delivering yachts. He and Kameela are officially engaged and hoping to marry soon.

* * *

REBECCA and **RUFUS** had a quiet civil wedding at the *mairie* in Antibes and a romantic ceremony and party with all their friends at Villa Sésame, followed by a honeymoon in Sydney. On their return, they purchased a four-bedroom villa on Cap d'Antibes, with a cottage in the grounds for Delphine. They make regular visits to Menton to see Brenda and Lionel who adore the fact that Rebecca and Bart are now part of their family.

* * *

As for **VILLA SÉSAME**, Rebecca is hopeful that under the management of the new independent owners (she refused to sell to a chain), Villa Sésame will continue to work its second-chance magic on the guests who stay there. Both she and Rufus are firmly of the opinion that everybody needs a second chance sometimes in their lives.

AUTHOR'S NOTE

Many years ago, there was an iconic hotel on the banks of the River Dart at Dartmouth called The Gunfield Hotel and I have taken the liberty of placing that hotel in this story in loving memory of a place that was special to so many people. Sadly, it ceased to be a hotel before the end of the twentieth century, but people still remember it and talk about it fondly.

ACKNOWLEDGMENTS

As always, everyone in the Boldwood Team has my unreserved gratitude for everything they do for me and my books. Caroline Ridding, my editor, has again had the patience of a saint as I struggled to get this story down. I'm not a planner of my stories, I make it all up as I go along, but this time I fell down a few holes. I also owe Jade and Rose a big thank you for their copy-editing and proofreading skills, thank you.

Thanks go this time as well to my policeman nephew, Ed Bohnet, who sorted out my worries regarding road traffic accidents involving motorbikes – thanks, Ed.

So many supportive writing friends who have bolstered me up during the last few months, not naming names as I'd hate to forget anyone, but you know who you are.

Thanks are due to all the bloggers out there who support and promote not only me but so many grateful authors. A special thank you shoutout to Rachel Gilbey, organiser extraordinaire.

Thanks, as always, to Richard, my husband, who cooks, does the housework I fail to do, does the shopping, drags me out for two walks every day, because otherwise I'd never leave the house, and, above all, lets me use him as a sounding board when I get stuck.

And I mustn't forget to thank all my readers who make it all worthwhile. Thank you one and all.

Love,

Jennie
x

MORE FROM JENNIFER BOHNET

We hope you enjoyed reading *Villa of Second Chances*. If you did, please leave a review.

If you'd like to gift a copy, this book is also available as an ebook, digital audio download and audiobook CD.

Sign up to Jennifer Bohnet's mailing list for news, competitions and updates on future books.

http://bit.ly/JenniferBohnetNewsletter

Explore more gloriously escapist reads from Jennifer Bohnet.

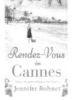

ABOUT THE AUTHOR

Jennifer Bohnet is the bestselling author of over 10 women's fiction novels, including *Villa of Sun and Secrets* and *The Little Kiosk By The Sea*. She is originally from the West Country but now lives in the wilds of rural Brittany, France.

Visit Jennifer's website: http://www.jenniferbohnet.com/

Follow Jennifer on social media:

f facebook.com/Jennifer-Bohnet-170217789709356

🐦 twitter.com/jenniewriter

📷 instagram.com/jenniebohnet

BB bookbub.com/authors/jennifer-bohnet

ABOUT BOLDWOOD BOOKS

Boldwood Books is a fiction publishing company seeking out the best stories from around the world.

Find out more at www.boldwoodbooks.com

Sign up to the Book and Tonic newsletter for news, offers and competitions from Boldwood Books!

http://www.bit.ly/bookandtonic

We'd love to hear from you, follow us on social media:

 facebook.com/BookandTonic

 twitter.com/BoldwoodBooks

 instagram.com/BookandTonic